The Year Shakespeare Ruined My Life

THE YEAR
SHAKESPEARE
RUINED MY LIFE

DANI
JANSEN

Second Story Press

Library and Archives Canada Cataloguing in Publication

Title: The year Shakespeare ruined my life / Dani Jansen.
Names: Jansen, Dani, 1980- author.
Identifiers: Canadiana (print) 20200208756 | Canadiana (ebook) 20200208764 |
ISBN 9781772601213 (softcover) | ISBN 9781772601220 (EPUB)
Classification: LCC PS8619.A67826 Y43 2020 | DDC jC813/.6—dc23

Cover by Liz Parkes
Edited by Kathy White
Design by Melissa Kaita

Printed and bound in Canada

*Second Story Press gratefully acknowledges the support of the
Ontario Arts Council and the Canada Council for the Arts for our
publishing program. We acknowledge the financial support of the
Government of Canada through the Canada Book Fund.*

ONTARIO ARTS COUNCIL
CONSEIL DES ARTS DE L'ONTARIO
an Ontario government agency
un organisme du gouvernement de l'Ontario

Canada Council   Conseil des Arts
for the Arts   du Canada

Funded by the Government of Canada
Financé par le gouvernement du Canada

Canadä

MIX
Paper from
responsible sources
FSC® C103567

Published by
SECOND STORY PRESS
20 Maud Street, Suite 401
Toronto, ON M5V 2M5
www.secondstorypress.ca

To all my students, past, present, and future.

CHAPTER 1

I took a short detour on my way to Mrs. Abrams's classroom after school. I wanted to do something I was too embarrassed to be seen doing during regular school hours. As I approached the trophy case, I glanced around. Just five minutes after last bell and the hall was quiet. I stopped in front of the glass case. At last, I was alone with my pretties. The sports awards weren't really my bag, though I could appreciate the happy little statue-people poised mid-athletic feat. What I wanted to see was the Valedictorian Award. The names etched on little gold plaques had reached legendary status in my mind: Ava Matheson, Charles Ling, Adam Goldstein. They were all scholarship winners whose futures were as shiny as the trophies in this case. My name would be next; I just knew it: Alison Green, written in Copperplate Gothic on its own plaque (yes, I knew what font they used—the trophy store was surprisingly open about such things if you called them).

I pressed my palm and splayed fingers against the glass case. Which is when Charlotte Russell turned the corner at the end of the hall. I jerked my hand back, but I'm pretty sure Charlotte had already seen me petting the trophy case. I mean, we were the only two people in the hall, so I was hard to miss. I could not believe my luck. Of all people, Charlotte Russell, the very coolest person in our school, had just seen me at my geekiest. Charlotte wore her wavy, dark-brown hair short in what I was pretty sure was called an undercut. Her T-shirt sleeves were rolled up, and you could see the suggestion of a tattoo peeking out underneath her right sleeve. Two small black spacers stood out in stark contrast to the fair white skin of her earlobes. She didn't exactly fit into a school full of girls with long hair who all loved to wear leggings and the latest trends. Me? I was a sad compromise of the two. My mousey hair hung mid-length, and I wore jeans with Converse sneakers. I was Average Teenager from any high-school movie produced in the past five decades. Charlotte was badass. And she had seen me petting a trophy case.

I started preparing a series of excuses for what she'd witnessed. "Hi, Charlotte. I was just killing a spider. I'm tough like that." "Oh, hey, Charlotte, I was thinking how lame awards are. I'm planning to vandalize the trophy case. Just doing some recon now." Obviously, I had nothing. So I was mostly relieved when Charlotte turned the other way. Mostly. Another part of me was disappointed not to have an excuse, even an embarrassing one, to talk to her.

I glanced at the Valedictorian Award one last time, then headed to the stairway. I couldn't let my shameful little moment in front of Charlotte distract me. I had a plan, and this meeting was a big part of it. Mrs. Abrams had told me at lunch that she wanted to talk to me. She said she had a favor to ask. Whatever that favor was—walk her dog, clean her car, donate a kidney—I was going to say *yes*, because that yes would get me one step closer to seeing my name on that plaque. I knew this would be a pivotal moment that I would remember in years to come.

I took long, purposeful strides into the room. The chairs were up on the desks and the whiteboard was wiped clean. The only sign the room had played host to teenagers all day was an overflowing garbage can beside the door. Mrs. Abrams, her gray hair swept up in a messy bun, motioned me over to her desk. I took a deep breath before approaching.

"Alison, I wanted to talk to you about the school play."

"What about the school play, Mrs. Abrams?"

"I've helped produce the school play for the past fourteen years now, and I thought it might be time to let someone new learn from my experience. Your teachers speak highly of you."

I could feel myself blushing. "Thanks."

"Not many young people could take on the responsibilities of being a coproducer, but I think you can. I could use your help."

"I'd be happy to help out." I was worried I sounded a little too enthusiastic, a little too much like a brownnoser.

"Excellent!" Mrs. Abrams didn't seem to find my enthusiasm off-putting. Instead, she plopped a giant red binder overflowing with loose papers on the desk in front of me. "Here's the production book with all the information from last year's show. You should read it through tonight. I know the show is four months away, but there's a lot for you to do. You need to get started right away."

I picked up the Red Binder and some papers slipped out. I bent down to gather them and looked up at Mrs. Abrams as she spoke. It felt a bit like I was kneeling to her. I had to get ahold of myself. I straightened. "Ah, Mrs. Abrams, I was hoping that maybe you could put a word in for me when the time comes for the teachers to start discussing valedictorians. I know I haven't done anything yet, but I promise you, I will be a great coproducer and I'd—"

"Sure, sure. Anything you want, Alison. Now remember to read through that binder tonight."

Mrs. Abrams shooed me out the door. I left, clutching the binder to my chest, some loose papers gripped in my right hand. I could feel the tight smile I'd plastered on start to slip, just a little.

CHAPTER 2

That night I did as Mrs. Abrams had asked and read through the Red Binder, even though I found a lot of it (okay, most of it) difficult to understand. I made a list of questions, then hole-punched and organized all the loose pages. I felt like I was off to a good start as a coproducer. By the time I walked into Mrs. Abrams's class the next day, I was smiling again and ready to work.

"Oh, Alison, I'm glad you were able to look over the production book. You should start assembling your crew. I have an appointment outside of school today, so I must run." With that, Mrs. Abrams swept past me, jacket slung over her forearm. I'd like to think she paused for a moment in the doorway, some whisper of guilt making itself heard, but I think it's more accurate to say that she walked out swiftly, her gray hair swishing and a bounce in her step. I followed her more slowly out the door.

I met up with my sister and my best friend in the gym, where the school's basketball team, the Otters, were being soundly beaten by a visiting team. Though their players were all shorter than ours, they probably practiced together sometimes, given that they knew how to do things like pass the ball. Becca, the aforementioned best friend, was grinning and clapping, her curly brown hair bouncing gleefully. Annie, my younger sister, was shouting at our team, "Defense!" Though she was smaller than almost everyone in the stands, her voice cut through the noise. That's how enthusiastic she was. The opposing team's fans seemed a bit confused by all the cheering and general merriment coming from the students in our section of the stands. I guess they didn't know our reputation. The Otters had lost every game so far this season. This losing streak was itself a source of great pride, but what really filled the stands was the fact that the Otters boasted the most fights in the league. Nobody from our school came to a game to see skilled athletes. They came hoping for a fight. Given the dour faces of our Otters, it looked like they would not be disappointed.

I squeezed in next to Becca, and she screamed "Whoo!" as the opposing team made another basket. I sighed and tried to find a way to balance the Red Binder on my knee without knocking into either Becca or the fan to my right. Without looking at me, Becca said, "Weren't you supposed to be meeting with Abrams? I thought for sure the game would be over before you were done. If you want a drive home, I can give you a lift once the slaughter is over." Becca knew I was one of the few people who didn't like cheering our team on to violence, but she also knew I hated taking the bus. I appreciated that she drove me and Annie home almost every day, so I tried not to complain about having to stick around for the occasional game/brawl.

"Thanks, Becca. Yeah, I met with Mrs. Abrams. It was a short meeting." I gave up trying to open the binder in the packed stands and glanced at the scoreboard. I winced: 60–4. The fight today was bound to be bloody.

"Yeah?" Becca kept her eyes on the game and rubbed her hands together. Annie was cheering louder than ever.

"Well, it wasn't really a meeting. She just said she had an appointment and left. But she did tell me I should get *my* crew together soon," I told Becca. I practically had to shout to make myself heard.

"So?"

"Shouldn't they be *our* crew?"

"Al…" Becca put a lot of emphasis on that one syllable of my name. I knew it meant she thought I was overthinking things. Again.

"What?" I picked at a corner of the binder.

"Al, she had an appointment. Don't read too much into it. HEY! HE CAN'T DO THAT TO YOU!" Becca shouted this last part at one of our players who had lost the ball to a kid who looked to be a good three years younger and fifty pounds lighter than him. Someone behind us threw popcorn in the general direction of the basketball court. It mostly landed in our hair. Becca picked the kernels out of her hair and popped them into her mouth while I shook out my hair and let the popcorn land on the ground. I had to give the fans credit—they came prepared. I just hoped someone wasn't hiding rotten fruit or eggs to throw if the game got too boring.

"Speaking of getting a crew together—"

Becca whipped her head around to glare at me. "Oh no. You are not dragging me into another activity I don't care about. Wasn't it bad enough when you got me to cover those basketball games for the school paper last year? Don't you remember how that ended?"

It was hard to deny that it had been a disaster. Apparently, Coach Isaacs hadn't known that the student body was proudest of the Otters' headlocks, not their free throws. Isaacs had demanded that we not only print a retraction, but that I also resign as editor. Thankfully, Ms. Merriam, English teacher, newspaper faculty consultant, and diplomat extraordinaire, had intervened, and I was allowed to stay on as editor, though Becca was more than happy to resign as sports reporter.

"It won't be like that this time! I'm sure we can find you a job you'll love!" The crowd groaned and clapped half-heartedly as one of our players made a shot that went into the basket. Even he seemed surprised when the scoreboard changed to 60–6. In fact, he was watching the scoreboard when the player he should have been guarding dribbled right by him.

"Yeah? What job would that be?" Becca raised one bushy eyebrow.

"What about assistant stage manager? You get to, um, work backstage. And you get to help me since I think I may be both the producer and the stage manager." Even after googling "role of producer" and "role of stage manager," I still couldn't quite tell the two jobs apart. I just knew that the Red Binder seemed to want me to "interface with the director" and "organize technical aspects of the show." Whatever that meant.

"Why would I want to do that?"

"Life experience?" My voice went up an octave as I tried to sound persuasive.

"Pass."

"Looks good on a university application?"

"Nope."

"Favor for a good friend?"

Becca snorted. "If we were keeping track of favors, you'd owe me at least fifty by now. Sorry. Not biting."

I was desperate, so I pulled out the big guns. "Because Jack is going out for the lead and we all know he'll get it, and you've had a crush on him since the ninth grade and this could be a chance to spend time with him?"

"I don't know what you're talking about." Becca stopped watching the game long enough to make sure Annie, who was seated on her other side, wasn't listening in. Becca's tawny skin hid any blushing, a fact I envied, but it was still obvious she was uncomfortable.

Annie chimed in, "Oh, come on, Becca. Even I know you have a crush on him. It's not exactly a secret." Apparently, she *had* been listening to us, even though she had seemed completely mesmerized by the disaster on the court.

I decided to use this opportunity to change targets. I leaned forward so I could see around Becca and get a good look at my sister. Annie calmly met my gaze, ice-blue eyes and dark eyeliner adding emphasis to her no-way-will-you-play-me-like-that look.

"You know, Annie, I'll also need a prop master."

"Hell no."

"Mom's car." I knew I only needed those two words.

"You wouldn't." Annie glared at me.

I coolly turned around and feigned interest in the game. "Wouldn't I?"

We watched the game in silence for a while. Even a brief shoving match, which had most of the Otters' fans on their feet, went unnoticed. Becca was probably mulling over the fact that her secret crush wasn't so secret, while Annie was surely doing some complicated math in her head. Had enough time passed that it wouldn't seem like such a big deal anymore? How long would she be grounded if Mom did find out? Did she have enough in equivalent blackmail to keep me quiet? I'd done the math. I knew I had her, but I didn't want to press too hard. Let her do the work and arrive at the same answer I had.

"What do you think, Becca? Assistant stage manager? You get to feed actors lines and hang around backstage." I could see that Becca was still hesitant. "What if I promised not to ask you to do any other activities for the rest of the year? I won't even ask you to join the grad committee."

"Swear on the Valedictorian Award, and you've got yourself a deal." Becca jabbed her index finger in the general direction of the lobby for emphasis.

I raised my right hand. "I, Alison Mary Green, do solemnly

swear on the Valedictorian Award that I will not make Rebecca Choukri-McArthur join any other activities for the remainder of this—our graduating—year, so long as she promises to fulfill the duties of assistant stage manager for the school play." I was glad the people around us were wrapped up in the game. It was one thing for your best friend to know about your obsession with becoming valedictorian; it would be quite another for the whole school to know.

Becca nodded, turned her attention back to the game, and said simply, "Okay."

"Don't you think it's weird that you know my middle name, but I still don't know yours? How bad could it be?"

"Don't push your luck, Al." Becca was smiling, so I knew we were okay.

I chanced a quick look at Annie. She was scowling, her blue-for-now hair half covering her face. I could tell she'd done the math and didn't like the answer. Maybe it was time to give her ego an out.

"You know, it's mostly seniors who work on the play, Annie. You'd be one of the few grade nines." Annie grunted. "You'd also get to miss some classes for dress rehearsals," I added.

"Whatever. Fine." Annie jumped to her feet with the rest of the crowd as two forwards wrestled on the ground and an exasperated referee blew his whistle over and over, to no avail. I let her save face and hoped that she'd end up liking the job enough that she wouldn't want to find a way to get even with me.

CHAPTER 3

"You didn't tell me it was going to be Shakespeare!" Annie tossed the photocopied script on the table. Becca kept flipping through her copy as if there were some kind of mistake.

"Why does it matter?" As if I didn't know. Shakespeare made an already difficult task practically impossible. Our school wasn't what you'd call "artsy." After all, the only reason the student population came out to basketball games was because they hoped for a good fight. No one was going to come see some play in "Old English," as many of my classmates called it. I remembered Mr. Kay's repeated attempts last year to explain that Elizabethan English was actually modern. It was like watching someone smash their head repeatedly against a brick wall—oddly fascinating, but you also worried about them. The English department had a hard enough time selling Shakespeare to a captive audience. What hope did we have?

"You know damn well why it matters," Annie muttered as she went back to opening cardboard boxes.

Annie and Becca had agreed to help me take inventory in the drama department's storage room after school. We were supposed to figure out what props, backgrounds, and costumes from previous shows could be reused. So far, we'd found a few spiders' nests, which Annie had refused to approach until the spiders were safely removed, some ripped costumes, most of which smelled like old BO, and a box of foam swords, all of which were mysteriously bent. The dust was bad enough that our hands looked like we'd been digging through dirt. I had a hard time believing that anyone had been up here in recent years. Annie and Becca were discouraged enough at the prospect of helping produce "Ye Olde Shakespearean Disaster," as they were now calling it, so I felt it was my duty to stay positive about, well, everything. At least on the outside. On the inside, I was panicking a little.

I checked the Red Binder again, hoping to find an answer there. I stopped flipping when I found a page titled *First Steps to Putting on a Show*:

1. **Choose a script.** (Already chosen by Mr. Evans, our enthusiastic, if eccentric, drama teacher/director. It might not have been a popular choice, but—as Mr. Evans had pointed out to me earlier that day—it was a cheap one. You don't have to pay royalties to a playwright who's been dead for more than four hundred years.)

2. **Get your team together.** (Mr. Evans would be holding auditions early next week, but in the meantime, I'd at least found my assistant stage manager and my prop master. Though my assistant stage manager might quit soon if my prop master didn't stop poking her with a foam sword.)

3. **Create your budget.** (Mrs. Abrams's "budgets" for past years consisted mainly of receipts stapled together and a note from the school principal to "be reasonable, damn it." Not exactly the detailed, itemized list I'd hoped for. However, I did have a pretty good sense that we would need to do things on the cheap, which was why we were digging through the drama department's castoffs instead of studying for a math test or watching paint dry—either of which would have been more fun.)

4. **Make a schedule.** (The Red Binder included a lot of notes on past productions, but nothing so mundane as a straight-forward schedule. There was a Puppies of the World calendar from ten years ago in which Mrs. Abrams had written help-ful notes like "dir. mtg" and "check pst." Unless Mrs. Abrams stopped changing direction every time I saw her in the hall-way, I didn't think there was much chance that I'd be able to crack the code.)

5. **Have fun!** (I resented the exclamation point at the end of this step. It felt like some sadistic coach who yells at you from the sidelines to get your act together while you're

limping with a sprained ankle and the opposing team is twenty points up. You can't order someone to have fun, can you?)

"You know how I said you were being paranoid about Mrs. Abrams?" Becca held a stringy object that might have been either a mop or a wig at one point, her nose wrinkling.

"Yeah?"

"I take it back. That old bat totally knows what she's doing. She got out while the getting was good." Becca tossed the mop/wig into the discard pile.

"I think the drama department also knows what it's doing. Free labor! That's what we are," Annie piped up. She was crouched in the corner opening unmarked garbage bags and emptying out what looked to be strings of Christmas lights. To protect against the dust and spiders, she had pulled the front of her hoodie over her mouth. With the hood up, she looked a bit like a Jawa from *Star Wars*.

"There's bound to be something we can use in here," I said, trying to sound positive. That was when I found a box of moldering clown noses. I don't know if mice had been eating them or if that weird spongy material naturally disintegrates over time, but the noses were pockmarked and discolored in a way that made me think this was what post-apocalyptic clowns would wear.

"First spiders and now creepy-ass clown shit? I am done." Annie pitched the string of lights she'd been untangling onto the floor, then wiped her hands on her jeans, leaving a smear of gray-brown dust down the length of her thighs.

"I can't believe you're still afraid of spiders," Becca said to Annie.

"Oh yeah? So you don't mind that there's a spider in your hair?" Annie asked.

Becca's whole body shuddered, then she dumped her curly hair upside down, all the while screeching, "Is it gone yet? Is it gone yet?" Annie's laughter must have clued Becca into the joke because she stopped shaking out her hair. She was about to say something else to Annie when she looked over at me.

The thing about best friends is that they know how you're feeling just by looking at your face, even if you think you're doing a good job of hiding your emotions. So Becca must have known I felt like crying when she said, "Maybe *it is* time for a break, Al. Why don't we go to the caf and get some of that gross tea you like so much?"

"Green tea isn't gross," I mumbled as I followed her out the door and down the corridor to the caf. Annie followed behind, digging her phone out of her pocket and texting someone— probably about how her overbearing older sister was using her as slave labor. I should have been annoyed, but I was feeling too hopeless to care.

We entered the cafetorium and I was grateful to notice that it was mostly empty—fewer people to avoid. Unfortunately, it still sounded like it was full to bursting. The space had been designed to act as both a cafeteria and an auditorium, so the dozen or so voices echoed and reverberated. The acoustics would be great for the play, but right now they were not helping calm my sense of dread.

Becca steered me to a table at the edge of the caf. She dusted off her pants and shook out her hair. I took her cue and tried to do the same, though I didn't put much effort into it.

Annie flopped into a chair and used her phone camera to get a good look at her own hair. As she ran her fingers through her blue strands, she grumbled, "I cannot believe I touched spiderwebs for Willy Shakespeare. Isn't it bad enough I have to read about those twitterpated idiots Romeo and Juliet this year?" I sat down beside her and rested my head in my hands.

Becca sat down across from me. "Annie, maybe you could lay off right now?"

Annie stared at her. "You're telling me you like all this 'thou' and 'doth' crap?"

Becca sighed. "I'm not saying that, I'm just saying…" She suddenly stopped talking and I lifted my head, following her gaze. Ah. Jack Park had just entered the caf. He was taller than most other people in the room and walked with a confidence that came from being well-liked. He wasn't the cutest guy at school, but there was something about Jack that drew people to him. It might have been that he was always quick to smile or that his dark-brown eyes seemed to see the best in the world. When he spotted us, he walked over. Not good news for Becca.

"Hey! What are the three of you still doing here?" Jack sat down beside Becca, facing me.

I couldn't bring myself to talk about the play, and Becca was now staring down at the table, so Annie answered for us.

"We're digging through boxes of useless crap in the drama department's chamber of doom."

I tried to stop her. "Annie—"

She cut me off. "What? That's what we're doing, isn't it? Whatever. I'm going to get a drink." Annie stalked off to a row of vending machines at the other end of the caf.

Jack chuckled. "She doesn't seem happy."

"Yeah, well, she's kinda right. We are digging through a lot of useless crap."

Jack tilted his head. "Yeah? Why's that?"

I wished Becca would answer, but she stared at her fingernails. This was on me. "We're helping out with the school play. Actually, I'm producing or stage managing the play. I don't really know what the difference is, but it seems like I might be doing both things."

There was Jack's trademark smile, genuine and warm and completely disarming. "That's awesome!"

I tried to smile back, but I couldn't. "Is it?"

"For sure! I heard Mrs. Abrams refused to produce the play this year, and Mr. Evans kept saying he wouldn't put on a play without a producer, so I was afraid there'd be no show. It's senior year—my last chance to maybe get a lead role." Jack ducked his head, maybe a bit embarrassed to admit he was hoping to get a leading part. He deserved it. Jack had been in a school play every year, going all the way back to *The Little Chicken That Made a Friend* in Grade 2. He was always cast in an important supporting role, but he never got the lead. I suspected it might have had something to do with the fact that his parents were Korean and that Jack didn't look like a "traditional lead," but we'd never talked about that possibility.

I was about to reassure Jack that I was certain this was his year when something he said sunk in. "Wait. Mrs. Abrams said she wasn't going to produce the play?"

Jack seemed confused. "Yeah. Why?"

Suddenly I was furious. "She lied to me! I cannot believe she lied to me!"

"Al, what are you talking about?"

"She told me we'd be *co*producing the play—together. She lied!"

Jack chuckled. "Ever notice how often Mrs. Abrams has student teachers? She kinda has a rep for passing work on to others."

How could Jack laugh? "This isn't funny!" I told him.

Jack smiled gently. "It kinda is."

I pointed at him. "Maybe to you, but I'm the one stuck doing a job I don't know how to do! It *is* going to be a Ye Olde Shakespearean Disaster!" I could hear the whine in my voice, but I couldn't stop it.

Jack ran a hand through his messy black hair. He looked nervous. "Did you say Shakespeare?"

"Oh, I definitely did." I was being petty. I was happy Jack felt nervous. Misery loves company, right?

"Which play?" he asked.

"*A Midsummer Night's Dream.*"

I could see him relax just a little. "At least it's a comedy,

19

right? And lots of great actors have played the role of Puck. So the language is a little—"

"Inaccessible?"

"I was going to say difficult. But difficult isn't a bad thing. It's a challenge, sure, but that's how we grow, right?" Jack was smiling once again. Good old Jack. Forever an optimist. When we were in first grade, Miss Sefina told us that our class pet, an aged hamster who'd been traumatized by less-than-gentle caregivers for three years straight, had escaped his cage and was missing. I was convinced Miss Sefina just didn't want to tell us the hamster was dead, but Jack looked for it every lunch hour for a week. The following Monday the hamster reappeared, and Jack declared he'd been right all along. Even back then I suspected Miss Sefina had replaced the beleaguered rodent, but if she had, it had been a convincing stand-in. Maybe Jack had been right to believe.

"Yeah," I said. I put a little more conviction in my voice. Fake it till you make it, right? "Yeah, you're right. Thanks, Jack. I think we better go sort out some of the mess in the storage room before we leave."

Jack wished us luck, and Becca waved good-bye, though only after he'd turned his back. Oh, Becca.

I'd gone to school with Jack since kindergarten, and I'd known him even longer. Our moms worked at the same law firm, and they liked getting us together for "play dates" whenever they wanted to complain about work. We'd played games of tag and fought over the last cookie on the plate for so many years that I found it easy to talk to Jack. Unfortunately, Becca did not. She was not someone who was used to her emotions getting the better of her. It was like she was mad at herself for having a crush and had chosen to remain silent in order to preserve her dignity. I often wondered if Jack had ever even noticed that Becca never spoke to him, and if he did notice, what he thought of it. After a disastrous foray into his love life two years earlier, when I (correctly, but unadvisedly) informed him that his girlfriend was a snob, I had vowed to keep my opinions about whom he should or shouldn't date to myself. Actually, I hadn't so much decided as had been told that I should keep such opinions to myself or risk losing the friendship. As a result, I could not advocate on behalf of my best friend, whom I most definitely thought Jack should date. What are you supposed to do when two of the best people you know would be perfect for each other, but you've been forbidden to interfere? I was starting to think Shakespeare had it right, "The course of true love never did run smooth."

CHAPTER 4

Charlie Egan was stripping. Right now. Right in front of me. His shirt was already off, and his hand was on his belt buckle. His shoes were still on, so I wasn't sure how he planned to take off his pants, but I didn't want to find out. (Okay, a little part of me wanted to watch him hop around with his pants around his ankles, but that was a *very small* part.)

"Charlie, that's enough for today, okay?" I managed to stay professional. Becca, seated to my right, was trying to disguise her laughter as a coughing fit. Out of the corner of my eye, I could see her big, curly hair bouncing, as if it, too, was in on the joke.

Charlie stopped, his belt open and his fingers poised oh so precariously on his zipper.

"But I'm not finished with the monologue."

"You are finished with the monologue."

"But I have this whole vulnerability thing I'm—"

"Charlie, we'll let you know. We have other auditions." Charlie shrugged and headed for the door. "Charlie, don't you think you're forgetting something?" I motioned at his shirt on the floor. He turned around, scooped up the shirt, draped it over his pale white shoulder, and sauntered out the door, as if he hadn't just tried to win a role in the school play by stripping.

"You know what's crazy?" Becca asked as she wiped tears of laughter from her eyes. "That wasn't the worst audition today."

"I'll admit we've had a bit of a rocky start to things." I pretended to consult the audition list so I wouldn't crack. I couldn't start laughing now or I might not stop.

"Al, this is not just a rocky start. It's a disaster. Charlie tried to strip for us. I'm straight, and even I didn't want to see that shit. And Caroline actually spit on you."

"She didn't mean to spit on me. She got a bit worked up and had a hard time with one of the lines." I wiped at my face, remembering the wet feel of her saliva on my cheek. The worst part was smiling and pretending everything was just fine, even as I watched the slow arc of her saliva coming right at me.

Becca shook her head at me. "Sure. Caroline was just a bit nervous. Tell yourself that. If Mr. Evans had bothered to show up, even he would admit we've got nada so far."

Two excruciating hours earlier, Mr. Evans had rushed out of the drama room just after last bell, shouting to us as we walked in, "Girls, I have to go. Mr. Wigglesworth needs me! Just take lots of notes on the auditions and we'll talk tomorrow. The show must go on!" The framed photo of a cute lap dog on Mr. Evans's desk suggested Mr. Wigglesworth was a pet, though neither Becca nor I was willing just yet to discount the possibility of an imaginary friend. Whatever or whoever Mr. Wigglesworth was, he was obviously very important to Mr. Evans because here we were, auditioning actors, even though we didn't know what we were doing. The room reeked of institutional disinfectant and nervous sweat. Right now, I couldn't think of anything more hellish. Well, I guess Charlie could have started with his pants instead of his shirt. So there was that.

"I choose to be optimistic," I said to Becca. So far, not one of the "actors" could have played Dead Person #5 in an episode of *CSI*. But I am a firm believer that your luck can always change.

And then Ben Weber walked in.

"Well, hello, ladies. I hope I didn't just interrupt a make-out session." Ben waggled his eyebrows at us, then ran his fingers over his gelled-back hair, making sure every strand was in place. He wore a blue polo shirt that might generously be described as fitted, but was more accurately just plain tight.

In a school full of mostly decent human beings, Ben Weber had the distinction of being a bona fide jackass. He never missed an opportunity to be pervy, and he was well-known as a guy who still thought wedgies were funny. Back in elementary school, he'd called Becca "McChowder" for a few days. He'd seemed very proud of his "clever" play on Choukri-McArthur, taunting her at every opportunity until Becca punched him in the nose. Not many people in our school were ignorant enough to make fun of non-Anglo last names or suggest the only reason two girls would kiss is to turn on some straight dude. This was part of why I didn't feel like I needed to join our Gay-Straight Alliance or make some big coming out announcement. I mean, the decent people were already decent, and I didn't want to waste my time trying to educate the morons of the world, like Ben. Anyway, it's not like I was in the closet or anything. It's just that I didn't want my sexuality to be everyone's business. It's not like straight people have to announce their sexual preference.

"Hi, Ben. What part are you auditioning for?" The words were polite, but I'm sure he understood that my tone was contemptuous. Although that might have been giving him too much credit.

"The king, obviously."

"Oberon?" I asked.

"No, the human one. You know, the one who defeated the Amazons." Ben flexed his bicep and winked at us. How he managed to keep up in all our Advanced Placement classes was beyond me.

"You're an idiot, Ben," Becca said.

"You don't know what you're missing out on, Becca."

"Oh, I do. So does the whole senior class. That's why no one will go out with you," Becca retorted.

I thought this would be a good moment to get things back on track, before we ended up in some ridiculous argument that would end with Ben high-fiving himself. "Ben, Theseus is a duke, not a king. But whatever. Do you have your audition piece ready?"

"I always come prepared." Becca rolled her eyes at me as Ben cleared his throat and ran through some tongue twisters. He stretched his neck, shook out his hands, then recited Theseus's lines from Act 1 in a surprisingly warm tenor, looking down at the script only occasionally. He ended his audition with Theseus's romantic declaration to his would-be wife, taking Becca's hand gently in his own: "Hippolyta, I woo'd thee with my sword, and won thy love doing thee injuries; but I will wed thee in another key, with pomp, with triumph, and with reveling."

Becca and I were shocked into silence. Damn it all, Ben was good. He played the part of the duke with dignity and strength, but also with a certain sensitivity. I felt like maybe I had underestimated Ben all these years. And then he giggled as he repeated, "Woo you with my sword." We didn't need the hip thrust to understand what Ben found so funny, but he did it anyway.

"Okay, Ben. We have to discuss the auditions with Mr. Evans. We'll get back to you." Ben strutted out the door. I looked at Becca and said, "I know I'm not a good judge of these things, but Ben almost seemed attractive for a few minutes, didn't he?"

"I feel so dirty." Becca pretended to dry heave but stopped abruptly as Jack walked in the door. She started organizing some papers on the desk in front of us, and I hoped for her sake that Jack wouldn't notice that the pages were blank.

I'd deliberately put Jack's name at the end of the audition list so that Becca's inevitable awkwardness wouldn't affect the rest of the auditions. I also thought that it might naturally lead to all of us walking out of school together. Maybe Becca would offer to give Jack a lift home. Maybe after they'd dropped me off, they'd have a deep conversation and start dating. Maybe they'd both thank me in their wedding vows. Of course, that would only happen if Becca spoke.

"Hi, Jack. I'm assuming you're here to audition for Puck?" I asked.

"I am. Um, was that just Ben Weber in here?" Jack looked over his shoulder and out the open door, the space between his brown eyes wrinkling in confusion.

"It was. Don't ask."

Jack chuckled. "That bad?"

"No, that good. I think we're going to have to give him a part."

"Wow. That's…unexpected."

"Right? But enough about Ben. We'd love to see what you have prepared. Wouldn't we, Becca?" I nudged Becca, and she managed a twist of the lips that was probably meant to be a smile. *Oh, Becca, you are not making this easy,* I thought.

Jack closed his eyes for a moment and took a few deep breaths. He was obviously a little nervous, and I was just about to say something reassuring when he launched into Puck's famous monologue from the end of the play. Ben had been good, but Jack was great. Seeing him audition after an afternoon of "actors" who kept pausing awkwardly when they had to say unfamiliar words was like watching Patrick Stewart play Macbeth after having just watched the latest teen heartthrob play the dark, sensitive love interest in some forgettable drama about vampires or kids dying of cancer. Listening to Jack recite Puck's monologue, I felt like Jack might just be able to make Shakespeare accessible. He made it sound so easy, so fun, so… cool.

"That was amazing, Jack!" I didn't feel like I needed to hold back in my praise. This was Jack—one of my oldest friends—and obviously, he deserved the role. "We'll definitely recommend you for the part. Won't we, Becca?"

Becca gave a terse nod.

"You think so? I was worried I went overboard by memorizing all the lines, but I just really want this part, you know? I can get a bit too enthusiastic about things. Anyway, I'm glad you liked it." Jack was beaming. Then there was an awkward pause as I tried to wait out Becca. *Say something*, I thought at her. The silence must have gone on too long because Jack eventually said, "So, I guess I'll talk to you two later?"

"For sure. Great job again, Jack," I said as he grabbed his backpack and walked out the door. I looked at my best friend and said, "Oh, Becca."

"I know," Becca said, forehead now planted on the desk in front of her. "I know."

CHAPTER 5

I was more than a little surprised when I spoke to Mr. Evans the next day and he seemed unsure about casting Jack as Puck. My surprise might even have gotten the better of me. I *may* have said to him, "Are you crazy? He was great! You can't cast anyone else!" Not exactly the way a student traditionally speaks to a teacher, I know.

Thankfully, Mr. Evans seemed unruffled. After my little outburst, he explained, "I'm sure Jack was great. He's been in *my* drama class for three years, after all. That's why I want to use him to our best advantage. We might need to double cast some of the roles, so I was thinking of having him play Oberon and Theseus."

"But they aren't as cool as Puck!" Yup. That was some first-class arguing there. My two years on the debate team had really paid off.

"No, they aren't as 'cool' as Puck. But who else could we cast as Oberon and Theseus? It needs to be someone who can be regal and command the audience's full attention."

I knew then what I had to do, but I really, really didn't want to do it. I looked through my notes from the auditions, even though I knew there was only one solution. "Well, actually, Ben Weber was pretty good, and he auditioned for Theseus."

Mr. Evans's gray eyebrows shot up in surprise. "Is that so?"

"Yeah, but he didn't want to play Oberon. I don't know if he'd want to take on both roles. He kind of made fun of Oberon, to be honest. Plus, he's, uh, hard to work with." I couldn't give Ben a full-out endorsement. My conscience and gag reflex would not allow it.

"Now, Alison, I know you and Ben are rivals for valedictorian, but I wouldn't have thought you'd stoop to this."

My mind raced. How did Mr. Evans know who was in competition to become valedictorian? Wait. Had he just said that Ben Weber was in the running? Ben Weber, who often wore a T-shirt that said "Federal Boobie Inspector?" And was Mr. Evans accusing me of trying to sabotage Ben? Didn't any of the teachers know how stupid he was? "But, Mr. Evans, that's not—"

He cut me off with a smile. "It's settled, then, Jack can play Puck and Ben will play Theseus and Oberon. I'm sure you can convince him to play a double role. It's such a privilege, after all."

"I guess I can try." I didn't feel like I could tell Mr. Evans that I was possibly the last person who would be able to talk

Ben into doing anything. Any conversation between the two of us ran the very real risk that I might strangle him. Mr. Evans had all but accused me of being petty, so I didn't see a way to decline this task without seeming childish.

"Great!" Mr. Evans straightened his sweater vest, then sat down at his desk. "We have one more actor to audition today. She couldn't make the auditions yesterday, so I told her she could come by after school. She should be here any minute now. I'd appreciate it if you could stay to watch her."

"Sure," I answered half-heartedly, digging my phone out of the front pocket of my backpack. I needed to text Becca and Annie to let them know I was going to be late. They'd be waiting in Becca's car by now, since I'd told them I only needed fifteen minutes to speak with Mr. Evans. Normally I didn't like using text shorthand—I mean, it doesn't take that much longer to write in full sentences than it does to write like an illiterate ten-year-old—but I needed to be fast: *Gon 2 b late. Sorry. Plane laser.* I pressed send without fixing the autocorrect because the final auditionee had just appeared in the doorway. It was Charlotte Russell, looking just as cool and composed as ever. Her full lips were quirked into a half smile, which looked both self-deprecating and a bit ironic, as if she knew how ridiculous all of this was and was sharing the joke with us.

Charlotte leaned against the doorway and said, "Hey, Mr. Evans, thanks for letting me come in to audition today. I appreciate it."

Mr. Evans grinned broadly at Charlotte, his high, bald forehead folding into a series of happy wrinkles. "Not a problem at all. I'm glad you decided to finally audition for one of my plays." Mr. Evans waved her in, and Charlotte tossed her bag on the floor next to the door as she made her way to the center of the room. I suddenly noticed that I was standing next to Mr. Evans's desk like a servant waiting on her master. I decided to casually lean against the desk, but I kind of miscalculated the distance.

"Alison! Are you okay?" Mr. Evans seemed genuinely worried for me as he bent down to help me to my feet. I took his hand and pulled myself up.

"I'm fine," I lied. My butt felt like it must be turning black and blue as we spoke, but I couldn't admit that in front of Charlotte. And now I was standing even more stiffly than before, too sore to sit and too nervous to lean. So that I would have something to do with my hands, I pulled the Red Binder out of my backpack. I opened it to a random page, pretending to be looking for something, and when I looked down at the page heading, it was like it was mocking me: "First Aid Protocols." *Har, har, Red Binder, you think you're so funny, don't you? See how funny you think it is when I toss you in the garbage after this is all over. See if you laugh then.*

"What do you think, Alison?" Mr. Evans asked me. Both he and Charlotte were looking at me.

"Um, seven?" Why had I just said that? Why would seven be the answer to his question? Unless he wanted to know how many dwarves Snow White lived with. *Please let him be a big Disney fan. Please let him be a big Disney fan.*

"Alison, I asked you who else had auditioned for the role of Hippolyta. Are you sure you're okay?" Mr. Evans cocked his head to the side. Charlotte seemed to be on the verge of laughing. I couldn't blame her. I was both mortified and a little angry. I mean, I could have been hurt, and here she was practically laughing at me.

"Sorry. Yeah, I'm fine. No one has auditioned for the role of Hippolyta yet."

"It's fate! You must audition for the role, Charlotte. Just give me a moment to get settled and you can begin." Mr. Evans sat in his chair, his pale, freckled hands folded together on his desk. I shifted my weight to my other foot, trying (and failing) to stay comfortable.

It turned out that Charlotte was one of those actors who seem to just play themselves, but it worked for her. Maybe it worked because Hippolyta, the former Amazonian queen, is proud and strong like the real-life Charlotte, but I suspected it was because Charlotte was so charismatic that you wanted to keep watching her no matter what role she was playing. Plus, she was fearless. When she made eye contact with us—her audience—it felt like she was daring us to try to turn away. Her eyes were a cool blue, I noticed, before I had to break eye contact. She had barely finished her audition when Mr. Evans was on his feet, applauding. "My Hippolyta! I've found you! I want you to learn Titania's part as well, because I'd like to cast you in both roles. I'm sure you'd make an excellent fairy queen."

Charlotte's ironic half smile had returned, and she said, "Queen of the fairies, huh? I think I can get behind that." And then she looked right at me and winked. Winked! I felt myself blushing and cursed my capillaries for betraying me yet again.

Charlotte told Mr. Evans she'd study Hippolyta and Titania's lines, then both she and Mr. Evans started walking to the door. He had to turn back to say to me, "Alison, you can't stay here."

I shook my head, slung my backpack over my right shoulder, and tried to hide a wince when the bag hit my butt, which was still feeling sore from the fall. I was grateful when Charlotte and Mr. Evans turned right and headed for the front doors of the school. I turned left instead, making my way to the student parking lot at the back of the building. It gave me time to worry obsessively about what Charlotte had meant by the wink. I wondered if I had imagined it, though I was pretty sure I hadn't. Then I wondered if it was just another way to show she didn't take all of this too seriously; I should have found her too-cool-for-school attitude annoying, but it seemed so light-hearted that I didn't. I hoped she wasn't making fun of Mr. Evans, who might be a bit self-important, but who obviously loved what he did and seemed to think highly of her. I didn't *think* she was making fun of him, since it hadn't exactly happened behind his back. So what else could it mean? Was it possible she was flirting?

I was still contemplating the wink when I reached Becca's car, a thirteen-year-old Honda Civic named Harvey. Harvey didn't look like much, but he saved us from a loud thirty-minute bus ride home, so we treated him with great reverence. As soon as she spotted me, Becca called out of the driver's-side window,

"Glad you made it out alive. Those plane lasers sounded dangerous. I was starting to think I'd be able to listen to all of *Ghost
Stories* before you got here."

"Yeah. So disappointed that didn't happen," Annie muttered from the backseat. Becca was obsessed with Coldplay, a
fact I found endearing and which my sister found aggravating.
Only the threat of public transportation kept Annie from muti-
nying against Becca's tight control over the aged CD player.

"Sorry I'm late," I said, climbing into the front passenger
seat.

"What took so long?" Becca asked as she performed the
many rituals Harvey demanded before he'd start up: She rubbed
the dashboard three times counter-clockwise, patted the steering wheel, and then quickly pressed on the gas pedal as soon
as the engine turned over. The rituals performed, she pulled
Harvey out of the student parking lot and onto the road.

"Oh, there was one more audition. Someone who couldn't
make it yesterday," I said, trying to sound casual.

"Yeah? Who?" Becca asked.

"Charlotte Russell," I said, looking out the side window
and making brief but awkward eye contact with the driver stuck
in traffic beside us.

I probably shouldn't have turned my head. I also should
have moderated my voice better so that I didn't sound like a
prepubescent boy. But it was too late. Becca had caught on that
there was more to this story. "Charlotte Russell, huh? You mean
the girl with the tattoo?"

"Does she have a tattoo?" I asked, hoping to sound non-chalant. I failed. Miserably.

"Everyone knows she has a tattoo. Oh my god. You like her, don't you?" Becca grinned at me, her brown eyes twinkling in delight.

"Becca! The road!" Becca slammed on the brakes just in time to keep from rear-ending the SUV in front of us, but only barely.

"Don't change the subject," she said, not a trace of concern in her voice.

"I don't think basic road safety is a change of subject, Becca." I took a few deep breaths. No matter how often I drove with her, I could not quite get comfortable with her laid-back approach to driving.

"You're still avoiding the question."

"No, I don't like her. She's just really interesting." I picked a hair off my jeans.

"Just really interesting?" Becca sounded unconvinced. "So did you speak to her?"

"I…well, I didn't speak to her directly," I admitted.

"You totally have a crush on her," Becca concluded, smile growing.

"I don't even know that she's gay," I said lamely.

"You're both such losers," Annie added helpfully, poking her head between our two seats. "Obviously Charlotte is gay. Just look at her haircut."

I craned my neck to glare at her. "That is such a stupid stereotype."

"Stereotypes have to come from somewhere. With a haircut like that, she has to be at least bi," Annie replied, totally unfazed by my stern look. "Neither of you can even talk to your crushes. It's so sad."

"Annie?" I said.

"Yeah?"

"Mom's car."

"You're going to have to stop using that some time, you know." Annie retreated into the backseat. She was angry. I could tell by the way she hunched her shoulders.

"Maybe. But not today. So just shut up, okay?"

Becca turned up the music and we listened to Coldplay the rest of the way home.

CHAPTER 6

That night, I closed the door to my bedroom, lowered the lights, and played some yoga videos from YouTube in an attempt to relax. When deep breathing and downward dog didn't do the trick, I cleaned my room, a time-tested cure for stress. While my sister liked to make a cocoon of all her earthly belongings, curling up comfortably in a bed littered with dirty clothes and crumpled homework, I felt most clear-headed in a tidy room. I started by changing my sheets and fluffing my pillows, but I couldn't stop thinking about Charlotte's wink and my sister's stupid comment about her hair. I hated those kinds of stereotypes, which was part of why I kept my own hair ponytail length. As much as I hated the stereotype, though, a part of me wanted Annie to be right. This is one of the problems with being an "invisible minority." People don't know you're gay unless you tell them. I wasn't about to ask Charlotte if she liked girls, so I could only play a ridiculous guessing game based on a hairstyle and a twitch of the eye. It felt unfair. Yes, everybody has to wonder if the person they like likes them back. But when you're gay, you have to first wonder whether or not that person even likes your gender. And whether they know *you* like your gender. Anyway, I did not have time to obsess over some girl who might or might not be gay or bisexual, not if I wanted to be valedictorian.

I needed to do something more active to keep my brain from spinning in circles, so I decided to tackle my desk, the one place where I couldn't seem to maintain order. I kept my clothing organized by season, I limited myself to one wall poster (Rosie the Riveter), and I worked hard to keep my books contained in the tall Ikea bookshelf squeezed into the corner of my room, though there was some double-stacking to make them all fit. But when it came to my desk, it seemed like all my organizational powers failed. There was never enough space for everything. I couldn't even fit my laptop on the desk anymore. I did most of my work on my bed these days, using my desk less as a workspace and more as a storage container. The Red Binder took up a goodly amount of space, but there were also smaller binders full of handouts and homework for my classes, as well as Post-it notes with to-do lists. There was a pile of university brochures, which I had been slowly accumulating for three years now, as well as various drafts of essays I'd been writing for scholarship applications. I liked to write on my laptop, but I needed to print my work to edit it, and I was too scared of computer crashes to throw out old drafts. My desk looked like the workaholic's version of my sister's bed.

I began by sorting through the Post-it notes, throwing away the ones that had every item on the list checked off. (Don't you just love the feeling of checking off the last item on a to-do list?) Then I started shuffling through loose papers, which is when I spotted a small rainbow pin, one of the little tokens my parents would leave in my room from time to time to show their support. My parents weren't ones for grand gestures, so instead, they showed that they accepted me by bringing home pins and talking about the great gay couple who worked at their law firm. I had come out to my parents only last year, after Becca had insisted that coming out to just her wasn't enough.

We had been eating supper at the kitchen table. It was unusual for all of us to be home at the same time, especially on a weeknight. My parents are both lawyers, and they love what they do, which means they often work late. With my extracurriculars and Annie's busy social calendar, we usually eat alone or in twos. That night, though, we were all there, and we were having a good laugh about Grandma's new obsession with memes.

"She also sent me the Grumpy Cat one! I didn't have the heart to tell her everyone knew about Grumpy Cat years ago," I told my mom. My lasagna was getting cold, but every time I tried to take a bite, someone else mentioned a ridiculous e-mail from Grandma, and I'd be laughing again. Things had gotten a bit competitive.

"Wait. Wait. I beat all of you," my sister said. Annie was laughing hard enough that her eyes were watering, smudging her eyeliner. "She sent me the one with a scared-looking cat that said, 'Wait. Lesbians eat what?' I mean, she's like, ninety! Why is she sending sex jokes to her granddaughter?"

"You win, Annie," my father said, blushing deep red, but still laughing. My mother was giggling so much that she couldn't even sip her water. Annie took a little bow, acknowledging her win.

Now, a person with better timing than me—and let's face it, most two-year-olds have a better sense of timing than I do—would not have chosen this exact moment to come out to her family. A bad lesbian joke is not exactly the best conversation starter, but I'd been waiting for weeks for an opening. So I jumped in. "Actually, guys, I have something I want to tell you."

"If your grandmother sent you a sex joke too, I don't want to know." My father smiled at me as he raised his hands, signaling his surrender.

"Well, she also sent me the meme about oral sex, but that's not what I wanted to tell you." Yes, I said *oral sex* in front of my parents. I sounded like an uptight gym teacher who's been roped into giving the sex talk to a group of freshmen. My dad choked on a bite of garlic bread, and my mother patted him hard on the back. When it was clear he was breathing again, I decided I'd come too far to look back, so I continued. "Sorry. I didn't mean to…. Listen, I've been meaning to tell you that, well, I'm gay."

They were all silent. I think they were trying to figure out if I was being serious. To be fair to them, we had all just spent half an hour telling increasingly ridiculous stories about Grandma's awkward e-mails. Who could have seen this abrupt change of tone coming? It was Annie who spoke first, and for once I was grateful for her bluntness. "Al, you have the worst timing of anyone I know." She smiled as she shook her head at me.

My parents took another couple seconds to recover from the shock, then they tripped over themselves trying to make up for the awkward silence. Mom said, "Thanks for sharing that with us."

Dad got serious and went into lawyer mode, asking me how long I'd known, whether I'd been facing any trouble at school as a result, and how I'd like to proceed. I told him I'd only known for sure for a few months, that no one at school knew except Becca, and that I had no idea how to proceed. Other people might have taken his questioning as cold, but I knew it was his way of showing he cared, and I appreciated the fact that I wasn't the one leading the conversation anymore. Obviously, I could not be trusted to be in charge of things.

After I'd answered his questions, Dad said, "You'll tell us if you face any kind of discrimination or bullying at school, right?" My father's sense of justice was part of what made him a great lawyer and one of the things I most admired about him. I nodded, tears threatening at the corners of my eyes.

My mother stood up from the table then, walked over to me, pulled me from my chair, and hugged me tight. My mother is a marathon runner who works out regularly. Her hugs are

42

no joke. After an awkward yet comforting minute of intense hugging, she held me at arm's length and said, "We love you no matter what, and we're here for you. We're incredibly proud of you. You're so brave." I admit that I cried at this point, both because I felt protected and loved but also because I felt a bit guilty. What was brave about coming out to parents you knew would be there for you? Coming out is brave when your parents are fundamentalist Christians who you know will kick you out of the house for telling them the truth. I didn't deserve that kind of credit, but it wasn't like I could explain that to my mom and dad, who were both hugging me now.

Annie was using this as an opportunity to eat the last piece of garlic bread. Later, though, she gave me a quick side hug and said, "It's cool that you told us."

And that had been it. I'd come out to my parents and sister, and life went on much the same as it had before. Since then, we hadn't had any deep conversations about it, though Mom had given me the rainbow pin, some pamphlets, and a book titled *The LGBTQI Survival Guide for Teens*. Over the summer, my parents asked if I wanted to go to the Pride Parade, and I declined. Mom also sometimes asked me if there were any girls I liked, just as she asked Annie if there were any boys she was interested in. I politely told her "No," while Annie just rolled her eyes and whined, "Mom!" I didn't know what I'd say if my mom asked me now if there were any girls I had a crush on at school. Obviously, there was one. But I wasn't planning on doing anything about it, so what would be the point in admitting it? Part of me wondered how out and proud I could really be if having a crush seemed so ridiculous to me. It was an uncomfortable thought, so I tried to ignore it as I arranged and rearranged the piles of paper and binders on my desk.

CHAPTER 7

Now that the play was cast, Mr. Evans started issuing commands regarding the set, costumes, and props. I needed to find people with actual artistic talent if we were going to create the "magical, but edgy atmosphere—something like a cross between Lady Gaga and Disney" that Mr. Evans wanted. (At least, that's what he wanted now. Only a few days before, he'd wanted "understated.") I couldn't draw a stick figure, I didn't know much about fashion, and I couldn't be trusted with power tools, so it was time to do some more recruiting. The Red Binder suggested I start by speaking with the art department, so I headed there after school with Annie, who had reluctantly agreed to be my tour guide. She was the only person I knew who continued to take art classes once they became optional, and I was hoping she could help me communicate with the locals.

The art room smelled pleasantly of dried paint, a scent I associated with kindergarten and sunny afternoon naps. Along with the gym, this was one of the few corners of the school that remained busy after last bell. The artsy kids stayed late most days to work on paintings, sculptures, and weird multimedia pieces under the watchful eye of the much-beloved Ms. James. When we walked in, not a single student looked our way. They were concentrating too hard on what they were doing to be bothered by a stranger passing through their land.

"Hey, Ms. J," Annie said as we wound our way through stacks of art supplies to the teacher's desk in the far corner. It was clear that Annie felt comfortable here, and I wondered how many afternoons she'd spent in this room. I always just assumed that she waited for me impatiently in the gym or caf when I stayed late for an extracurricular, but I was starting to think I might have been wrong.

"Hi, Annie." Ms. James smiled but didn't look up from a painting she was closely inspecting. We stood at her desk next to a goth girl who I was pretty sure was the painter, given the dark tones and blood-like splashes in the piece. Ms. James took off her purple cat's-eye glasses and let them dangle on the chain around her neck. She said to Goth Girl, "I like what you're doing with texture here, but you need to think about creating more contrast." Goth Girl nodded and took the painting back to her workstation without looking at us even once.

Ms. James turned to us, wiping her hands on a paint-splattered apron. Her skin was a rich black, and she wore a beautiful teal-and-yellow head wrap that only an art teacher could so perfectly pair with purple eyeglasses and a deep coral tunic. "What can I do for you?"

Annie dived in. "We need to find people who can help out with the school play. My sister," she nodded at me, and I tried to give my most winning smile, "is producing the play, and we need people to do sets and costumes. I'm acting as prop master or I'd do some scene painting myself. Anyway, we were wondering if you could recommend some people."

Ms. James looked at me and cocked her head to the side. "I heard Mrs. Abrams asked a student to take over producing the school play this year. It's a lot of work." She sounded a little like she pitied me. Or maybe it was that she didn't entirely approve of Mrs. Abrams. It was hard to tell.

"It is a lot of work, but I like being busy," I answered, not wanting to let on how overwhelmed I felt. The valedictorian wasn't going to be some whiner who complained about too much work. I had to keep it together.

There was something about the way Ms. James looked at me that made me think she knew this was an act of bravado, and I appreciated that she didn't press the point. "So you need help finding people. What exactly needs to be done?"

"We need a costume designer and a set painter." I looked around the room at the potential candidates. I was not filled with confidence. Besides Goth Girl, who had just shot us a dirty look, there were a couple of boys dressed like hipsters wrestling with a wire sculpture, a group of girls wearing T-shirts with political statements like "Good planets are hard to find!" who were gluing things to a large canvas, and a guy wearing a red blazer and oversized glasses working on a laptop. These were not my people. I felt self-conscious in my boring long-sleeve T-shirt and clean black sneakers. Annie, with her blue hair and knee-high, multicolored socks, fit in much better.

Ms. James seemed to guess what I was thinking because she said, "Annie knows most of the regulars here, but why don't I introduce you to some people who might be able to help you? Zach, can you come here?" The boy in the blazer put up a finger to ask for a second, finished something important on the laptop, then walked over to us. Up close, his outfit looked even more unusual for a high-schooler. He'd pushed up the sleeves of the blazer, and his black T-shirt was only half tucked into his dark skinny jeans. The whole look seemed purposeful and sophisticated in a way that I associated with teens on TV shows, the ones who are dressed by stylists.

"What's up, Ms. J?"

"This is Annie's sister. She's producing the school play, and she wants to speak to you." Having made introductions, Ms. James left us to see to a student who wanted her help.

"Hi, I'm Alison." I reached out a hand. Zach looked at it for a second before shaking it. Of course, I know it isn't normal for teenagers to greet each other with handshakes, so I couldn't blame him for hesitating. "I don't usually go in for handshakes," I explained, making things even more awkward.

Zach laughed. "I'm very pleased to make your acquaintance, Miss Alison, play producer. How may I be of assistance?"

I looked at Annie for help. She got right to the point. "We're looking for a costume designer for Ye Olde Shakespearean Disaster."

"What? I'm the one gay guy you know, so obviously I have to be the costume designer?" Zach frowned at Annie and crossed his arms.

I was horrified. What had Annie just done? I had to fix this. Fast. "Um. No, that's not…It's just…you're the best-dressed person here, so Annie must have…I mean, would you like to build sets?" I finished lamely.

Zach snorted. "Hell no. What do I know about building things? Clothing, I know. I'd be happy to help out with costumes." Annie, who must have known Zach was into fashion, was having a good giggle beside me. Yup, I was making a real impression here.

"That would be great," I said to Zach, after I had properly glared at Annie. "Production meetings should start in a few weeks. They'll be Wednesdays after school. Will that work for you?"

"It will. Annie can give you my number, and you can text me when the first meeting is set up." Zach nodded at Annie in what I now suspected was a conspiratorial way, then returned to his laptop.

Ms. James came back to check on us. "I'm assuming Zach agreed to do costumes?" I nodded. "Great! So that means you still need a set painter. I think Jenny would do a wonderful job with sets."

"Jenny?" Annie asked. She looked a bit nervous; she was even biting her lower lip, a habit she had mostly given up ever since I'd teased her about it being her "tell."

"Jenny is a great painter, and she can work on a large scale," Ms. James told us.

"I know, it's just that she…" Annie was looking for the right words—words she could use with a teacher, "she can be difficult to work with."

Ms. James nodded. "She can be, but she's also very talented, and I think this would be good for her." I could see why the art kids liked Ms. James. She was honest, and she obviously cared about them.

"Okay." I could tell Annie was still hesitant, but she trusted Ms. James, so I decided to as well.

"Great!" Ms. James's smile was warm and wide. It was the kind of smile that was contagious, like a yawn. "Jenny? Can we speak with you?"

Goth Girl looked up from her work, which was when I understood she was Jenny. I'd like to say that I decided then to give her a real chance, that I chastised myself for judging her based solely on her appearance, but I didn't. What I did was stare at Annie and try to communicate telepathically *How are we going to get out of this?* Annie must have understood the desperation in my eyes because she shrugged her shoulders as if to say *I have no idea. We're in for it now.*

Jenny made her way over to us, her combat boots thumping ominously with every step. She stopped a few feet away, keeping an awkward distance between us. I could see that she was giving me the once-over and she was not impressed. As I got a good look at her, I realized that I had grossly underestimated just how much dark eyeliner a person could wear. I'd always thought Annie was much too liberal with her eyeliner, but this girl looked like she must go through a new eye pencil every week. Her eyes were a dark brown, and the whole effect, especially against her pale skin, was a bit intimidating. Which I suppose was kind of the point.

Ms. James made the introductions, and this time I didn't try to shake hands. "Jenny, Alison here is producing the school play. She's looking for a set painter, and I recommended you."

Jenny continued to glare at me. I looked at Ms. James, desperate for help.

"I think adding set painting to your portfolio could help with your applications for art school," Ms. James explained. At this point, Jenny finally blinked.

"What's the play?" Jenny asked, looking at Ms. James and ignoring me completely.

Ms. James turned to me for the answer. "*A Midsummer Night's Dream*," I croaked.

"A comedy? I don't think so." Jenny started to turn away from us, which is when Annie finally spoke up.

"Mr. Evans wants to do something different with the design," Annie said, her voice much steadier than mine. "I think he'd be open to suggestions."

"*My* kind of suggestions?" Jenny challenged Annie.

"Why not? You'd just have to help him see things your way," Annie answered.

Jenny locked eyes with Annie, who was much better at holding eye contact than her older sister. "Okay, then. I'll do it. But only if Mr. Evans will agree to my designs." I did *not* like how she said that. I was pretty sure she was going to design something freaky that not even Mr. Evans would like. But I didn't have a better alternative, or any alternative at all, so I just stood there, completely useless.

Ms. James clapped her hands together. "I'm so excited about this! I think you're going to make something memorable together. There's a lot of potential in *A Midsummer Night's Dream.*" Ms. James grinned at all of us. At least one person was happy with this arrangement.

CHAPTER 8

During AP English the next day, instead of listening to Ms. Merriam's lecture on the psychological significance of monsters in Victorian literature, I grappled with my own monster, the grotesque Ben Weber. I split the page in my notebook into two columns: Things I'd Rather Do Than Ask Ben to Star in the Play and Reasons I Have to Ask Ben to Star in the Play. One list was longer than the other. Guess which one.

Things I'd Rather Do Than Ask Ben to Star in the Play
1. Tell Becca I think Chris Martin is overrated.
2. Explain Grumpy Cat to Grandma.
3. Take the blame for Mom's car.
4. Break up a fight between the Otters and their nemeses, the Bridgetown Bears.

5. Finish watching Charlie Egan perform his striptease.
6. Eat the surprise casserole from the caf.
7. Set fire to my own hair.

Reasons I Have to Ask Ben to Star in the Play
1. There's no one else who's even half as good as him.
2. If I refuse to ask Ben to play Oberon, I can kiss good-bye any chance Mr. Evans will recommend me for valedictorian.
3. I said I would do it.
4. Rehearsals start tomorrow.

At the end of class, I fearfully approached my monster. Though he wasn't breathing fire or making a feast of a village, he was doodling boobs all over his binder, so I was repelled already.

"Ben, we need to talk." No time for pleasantries when you're dealing with a monster. Best to just get to the point.

"Yeah?" He didn't even bother to look up from his "masterpiece," too focused on his shading to make eye contact. It was probably for the best. Many monsters have the power to immobilize their prey with their eyes.

"Mr. Evans wanted me to ask you to be in the play. You in?"

"Who am I playing?" Damn. I had hoped that Ben would be too distracted to ask any pesky questions.

"Theseus, just like you wanted."

Ben looked up now. He squinted his rat eyes at me. Classic monster intimidation. "And?"

"What do you mean?" I tried to sound casual. I failed.

"You're being way too weird about this. You're leaving something out. I can tell." Ben could be perceptive at the most inopportune moments.

"Fine. Mr. Evans wants you to play two roles: Theseus and Oberon."

"The king of the fairies?"

"Yes. It's one of the lead roles."

"No thanks." He closed his binder.

"What do you mean, 'no thanks?' You auditioned!" I was losing my cool. He was being so infuriatingly blasé about the whole thing. How could I do battle with a monster who coolly said, "No thanks?"

Ben stood up and started packing his bag. He spoke to me slowly, as if I was too stupid to understand him. "I mean, I don't want to play Oberon."

"Why not? Afraid you won't be 'manly' enough to play the part?" I knew I was taunting the beast. I didn't care.

"I can show you how manly I am." Ben stepped into my personal bubble, angling his face down toward mine.

"Get. Out. Of. My. Space." I stood my ground, though I wanted to take a big step back.

"Don't be so sensitive." Ben rolled his eyes.

"If a guy told you to get out of his space, you'd respect that. You're being sexist." I issued this as a challenge.

"Yo! Ben, you coming?" One of Ben's friends poked his head around the corner of the classroom door. I could see I'd lost Ben's attention. I no longer felt like a knight nobly fighting a monster. I felt like a producer who had let her personal feelings get in the way.

"Yeah, bro. I'll be there in a second." Ben nodded to his friend and went back to packing his bag. He wouldn't even look at me, and I didn't know what to say. He was still an idiot, and I couldn't apologize for something I didn't feel sorry about. But I could also feel my chance of making this happen slipping away.

Ben walked around the table, still avoiding my eyes. When he was nearly at the door, I half-shouted, "What about the play?"

"What about it?" He turned to look at me, slouching against the doorjamb, cool and nonchalant.

"Are you going to do it?"

"I won't play Oberon."

"You have to." I could hear the whine in my own voice.

"No, I don't." Ben sneered at me.

Ms. Merriam chose this moment to step in, and I have never been more grateful to a teacher in my life. "You know, Ben, Oberon is a great character. He's actually got more lines than Theseus." I could see Ben was listening to Ms. Merriam, so I kept quiet.

"Yeah?"

"Absolutely. And you know that universities like to see that students are well-rounded, right? I know you're a strong hockey player but showing scholarship committees that you're also involved in the arts could go a long way to making your application stand out."

"I guess so," he said slowly. I had tried fighting the monster. Ms. Merriam was charming it instead. Her tactic was working much better.

"Why don't you go to the first rehearsal, just to see what you think? Alison, when do the rehearsals start?" Ms. Merriam looked at me, her brown eyes radiating warmth. She was giving me a chance to smooth things over.

"Tomorrow. I know Mr. Evans really wants to see you there, Ben." I tried to follow Ms. Merriam's lead. I couldn't say I wanted Ben there, but I could honestly say he was wanted.

"I guess I could come to the rehearsal." Ben sounded like a toddler who's been convinced to try a bite of brussels sprouts but is ready to spit them out if they're as disgusting as they look. "See you tomorrow." I wasn't sure if this last part was for Ms. Merriam or for me, or maybe for both of us.

After Ben left, I stayed behind to thank Ms. Merriam. She sat on the corner of one of the tables. Her feet dangled, and it struck me that she was much shorter than me. She always commanded so much respect that I never thought of her as short. I leaned against a table opposite her. "Thanks for helping out. I told Mr. Evans I'd talk to Ben. I probably shouldn't have promised to do that. Ben and I don't exactly get along."

Ms. Merriam laughed. "So I noticed."

"It's just…he seems so smart sometimes and then he makes ridiculous sexist comments!" I could feel myself getting angry all over again.

"You know, Ben has his reasons for being who he is. Just like you have reasons for being who you are. He probably doesn't understand why you care so much about the play. And I can see you don't understand why he acts so…" Ms. Merriam played with her turquoise drop-earrings as she took her time picking the right word, "…*macho*."

I snorted. "Yeah. *Macho* is about right." I stood up to go. "Thanks for helping me out."

"Anytime. Good luck with the play." Ms. Merriam nodded at me as I headed out, and I wondered if maybe she was using the charm offensive on me as well. If she was, I didn't mind. Somehow, it always felt like Ms. Merriam was on your side, even when she was suggesting you play nice with a monster.

CHAPTER 9

"Be the tree!" Mr. Evans instructed us, his own short arms stretched high above his head, fingers splayed. "Feel the warm breeze in your branches, the sun on your leaves. Now the wind is picking up. Sway with the wind, my trees!"

I looked around me and was amazed once again that people were going along with this. A roomful of perfectly rational—or at least not certifiably insane—people were seriously pretending to be trees. And I was one of them, though I had to admit my arms still felt like arms and I wasn't keeping my eyes closed, as I had been instructed to do and as all the others seemed to be doing. I was humoring the deranged person who was apparently in charge of all of us. Maybe the others were as well? I could only hope this was the case as I watched them sway in the pretend wind.

"Now we're worms," Mr. Evans informed us. He dropped

to the ground, legs together and arms pressed to his sides. He squirmed around. Most of the actors joined him, but I was happy to see that some of them, like me, were hesitating. This was a school floor, after all. It was not going to be clean. If we were lucky, it was covered in regular bottom-of-shoes gunk like mud and gum. If we were unlucky, someone had stepped in dog doo that morning. One by one, even the hesitators eventually followed their director's lead. The last actor to join them was Charlotte, and she just squatted, her hands never touching the contaminated floor, waiting for the worm section of this game to end. My respect for her increased as I also squatted. She flicked her eyes sideways at me, smiled, then brought her focus back to Mr. Evans. I don't think she wanted him to know she was cheating, and neither did I, when it came down to it.

Fittingly, Ben Weber was the most enthusiastic "worm." I wished Becca was there to see him slither on the ground, but I was pretty sure she would have flat-out refused to join in this ridiculous exercise in the first place, and I wasn't sure what poor Mr. Evans would have done in the face of Becca's no-nonsense attitude. I wondered once again why the producer/stage manager had to join the warm-ups. I hadn't signed up to be an actor, so why did I have to "get in the creative head space," as Mr. Evans put it? When I had tried to stay seated, though, Mr. Evans had pulled me to my feet and told me I was part of the family. I didn't want to be part of this family now that I could see them writhing on the ground.

"Take a deep breath, open your eyes, and let's all make a circle," Mr. Evans told us, his voice far off and floaty. His face had taken on a definite pink hue and his forehead was beaded with sweat from the exertion of changing too quickly from tree to worm to human. We formed a ragged circle, and everyone waited for Mr. Evans's next instructions. "This exercise is called Look Up. It will teach you to focus and will help you all grow together as a group. You will start by looking at the floor. When I say 'look up,' you must look directly into the face of someone in the circle. If the person you are looking at is looking back at you, you are both out, and you must leave the circle. We'll keep going until there are only two people left."

This game sounded slightly less awful than rolling around on the floor. At least it seemed less likely that I would contract a communicable disease while playing it. Although it did mean I was going to have to make awkward eye contact with people.

"Ready?" Mr. Evans asked. I quickly scanned the group, making a mental note of where Charlotte was standing. I couldn't look her way. "Heads down, everyone." But what if she was looking at me? Wouldn't I want to know she was looking at me?

"Look up!" Mr. Evans sounded so excited that I thought he might have jumped up and down, clapping his hands, if the game had allowed for it. I looked in the opposite direction of Charlotte, at a girl in Grade 10 who was playing one of the fairy attendants. She wasn't looking at me, so unfortunately, I was still in the game. Apparently, no one had made eye contact during this first round, so no one was out. This game was going to last forever.

"Heads down." We all obeyed in a way that made me question whether teenagers were really so rebellious after all. "Look up!" This time I looked at Jack, safe Jack, who was grinning as he and one of the other actors were the first two to leave the game. They laughed together as they dropped out of the circle. *Lucky bastards.*

"Heads down. Now look up!" This time I peeked at the red-haired boy standing next to Charlotte. I strained my peripheral vision trying to decide if she was looking in my direction. Try as I might, I couldn't tell if her eyes were even open. This time four people were out. The circle was shrinking, which was not good. Not good at all.

"Heads down. And look up!" Mr. Evans's enthusiasm wasn't wearing off. He let out a loud guffaw as he made eye contact with a nervous junior who was playing a minor role in the play. I had looked to my left, firmly deciding not to look anywhere near Charlotte this time. Which is when I saw Ben cheating. He was looking at the floor, avoiding eye contact with everyone. I wanted to call him out on it, but then Mr. Evans instructed us, "Heads down. Look up!"

Things were moving too fast. My disgust at Ben's childish behavior had thrown me off balance, and I panicked. Which is how I found myself gazing into the cool blue eyes and long, dark lashes of the girl I was crushing on. She didn't break eye contact, and I felt a warm blush radiating from both my cheeks and my chest. My eyes started to feel dry, but I didn't want to be the first to blink. It was a bit like having a staring contest with a cat. A sexy, unattainable, sardonic cat. Just as my eyes started to water, Mr. Evans reminded the group, "Anyone who's made eye contact is out." Charlotte turned to leave the circle. I walked away as well, my pulse throbbing because I'd just made a fool of myself. *Stupid Ben. This is all his fault.* I was fuming as I watched the rest of the game unfold. Thankfully, Ben could no longer get away with cheating once the group had been reduced to only five students. He lost to a pair of sophomores who giggled excitedly at winning this ridiculous game. I wondered vaguely if Mr. Evans was brainwashing us by having us perform embarrassing tasks, but his gleeful congratulations to the final winners was too genuine. He loved every minute of this.

Warm-ups finally over, I was allowed to take a seat at a small, scarred wooden desk in the corner of the room. The actors dragged chairs into a circle, scripts resting in their laps. My job now would be to take notes as Mr. Evans ran the actors through the rehearsal. I pulled a perfectly sharpened pencil, a blue pen, and a yellow highlighter out of my pencil case, and arranged them next to my copy of the play. Grudgingly, I also took the Red Binder out of my bag and slid it onto the desk, thinking at it, *Behave yourself.*

Mr. Evans all but forgot me as he ran the actors through their lines for the first time. They had to stop often to talk about what the language meant. Some of the actors seemed a bit overwhelmed now that they were getting down to the work of not just parroting but understanding Shakespeare's words. Not Jack or Charlotte, though. They didn't trip over words or stop the rehearsal to ask Mr. Evans to explain what they were saying. To my great annoyance, neither did Ben.

I continued to listen and watch, underlining any passages Mr. Evans told me would require further scrutiny and highlighting any bits Mr. Evans thought we might be able to cut. I was able to relax into the role of notetaker, and soon Mr. Evans told us all, "Great job today, my thespians!" Ben smirked and threw a look at an immature junior who giggled in response. Mr. Evans either didn't understand why they thought this was funny or decided to ignore it. "Keep reading through the play. It will get easier. Give yourselves a round of applause for all your hard work today." The cast clapped, then dispersed to gather belongings, answer texts, and generally get ready to re-enter the world of the normal teenager. Jack came over to speak to me, pure joy radiating from him. I couldn't help but smile back.

"Thanks for recommending me for the role of Puck, Al. I owe you."

"You don't owe me anything. You deserve the role." Seeing Jack so pleased, I no longer minded having to ask Ben to take on the role of Oberon. One of my oldest friends was beaming. If I had to see Ben every week at rehearsals, so be it.

My happy little moment came to a standstill when I saw Charlotte walk toward us. Part of me hoped she would turn away, speak to someone else, but a bigger part of me hoped she was coming to talk to us, to talk to me.

"Hi. I don't think we've been introduced. I'm Charlotte." Her eyes were so blue, I couldn't think of anything else.

"Are you sure?" I asked. *Why? Why would you ask that, stupid brain?* Jack looked at me quizzically.

Charlotte laughed. "That's some existential shit. I don't think I'm up to questioning my own existence after that rehearsal. I mean, what if I'm actually a tree?"

Jack tried to help me out, adding, "Or maybe we're all worms."

I forced a laugh. "Sorry about that. It's been a long day, what with having to transform from a tree to a worm in a matter of seconds. Of course, you know your own name."

Jack took charge of introductions since I obviously could not be trusted to speak for myself. "Charlotte, this is Alison. She's producing the play."

"I know. She was at my audition. Plus, she kinda stands out in this crowd."

Jack nodded his head. "Yeah, Al's definitely not an actor-type. For one, she's quieter than the rest of us." He looked at me, giving me a chance to say something for myself. I couldn't think of anything, so he continued. "But don't let that fool you. Al's got big dreams too. She's a shoo-in for valedictorian."

I blushed. This was not how I wanted Charlotte to think of me. "I'm not a shoo-in."

"You're being too modest," Jack teased.

"No, I'm not."

Jack looked at Charlotte like they were in on a joke together. "She's being too modest."

"Jack, stop it!" Even I was surprised by my tone. I was suddenly angry and embarrassed.

Charlotte saved us. "You two must be old friends. Only old friends bicker like that."

I felt bad about the outburst. "Jack is one of my best friends. He's almost like a brother." I smiled at him, but Jack didn't smile back.

Charlotte elbowed Jack in the ribs. "Just what every guy wants to hear from a cute girl. Right, Jack?"

Jack rolled his eyes theatrically and forced a smile. "Oh, for sure."

I was trying desperately to think of what else I could say to make things up to Jack (and maybe also to keep talking to Charlotte) when my phone buzzed. I glanced at the screen and was reminded that I had a big test the next day. I couldn't waste time trying to talk to a girl who probably thought I was a complete nerd. "Sorry," I said. "I have to go. I told Becca I'd meet her to study for our biology test. You wanna come, Jack?" I hoped the invitation would smooth things over.

"No, thanks. I told my parents I'd be home for supper tonight." Jack finally smiled, and I hoped he'd forgiven me for being snippy.

I picked up my backpack and tucked my pencil case into a side pocket. I was fighting to get the Red Binder to fit into the bag when Charlotte said, "I better get going too. See you two around."

"Not if we see you first," I blurted out. I could not believe I'd ended our first conversation with a bad dad joke. I wanted to climb inside my backpack and disappear. Charlotte raised an eyebrow and smirked as she left.

"I'm such an idiot," I mumbled.

Jack gave me a little side hug and tried to reassure me.

"No, you're not. Though I don't think I've ever seen you so… flustered before. Is being a producer stressing you out?"

I didn't want to tell Jack why I was flustered so I just nodded my head a little. It wasn't exactly a lie. Being a producer *was* stressing me out. Jack gave me another gentle squeeze and said, "I should head out. Try to relax a little tonight, okay, Al?"

Once I was alone in the room, I sat back down in my chair and stared off into space. I replayed the whole conversation in my head three times before my phone buzzed and I remembered I had other priorities.

CHAPTER 10

She said I was cute. She called me cute. Me. Cute. I couldn't stop obsessing about that one throwaway comment. It probably didn't mean anything. Charlotte was just teasing Jack. But she could have said many other things, like I was well-organized. Instead, she said I was a cute girl. Which obviously meant I had to avoid her. She was trouble, a distraction. I was always saying the wrong thing around her, like asking if she was sure of her own name. I was grateful there was a whole week before the next rehearsal. Maybe I would contract some highly contagious virus and be excused from attending another practice. In the meantime, I would do my homework, hide in the library at lunch, and pray to any and all deities that I wouldn't run into Charlotte in the halls.

When Becca reminded me a couple days later that we needed to start work on designing the set, I was briefly excited at the prospect of spending time in the art room, a place I knew Charlotte didn't frequent. And then I remembered I would have to talk to Jenny, our friendly neighborhood goth girl. Becca suggested that we bring Annie with us to help communicate with Jenny.

I texted Annie, asking her if she could meet us in the art room. I got two words back, and I knew we were on our own: *b-ball game.*

."Damn," Becca said after reading the text.

"It'll be fine. Jenny's agreed to do the sets, so she's gotta be open to talking to us." I firmly believed that one of the keys to being a good leader was faking optimism so others wouldn't be put off by your panic. That might work with your average worker bee, but not with a best friend. Becca saw right through me.

She rolled her eyes. "Sure, Al. I'm sure she'll be totally open to talking with us."

Our short trip to the art room was completely silent. It gave me a chance to appreciate the late afternoon light streaming in the windows, to notice how heavy my bag was now that the Red Binder had taken up almost permanent residency there, and to wonder for the 2064th time if Charlotte really thought I was cute.

I nodded at a busy Ms. James as we entered the art room. Looking around, I was again struck by the atmosphere of concentrated creativity and quiet introversion the art kids had cultivated. It contrasted almost comically with the boisterous, nearly manic vibe of the first play rehearsal I had attended only two days earlier. I wondered what would happen if the drama and art kids switched places for a day. Would any of the people in this room pretend to be a tree, much less a worm? Spotting Jenny in the darkest corner of the otherwise bright room, I was sure there was at least one person who would not in a million years have followed Mr. Evans's instructions.

"Here we go," I said to Becca, who grimaced in response but followed me to stand beside Jenny's easel. We both waited while Jenny aggressively slashed black paint onto a canvas that looked like something Jack the Ripper might have hung on his wall. She made no sign that she even saw us standing there.

When it was obvious that Jenny either didn't notice us or had no intention of acknowledging that she knew we were there, I broke the silence. "Hey, Jenny."

Jenny's black-rimmed eyes stood out against her whiter-than-white skin as she glared at me in utter silence.

"This is Becca." I pointed at Becca.

"Hi." Becca didn't smile, but both her tone of voice and body language spoke of a polite willingness to engage.

Jenny still said nothing. Her body language said she wanted us to bugger off.

"Becca's the assistant stage manager."

"Good for her." At least Jenny was speaking, even if she was being sarcastic. Becca's eyebrows went up, but she let the comment pass, and I decided to ignore Jenny's rudeness as well. Challenging her wouldn't get us anywhere.

"We thought we could talk about the set design."

"Yeah?" Another slash on the canvas.

"Yeah. We were wondering if you'd thought about the design at all. Maybe we could brainstorm some ideas?"

Jenny turned her back on us, digging through a beat-up canvas messenger bag propped on a table beside her. I looked at Becca, who shook her head and shrugged her shoulders. I was just about to say something when Jenny turned back to us. She held a paint-spattered sketchbook out to me. I took it, waiting for some explanation or instruction. When none came, I opened the sketchbook to the first page.

As I think I've mentioned, I'm no artist. So anyone who can draw a hand that doesn't look like some lumpy claw-thing has my respect. But even someone with as little artistic skill or knowledge as me could appreciate the bizarre beauty of the sketches I was now slowly flipping through. Jenny was obviously most interested in the fairy section of the play, especially the night scene. Her sketches were dark, but fanciful. In one drawing, strange mosses dripped from the twisted branches of shadowy trees. A quarter moon tried bravely to peep out from behind this haunted forest landscape. In another sketch, a green, full moon took up almost the entire page, looming over a handful of spindly trees. Becca inspected the sketches from over my shoulder.

"These are beautiful, Jenny," I whispered. I felt the images deserved some sort of reverence.

"They really are," Becca added.

"Whatever." Jenny had returned to her canvas. She would have seemed completely unaffected by our compliments if it hadn't been for the slight blush peeking out from behind the layer of almost-white foundation she wore. Becca smiled then. Her sense of humor was too finely developed for her to find Jenny's angsty artist act anything but funny. I shot her a warning look, and she stifled the smile. I had the distinct feeling that Jenny wasn't someone who would take kindly to being laughed at.

"Could you recreate these on a large scale?" I asked.

"Obviously."

I didn't think that was so obvious, but again I let it go. I needed her on my side, or at least not angry with me, for what I had to say next. "I'm not sure this is exactly the vision Mr. Evans has for the play."

"Yeah? Well, that's *my* vision. If I'm going to be the set painter, that's what I want to paint."

"I get that. But is there some flexibility? Maybe in the colors?" I couldn't see the ghostly blues and sickly greens appealing to Mr. Evans, a man who wore bright purple and fuchsia on a pretty regular basis.

"No."

I looked at Becca for help. She shrugged.

"Okaaay," I dragged out the word, hoping that I could think of something else to say, something to change Jenny's mind. I couldn't. "I guess we can at least show these to Mr. Evans."

"Whatever."

"It was nice talking to you, Jenny." Becca's sarcasm nearly matched Jenny's.

"Whatever."

Becca took a deep breath. Time to get out of here before things got heated. "I'll let you know what Mr. Evans says. See you later." I gave Becca a gentle push. With one last exasperated look at Jenny, Becca headed toward the door. I followed her, sketchbook in hand. How on earth was I going to sell this dark vision of *A Midsummer Night's Dream* to Mr. Evans, a man who thought "darn" was a swear word?

At least Charlotte thought I was cute.

CHAPTER 11

At lunch the next day, Mr. Evans flipped through Jenny's sketchbook while I watched him and chewed on a hangnail. Becca, cool-headed as ever, played Candy Crush on her phone. I didn't like the way Mr. Evans's caterpillar eyebrows kept crawling closer together as he examined the drawings. I also didn't like his silence. Mr. Evans was a person who liked to smile big, whose freckled hands were always moving. He was oddly still as he contemplated the final sketch: the hauntingly beautiful green moon that Becca and I had both admired. I looked at Becca. She didn't even notice, engrossed as she was in her winning streak. I looked back at Mr. Evans, who gently closed the notebook and placed it on the desk between us. He tented his hands in front of his face, his elbows resting on the desk. He looked up at me, and I knew it was going to be bad news.

"Obviously your friend is quite talented," he started.

"She's not exactly my friend," I explained. As true as that was, it still felt a bit like a betrayal.

"I would love it if she could work on the show, whoever she is. But I was hoping for something a little more…peppy. Maybe something with a colorful, ethnic vibe."

"Ethnic vibe?" I repeated dumbly.

"Maybe something Native?"

"I don't understand." I looked at Becca again, hoping she might help, but she was still focused exclusively on her game.

"Or, maybe something inspired by Bollywood," Mr. Evans added helpfully, his enthusiasm for the idea evident in his massive grin.

"You mean, something Indigenous…or do you mean Indian…?" I was confused.

"I think the politically correct term is Native." Mr. Evans smiled knowingly.

At this point, Becca lost all interest in her game. She held her phone loosely in her left hand as she stared openly at him. This ridiculous game of teacher-does-not-know-best had finally caught her attention.

"I don't think so, Mr. Evans. Bollywood movies come from India," I said.

He flapped his hands in my general direction. "Well, wherever Bollywood cinema comes from, I think using some of its elements could make our production pop."

I made a noncommittal sound. I didn't know what to say to Mr. Evans that wouldn't be insulting.

Becca had no such compunctions. "I think that's called cultural appropriation."

Mr. Evans seemed genuinely surprised. "I don't want to appropriate anything! I just think our little fairies would look adorable in colorful kimonos."

"Kimonos come from Japan!" Becca looked at me to confirm both that she was right and that this was actually happening. I nodded at her, but I also tried to tell her with the piercing glare of my eyeballs to lay off and leave this to me. Becca did not suffer fools, and this was one fool I didn't want to insult. After all, Mr. Evans was ignorant—deeply ignorant, as it turned out—but he was the director of the school play, and I had to work with him one way or another. Given a choice, I would pick friendly over hostile any day of the week.

I tried to be diplomatic. "Mr. Evans, maybe we could add some color and pep without…using things from other cultures."

"I suppose so." Mr. Evans looked downcast, his high-voltage grin now only a whisper of a smile.

"What if we talked to Jenny about adding some brighter colors in her next round of sketches?" I opened the sketchbook to the full moon. "Imagine this with some blues, purples, and yellows."

"You don't think it's been done before?" Mr. Evans traced the outline of the moon with his index finger.

"Like stealing ideas from other cultures hasn't been done before?" Becca mumbled. I kicked the side of her foot, hoping Mr. Evans wouldn't notice.

I plowed on. "Mr. Evans, don't you want the focus to be on the performers? You're working so closely with the actors. You don't want the set to distract from their performances." I felt cowardly. Here I was trying to fool Mr. Evans into doing the right thing instead of just taking a stand for the right thing. First, I had to placate Ben's ego to get him to star in the play, then I had to stroke Jenny's ego to get her to hand over her sketches, and now I was outright fawning over Mr. Evans to get him to abandon his ridiculous plan.

I may have been disappointed in myself, but my strategy worked. Mr. Evans perked up. "That is true. So long as we have *some* brighter colors, I think these sketches could work." He cocked his head to the side as he re-examined the drawing. "Maybe she could also do something about these trees. I think they need some leaves. They look a little dead."

"I'm sure we can get Jenny to make some changes," I told him. Becca snorted, but I ignored her. I decided I had better get out now before I dug myself in any deeper. I held out my hand, and Mr. Evans passed me the sketchbook.

"Alison, you're doing a fabulous job as producer. I don't know what I'd do without you." I couldn't help but smile as Mr. Evans patted my hand. His enthusiasm was contagious. Mr. Evans loved "the theater" and he believed in everyone, even me. He was clueless about the world in a way that made me despair for our education system, but he also saw the best in people. I knew I didn't entirely deserve his praise, but I was going to take it anyway.

"Thanks, Mr. Evans." I smiled again. "We better get going. Class starts in ten minutes."

"Of course. See you later, girls." He waved us away, and we made our exit.

As soon as we closed the door to the classroom behind us, Becca stage whispered, "Did you forget that Jenny told us she wouldn't change her sketches?"

I groaned. "I remember." We walked down the busy hall to Becca's locker. She refused to carry around a backpack full of textbooks and binders like I did, so she always had to stop there between classes.

"So you just promised Mr. Evans something you can't do," Becca pointed out, none too gently.

"I know. But what else was I supposed to do?" I could feel my shoulders tensing as I grew defensive.

"I dunno. Maybe tell him his ideas are offensive and ridiculous? Say 'no' to someone for once?" Becca's comment stung, mostly because I knew she was right. She must have seen something in my face because she gently bumped me with her hip and said, "Oh, Al. You really know how to dig yourself into a hole, don't you?"

We stopped in front of her locker, and she opened her combination lock with one hand, then dug a textbook out of the precarious mountain of books, snacks, and gym clothing crammed inside. I slumped against a nearby locker and stared blankly down the hallway. Having retrieved the book, Becca was now busy trying to rebalance the mountain inside her locker. I didn't like her chances.

The bell was about to ring, so most people had already headed off to class. If the hall hadn't been so quiet, I probably wouldn't have noticed Ben. He was at the other end of the hall, where he seemed to be arguing with Zach, our costume designer. It was weird to see them talking, since they hung out in different crowds. Red-faced, Zach eventually threw up his hands and stormed off in the opposite direction. Ben ran his hands through his gelled blond hair as he watched Zach stomp away. He must have said something stupid or offensive to Zach. Of course. I was happy Zach had called him out on his shit. Ben got away with too much. He played the "free speech" card in class and acted like political correctness was a personal affront.

The bell rang and Becca slammed her locker shut, pressed a shoulder against it to keep it from popping back open, then quickly snapped the lock back in place. She tugged on my sleeve, hurrying down the hall. "Al, we have to get to class."

"Right." I shook my head, then hurried to fourth-period calculus. How Ben remained my main rival for valedictorian was a mystery almost as confounding as integrals.

CHAPTER 12

The Red Binder's advice on dealing with conflict between members of the production team was even less helpful than usual: "People want to be heard. Use a talking stick to allow each person to air his or her grievance. Encourage people to use 'I' statements instead of placing blame. When we listen to each other, any problem can be resolved!"

Oh yeah, Red Binder? You think I can just get a talking stick and Mr. Evans and Jenny will come together? More likely, Jenny will hit Mr. Evans with the talking stick.

I slammed the binder shut, but I could still hear it taunting me (it sounded oddly like my conscience, which sounded a lot like Becca right now): *There wouldn't be a problem if you hadn't promised them both something you can't deliver.*

If Becca hadn't sat down across from me just then, I feel almost certain I would have shouted at the binder. This would have been very, very bad given that we were in the crowded caf. I was grateful to Becca, both for saving me from making a public fool of myself and for the mug of green tea she shoved at me.

"It's not easy getting boiling water for your tea. Even the lunch lady judges you for drinking this stuff. That should tell you something, Al." Becca wrinkled her nose, maybe remembering the one time I'd convinced her to try some.

"It's full of antioxidants," I mumbled, playing with the tea bag's hanging tag.

"I'm just teasing you, Al. The lunch lady wears a hairnet, so who's she to judge?" Becca unpacked her lunch, munching on carrots dipped in hummus.

"Yeah." I blew on the tea as I scanned the room. Maybe I wouldn't see her. She hardly ever made public appearances, after all. I spotted someone dressed all in black, but when I took a closer look, it was definitely a guy. I was about to take a sip of tea when I spotted her: Jenny was in the caf. She was alone at a table in the far corner, her scowl plain even at this distance. I sighed and set the mug down.

"You're not going to drink that after all the trouble I went to?" Becca was now dipping cherry tomatoes in her hummus. I envied her the simple pleasure of enjoying her lunch.

"I don't deserve the tea yet. I have to go do something I don't want to do. I can have the tea when I get back." I stood up and shoved the mug over to Becca for safekeeping. She shook her head at me but continued to eat her lunch.

"You're weird."

"You know it." I gave Becca the best smile I could muster and then made my way through the crowded room, sidestepping juniors carrying trays of food and squeezing my way past a pack of giggling sophomores. I hoped Jenny might get up and leave before I made it to her table, but no such luck.

"Hey, Jenny." I sat down across from her, even though I worried that doing so would hamper my ability to make a quick getaway. It would be weird to conduct a conversation while looking down at her, so I perched myself on the edge of a hard plastic chair.

Jenny looked up at me, her mouth full. I could see that she was almost finished her lunch, even though lunch period had only started about ten minutes earlier. I guessed that she felt about as out of place here as she looked. The bright banter, fluorescent lights, and white-bread sandwiches were hardly a fitting setting for such a moody *artiste*. It's not as if I loved the cafetorium or anything. Cafeterias are always loud. And auditoriums are designed to carry sound.

Jenny swallowed her food and narrowed her eyes at me. "What do you want?"

So much for the pleasantries. "I need to talk to you about the designs for the set."

"What about them?"

I wished I'd brought my tea with me so I'd have something to do with my hands. Also, my mouth was feeling dry. I cleared my throat. "Well, Mr. Evans had a few notes he'd like me to pass on."

Jenny turned the full force of her scowl on me. "Like what?"

I considered just getting up and walking away then, but that nagging Becca-Red-Binder-conscience voice reminded me this mess was of my own making. "He thinks the drawings are beautiful. He has total confidence in your vision. It's just that he feels the sketches are a little too dark for a comedy. He'd like you to add some brighter colors."

"I told you I wouldn't change anything." Jenny wiped her hands on a paper napkin, crumpled it, and threw it on the tray in front of her.

"I know. It's just that Mr. Evans *is* the director." I left it at that, hoping Jenny could read between the lines.

Unfortunately, she was a little too good at reading between the lines. "So, everything you said to me basically meant nothing. Because *he's* the director, not you." Jenny said it with such contempt that it felt like she'd slapped me in the face.

I stared at the table. "I thought I could convince him to see how brilliant your designs are."

I heard the scrape of a chair being pushed back. I looked up as Jenny stuffed the remains of her lunch into a tattered canvas lunch bag. She was so upset that the knuckles clutching the lunch bag turned white. "I guess we're done, then," she said.

"Wait. Jenny, your sketches are great. Can't you just compromise a little?"

"No!" Jenny slammed her chair into the table, then marched off, the stomp of her heavy combat boots making so much noise that I could hear them over the din of the cafetorium.

I sat in shocked silence trying to gather my thoughts,

staring into space without even blinking. This was bad. This was very bad. I had just lost our set painter. The set painter I'd assured Mr. Evans would be amenable to making some changes. What was I going to tell Mr. Evans? How was I going to find another set painter? I couldn't go back to ask Ms. James for help. She'd want to know what had happened to Jenny. I didn't want to explain to her that I'd messed up. Royally.

I rested my forehead on the edge of the table and concentrated on breathing in through my nose and out through my mouth. I had to stay calm. I was not allowed to have a panic attack in the caf. I snorted. The idea of having a panic attack in this crazy mass of humanity all chowing down on lunch struck me as funny. Then it seemed really sad, and I had to hold back a rogue tear.

I felt a hand on my shoulder and turned my head to the side to see who was touching me. I saw Jack's worried face out of the corner of my eye. "You okay, Al?"

I turned my face back down to the floor. "No."

Jack sat down beside me. He rubbed my back and quietly waited for me to lift my head. I was grateful for the silent companionship. When I felt like I was no longer in danger of crying, I straightened my spine and turned to face him. "Thanks."

"Anytime. What's up? Or do you not feel up to talking about it?" Jack tilted his head as he looked at me. His brown eyes were clear, his eyebrows knitted together in concern. I rested my head on his shoulder, glad to call this good, strong person my friend.

"It's not worth talking about. I'll sort it out. I was just having a moment."

"Okay." Jack sounded unconvinced. "But you know you can talk to me about anything, right?"

"I know. Thanks, Jack." I reached over and squeezed his hand. He squeezed back.

"I think you need some cheering up. Why don't I take you out for dinner and a movie tomorrow?"

"That sounds great. I could use a night off from the play." I raised my head from his shoulder and smiled at him.

"It's a date, then!" Jack grinned at me, then looked a little confused as he glanced across the room. "Is Becca waving a mug at us?"

"Oh no! I totally forgot! I left her with my tea. I'd better go get it before she throws it out. I'll text you later, okay?"

Jack chuckled as he scooted his chair over so I could leave the table more easily. "Okay."

I smiled and waved back at him as I crossed the caf to collect a mug of lukewarm tea from a friend who had kept guard over it despite her personal distaste for it. I couldn't feel too sorry for myself when I had friends like this to watch my back. If only I could get them to fall in love, I would feel like I'd repaid some small part of what they'd done for me.

CHAPTER 13

"Have you ever come out to Jack? Does he know you're gay?" Annie shoved dirty dishes into the dishwasher haphazardly. It was her turn to do cleanup after supper.

"Not exactly. Why does it matter?" I rearranged the plates and pulled out a couple of bowls that needed to be rinsed. Either I would make sure the dishwasher was loaded properly now or Mom would do it later when she got back from the gym. I figured I'd save her the hassle.

Annie laughed and shook her head. "Because you just agreed to go on a date with him!" She answered a text, even though she was now holding a full garbage bag in one hand. The weird liquid that always seems to accumulate on the bottom of garbage bags dripped onto the floor.

"I did not agree to a date. I agreed to hang out with a friend." My sister could be clueless sometimes. She acted like she was more grown up than me, but she was still a kid in so many ways. She didn't understand that boys and girls could be friends. She also didn't seem to understand that chores go faster if you pause your texting.

"It's dinner and a movie. That's not a friend hangout. That's a date." Annie glanced up from her phone for a split second.

I was about to dismiss her comments again when I suddenly remembered Jack cheerily saying, "It's a date, then!" But that was just something people said, right? Just a turn of phrase. Nothing more significant than that.

I took the garbage bag from her and tied it off. I was about to take it out when something other than the gross garbage water on the floor turned my stomach. I didn't want Annie's judgment, but I had to ask someone: "Annie, what do you think it means when someone says 'It's a date'?"

Annie rolled her eyes at me. "If that someone just asked you out for dinner and a movie, I'd say it means you're going on a date."

"Oh god." The garbage bag hung in my hand. "Oh god. I can't go on a date with Jack."

"Obviously." Annie took a dishcloth and swiped it across the kitchen table a couple times, spilling crumbs on the floor.

"I have to fix this."

"And how exactly will you do that?" Annie wiped her hands on the kitchen towel. I noticed that she'd recently painted her short nails silver and purple. I liked the combo, though I'd never wear something so flashy myself.

"I don't know." I handed the bag of garbage back to Annie and contemplated the many ways I could get out of an accidental date. I could fake being sick, though that was only a temporary solution. Once the fake cold passed, I'd be expected to go on the fake date. I could tell Jack my parents wouldn't let me date, but he knew my parents too well to fall for that. I could tell him I didn't know that I was agreeing to a date, but that would be humiliating for both of us.

Annie interrupted my morose line of thought with a chipper reminder of just how messed up my life was. "At least there's one plus side to all this. You aren't worried about Jenny quitting the play anymore."

I heaved a sigh. "Thanks, Annie. Can you shut up now?"

"You know, maybe this is karmic retribution for all those times you blackmailed me over the thing with Mom's car." Annie swung the garbage bag back and forth as she headed out to the garage. She had a major case of Schadenfreude.

I had no energy to argue with my sister. Annie could be such a brat, but I had bigger fish to fry. And in some ways, I had to thank her for alerting me to the accidental date. Imagine if I'd gone on the date thinking it was just a friend hang! The idea of Jack leaning in for a good-night kiss at the end of the evening made my stomach turn. He was a great guy. But he was a guy.

In the midst of all this self-pity, I thought of Becca. If she found out about the "date," she would lose any progress she'd made. The other day, she'd smiled in Jack's general direction! She could never know that Jack liked me that way. She would never get up the nerve to talk to him if she thought he was pining for me. Leave it to me to create a mess of this magnitude without even being aware I was doing it. Becca was right. I had to learn how to say no.

And then I had a brilliant idea. There was one way I could salvage this whole fiasco. "I'll ask Becca to come with us," I whispered to myself. It was just crazy enough to work. Jack would realize I didn't think this was a date, and Becca would have a chance to spend time with Jack. It was the only way forward.

"Did you just mumble something about inviting Becca on your date?" Annie snorted. She'd come back from the garage without my noticing and was washing her hands in the kitchen sink. At least she had standards for her personal hygiene.

"Not that it's any of your business, but yes, I did. It's the perfect solution. Jack will understand I don't like him that way, and Becca will have to talk to him when it's just the three of us."

"You're delusional."

"Annie, it's not like you're some kind of expert on love. The last guy you dated borrowed your eyeliner without telling you, and you ended up with pink eye." Annie glared at me. I didn't need Annie's approval. I could feel in my bones that this was going to be a turning point. I climbed the stairs to my room and called Becca.

"Hey. Are you free tomorrow night?"

CHAPTER 14

When Becca pulled up to my house, I suddenly felt I should have told her more about the night ahead. I'd been worried she wouldn't agree to come if she knew we were meeting Jack, so I'd just asked her if she wanted to hang out. I didn't exactly know what I was going to tell her when we "ran into" Jack at the kitschy diner down the street from the movie theater. Maybe my brief time playing a tree had prepared me to improvise?

Becca honked to tell me she was waiting. It wasn't a good idea to stop Harvey once you got him going, so she idled in the driveway. To calm my racing heart, I tried some Lamaze breathing I'd learned from watching a trashy reality show about teen moms, but that only made me feel woozy. I steadied myself against the wall and caught a glimpse of myself in the hall mirror. I looked even paler than usual, maybe from lack of oxygen. My light brown hair was behaving itself, thanks to a last-minute spritz of my sister's favorite "dry oil" spray (whatever that was). The lipstick was definitely a mistake. You shouldn't wear lipstick to a fake date. That had to be rule number one of fake dates. (There had to be rules. I mean, there must be other people who find themselves accidentally agreeing to dates with people they think are just friends. Right?) I swiped at the rosy color with the back of my hand. Most of it came off, and I hoped what was left looked like my natural lip color.

As I climbed into Harvey's passenger seat, Becca said, "You look nice. Did you dress up just for me?"

Although I knew she was joking, I felt a little like I'd been caught out. "What? These old things?" I managed something that sounded more like a cackle than a laugh while pointing at my favorite pair of ripped jeans and the layered tops I'd carefully picked out. A date meant dressing up. I had purposely not dressed up. But maybe for me I looked a bit dressy, since I didn't usually bother "layering" anything. There was that woozy feeling again.

"You look nice too," I said to distract myself and Becca. It was true. Becca didn't think she was going on a fake (or even real) date, so she was dressed in her favorite baby-doll dress and opaque red tights. Curls escaped her bun in a casual way that most people would spend hours trying to accomplish, but which Becca just let happen. I liked that she'd used a little sparkly eye shadow to bring out her brown eyes. Jack would be a fool not to notice how beautiful this girl was.

"Thanks." Becca grinned. "You never know when I might run into a cute boy, right?"

I definitely cackled this time, nerves tightening my vocal cords so that I sounded like a pubescent boy whose voice was cracking. "Ha! So true, so true."

"Okaaay," Becca drawled. "You're acting weird. Everything okay?"

"Everything's great! Shouldn't we get going? Don't want to miss the movie."

"Aren't we grabbing dinner first?" Becca asked as she shifted Harvey into drive and pulled out onto the road.

"Yes! It's just that if we're late having dinner, then we'll be late for the movie." Even to my own ears, I sounded stilted. There was a reason I'd been asked to produce the play instead of star in it. I could not act. I needed an excuse not to talk anymore. "Wanna listen to *Coldplay Live?*"

Becca didn't even answer, just tapped the glove compartment to indicate where I'd find the CD. I fished it out, popped it in, and turned the volume up so loud that we couldn't possibly talk. Becca guided Harvey through busy suburban Friday night traffic as I chewed on my thumb. What was I going to say when Jack showed up at the diner? *Hey there, old pal. I didn't actually want to go on a date with you, so I tricked my best friend into coming so you could see how awesome she is.* I had the feeling this was one of those scenarios where the truth was not the best policy. Maybe the best policy was feigning food poisoning. Given that Becca was my driver, though, any hasty exit on my part would involve her also having to leave.

I tasted something salty and metallic. I looked at my thumb, which was bleeding. I pinched the skin around the wound, hoping to stop the bleeding. It was a welcome relief. It gave me something to focus on, a pinpoint of sharp physical pain that distracted me from the sweeping mental turmoil I had been experiencing only moments before. Unfortunately, the distraction was short-lived. As Becca pulled Harvey into the parking lot of the Sunshine Diner, the anxiety came crashing back. I spotted Jack's father's red sedan already parked in front of the diner. I wasn't sure whether it was better or worse that he was already here.

Becca parked Harvey, turned off the motor, patted the dashboard once, and opened her door. She paused as she was about to climb out, giving me a weird look. I still hadn't even taken off my seatbelt, so I pressed the release button. I paused with my hand on the door handle. Maybe I should tell Becca the truth now. I opened my mouth to say something, but I waited too long. Becca gave her door a final shove with her hip, just to make sure it was properly closed. I took a deep breath, pulled myself out of the car, and followed Becca through the diner's chrome and glass door.

As we entered the restaurant a wall of noise hit us: families squabbling, friends laughing, servers shouting orders to the kitchen. The Sunshine Diner had reproduced every detail of a fifties diner, from the jukebox to the checkerboard tiles to the red-vinyl booths. We stood inside the doors, and Becca waited for a server to come seat us while I scanned the room for Jack. I spotted him in a secluded booth at the back. It was the quietest part of the restaurant, perfect for an intimate date. Thankfully, it was a double-wide booth, so there would be room for all three of us. Time to make this happen. I waved at Jack and pulled on Becca's purse strap to get her attention. "Look who's here! Let's go sit with Jack."

I made my way through the busy diner, hoping Becca was following me. As I got closer to the booth, the confusion on Jack's face became clearer. His smile faltered. He looked back and forth between me and Becca. He was wearing a green T-shirt that showed off his shoulders. Jack wasn't a big guy, but he had the broad shoulders of someone who could have been an athlete if he'd wanted to be. His normally haphazard short hair was carefully combed. Jack had made an effort to look nice for our date. The thought made my stomach clench. I pinched the bloody hangnail, using the pain to keep me moving forward.

"Hey, Jack!" I slid into the booth before he could get up to hug or, worse yet, kiss me. I scooched over so Becca would know to sit next to me.

"Hey." Jack looked from me to Becca, who was hovering at the edge of the booth. I patted the red-vinyl upholstery next to me to encourage her to sit down. Reluctantly, she joined us. We sat in awkward silence. I knew it was my job to make this work, but I had greatly overestimated my improvisational skills.

I was flooded with a deep sense of relief when our waitress showed up to tell us the specials and give us our menus. I didn't hear a word she said, but I held on to the menu she handed me like it was a life preserver. I certainly felt like someone who was drowning. When I chanced a look at Jack and Becca, I noticed that neither of them had opened their menus. They were both just staring at me. I needed to break the ice.

"I love their onion rings, but I don't want a whole order for myself. Anyone want to share an order?" I saw Jack's shoulders sag as he realized that this wasn't a mistake. Becca was here to stay. I felt another pang of guilt twist my stomach, but I couldn't think of a single thing I could say that would save his hurt feelings. I could only comfort myself by hoping that he would thank me later when he fell in love with Becca.

Jack opened his menu, and I turned my attention to Becca. She wasn't just staring at me. She was out-and-out glaring. When I turned back to my menu, she stomped on my foot. I gritted my teeth. I deserved that.

"I was thinking we could catch the early showing of the new Wes Anderson movie," I said. I looked first at Jack, then at Becca. I needed to make sure they understood I meant all three of us. From Jack's almost imperceptible frown and Becca's angry scowl, I felt pretty sure they both took my meaning.

"Sure," Jack mumbled.

Becca said nothing. I was again grateful to our waitress when she showed up to take our orders. It was like she was an old hand at saving teenagers from awkward third-wheel dates. Maybe she was. Despite her perky ponytail and bobby socks, she looked to be somewhere in her forties. I focused on her kindly face as I ordered the veggie burger with a side of onion rings. I breathed a sigh of relief when Jack ordered a cheeseburger and Becca quietly asked for a club sandwich.

As we waited for our meals to come, Jack tried to build a house out of sugar packets while Becca took out her phone and scrolled through Tumblr. I pinched my injured thumb again and considered a list of possible conversation starters, topics on which we would all have opinions:

1. Reasons why Alison is a shitty friend. (List likely to be too long to finish at supper. Don't want to miss the movie.)
2. Things that are more awkward than this supper. (List likely to be too short to even fill the silence while we wait for our food to come.)
3. Ways to get revenge on Alison. (List likely to be dangerous to health.)
4. The one thing we all have in common: the play.

Here went nothing. "I think the cast is pretty talented. This might be the best school production in years. Don't you think?" I kept my tone peppy, as if I didn't notice the awkward vibe enveloping our booth like a noxious gas. If I wasn't mistaken, the man at the booth across from us was giving us side-eye. Even our neighbors could sense the awkwardness.

"I guess so," Jack said.

I looked at Becca, and she made a noncommittal *huh* sound while continuing to stare at her cell phone. It was a starting point, I figured, so I pressed on. "If you're going to do a Shakespeare play, it may as well be *A Midsummer Night's Dream*, right? I mean, all those crazy love triangles have got to keep the audience interested. She loves him, but he loves her, and they all end up in the woods together with some fairies! The story may be weird, but it's not boring."

Our food arrived and Jack and Becca dug in, maybe as a way to avoid having to contribute to my fevered analysis of the play. But I felt like I'd struck on something. Maybe I could use the play to help explain what was happening between us. "You know, Ms. Merriam is always saying Shakespeare's plays have survived because they're universal. Maybe she's on to something. I mean, love triangles still happen to this day. People are always falling in love with the wrong person. Or they don't notice the right person is right in front of them." I paused to let my deep words sink in, and I decided to reward my fast thinking with an onion ring. As I chewed my onion ring, I looked at Becca. She was glaring at me again. She obviously did not care for this line of conversation. In fact, she was so displeased that I could swear her right eye was twitching a little. I tried to swallow the onion ring, but I was now so nervous that I had no saliva left in my mouth. I couldn't swallow my food. The harder I tried, the worse it got. I felt like I might start choking. So I did the only thing I could think of: I stashed the food in my cheeks like a chipmunk. Like a nervous, idiotic chipmunk who thinks it's been planning for the winter, but it turns out it's just been lying to itself and its friends, but it's too late now to do anything about it. Oh, little chipmunk, I really do feel sorry for you.

I made sure the onion ring mush was carefully stashed in my cheeks and mumbled, "Excuse me. I have to go to the bathroom." Becca reluctantly let me out of the booth only after I shoved her a couple times.

I sped to the washroom, knowing that I couldn't leave Becca and Jack alone together for long. Becca still seemed to be taking the strong and silent approach with Jack. If he got over his funk enough to try to engage in conversation with her, the awkwardness might reach a dangerous level that could threaten any possibility of the two of them ever being in the same room together again.

As soon as I got into the washroom, I made a beeline for the paper towel dispenser. I did a quick inspection of the room. There seemed to be someone in a stall, but otherwise I was alone. I grabbed a paper towel and spat the onion ring mush into it, pleased that one thing had gone right tonight. No one had caught me spitting out my food like some picky toddler. I threw out the paper towel and went to the sink to wash my hands. I leaned on the counter and looked at my reflection in the mirror. The pale girl I saw looked like she'd just been chased by a rabid dog and hadn't quite made it out unscathed. I took a steadying breath and tried to turn on the water to wash my hands. The automatic sensor didn't seem to be working, no matter how close or far away from the tap I moved my hands. I stepped over to the next sink as I heard a toilet flush behind me. The sensor on this one must have been broken as well, because I tried sneaking up on it, then slowly waving my hands back and forth, but nothing worked. With a shake of my head, I moved on to the last sink. Nothing. What were the odds of all the taps in the women's washroom being broken? I was about to warn the woman who'd just exited the toilet stall when she came up beside me and helpfully Turned. The. Tap. On.

I rubbed my soapy hands in the stream of lukewarm water and tilted my head up to look at my savior in the mirror. I wanted to thank her and laugh off my space cadet moment, but the smile froze on my face when I saw just who had witnessed my inability to work a simple faucet. Charlotte was grinning at me as she washed her hands, her eyes crinkled in amusement, her long lashes partly obscuring the blue of her irises. I opened my mouth to say something, but my saliva had dried up again. I couldn't talk. I just stood there gaping at her like a fish out of water.

Charlotte finished washing her hands, grabbed a paper towel, and winked at me as she headed out. I banged my forehead against the mirror and thought this must be some kind of karmic retribution for dragging my best friend along to be a third wheel on my date with her crush. Yup, being humiliated in front of my own crush seemed fair. I turned off the faucet, dried my hands, and followed Charlotte out the door. She was nowhere to be seen as I made my way back to the booth. I scanned every part of the diner, but it was so crowded that it was possible I had missed her. Surely my overwrought mind hadn't just made her up?

I was so caught up in my worries about Charlotte that I didn't notice that the booth was half empty until I walked by it. "Where do you think you're going?" Becca asked in a low voice.

I turned around. Becca was seated exactly where I'd left her, her club sandwich only half-eaten. Jack's seat was empty, a mostly unfinished burger congealing on his plate. "Where's

Jack?" Becca didn't move to let me into the booth, so I sat down on Jack's side to let a busy server get by me.

"He left."

"What do you mean, he left?"

"What the hell do you think I mean, Al? He made up some excuse about not feeling well and left." She practically spat the words at me as she shredded her paper napkin.

"Oh."

"Oh? Is that all you have to say? Oh?" Becca was almost shouting as she dug through her purse to find her wallet. She threw a twenty-dollar bill on the table and stood up. "I'm leaving too. I would have left already, but I couldn't leave my so-called best friend to hang like that, even if she deserves to have to walk the four miles home."

I'd never seen Becca so angry. I hung my head, too embarrassed to look her in the eye. "Sorry."

"Damn right you should be sorry! What the hell gives you the right to toy with people like that? Jack looked fucking heartbroken. And I felt like such a fucking idiot!" I chanced a glance at Becca but had to look away again as I caught her swiping at a tear. I couldn't handle seeing my best friend so vulnerable and angry. I couldn't bear the weight of knowing it was all my fault she felt this way.

"Becca, I—"

"Don't! Don't you dare say a thing to me right now. You can't handle your own love life, so you think you get to interfere with mine?" Becca took a breath and turned away from me. When she turned back, she seemed calmer but sadder. "I'm

going to wait in Harvey. Pay your bill, and I'll drop you home."
I nodded to tell her I understood, glad that my downcast eyes
would hide the tears that were threatening to spill over.

I signaled our server and handed her Becca's cash and
my debit card. As she handed me back the change, she said,
"Honey, things are never as bad as they seem."

"Sometimes they are," I told her as I pushed myself up
from the booth.

We drove home in silence.

CHAPTER 15

I couldn't sleep Friday night. I wrote and rewrote texts to Becca, but none of them seemed right. I deleted at least two dozen, delighting in the speed with which I could make the useless words disappear, but then feeling that anxious emptiness again when the screen was blank. In the end, I settled on texting something simple but true: *I'm so very sorry.*

I didn't hear from Becca Saturday, and by Sunday I was so tired of cleaning my already spotless room that I decided to tackle the family room in the basement. My mother popped down once or twice in her weekend-wear designer jeans to see if I needed help, but we both knew the offer was just a gesture. I didn't want help, and she didn't want to spend what little free time she had scrubbing an already clean room. I was happy to pull all the DVDs and Blu-rays down from their shelves and then dust. Well, I wasn't exactly happy, but the work kept me distracted from the guilt that kept me from sleeping at night.

When my father came down, I knew my parents were really worried. My father liked to spend as much of his weekends outside as he could. He would go for a long run in the morning, then putter around his garden, and "read" (aka nap) in his hammock in the afternoon. Hanging out in the dark basement was about as far away from his weekend routine as he could get. I appreciated both his effort and what I was sure was my mother's gentle prodding to get him to check in on me.

I was swiping at cobwebs with a broom as he pretended to look for a book. He cleared his throat a few times before managing to say, "Alison, you know you can talk to us about anything. If there's something bothering you, we want to help."

I rested the broom on the floor, my back to my father. I thought about turning around and telling him the story of my stupid plan, but I was too embarrassed. I didn't want my father to know how much I'd screwed up. I'd never before done something that I felt too ashamed to tell my parents about. I'd even confessed to them when I cheated off of Billy Simcoe on a Grade 3 spelling test. They helped me tell my teacher and apologize to Billy. They helped me clear my conscience. But I couldn't see how they could help me out of this mess. My conscience wouldn't be so easy to clear this time.

"I know, Dad. I'm just stress-cleaning. The play and all my schoolwork are getting to me. I'll be fine." I raised the broom again at the invisible cobwebs, hoping my father wouldn't hear the hitch in my voice.

"Okay, but if you change your mind about talking, you know you can come find me." I was a little disappointed when I heard the wood stairs creak as he left the basement. I knew my father couldn't fix this problem for me, but that didn't keep me from irrationally hoping he would anyway.

I sat on the couch and checked my phone again for messages. Nothing. I flicked through old photos. Looking at all the happy pictures of me and Becca felt like penance. *This is what you've ruined, Alison. This is what you get for being a coward.* I stopped at a photo from the year before. We were holding miniature golf clubs and laughing at a windmill missing three of its five blades. I was grinning like an idiot, but my eyes were still red and puffy from crying. The day before, I'd seen my first real crush, Jessica, kissing another girl. The jealousy and hurt I'd felt had finally spurred me to admit to myself that I was gay. The next morning, I went to Becca's house and came out to her, then cried on her shoulder about the girl I liked kissing someone else. Becca didn't ask a lot of stupid questions. Instead, she fed me chocolate and then insisted we go play mini putt. We drove to the next town over because she knew how much I'd appreciate the ramshackle course with its crooked paths and cracked concrete. Harvey didn't like highways, but Becca had chanced going almost sixty miles an hour just to cheer me up. She didn't pressure me to talk to Jessica about my feelings. She didn't try to create awkward opportunities for us to be together. She didn't judge me for keeping my feelings secret. Unlike me, she was supportive without being pushy. Basically, she was just a better friend.

I swiped at the tears now coursing down my cheeks. What right did I have to be sad? I had brought this on myself.

Obviously, cleaning the family room wasn't going to help me fix anything. I needed a plan, so I packed away the cleaning supplies and returned to my room. I paced back and forth, considering possible scenarios. I could call or text Becca again to apologize for the massive blunder, but I didn't feel like I had the right words to help her understand. I wasn't even sure I could explain it to myself.

What had I been thinking? Did I think I could make two people fall in love just by shoving them at each other? Becca was right. I was trying to avoid my own crap. Last year I had been too afraid of my feelings to even admit to myself I had a crush on Jessica. I only came to terms with my feelings when she was no longer available. And now, instead of pursuing Charlotte, I was trying to set Becca up with Jack. I was technically out, but I wasn't ready to be open about my feelings. So where did that leave me?

I stopped pacing and spotted the Red Binder on my desk. It was always there, reminding me of the thousand impossible things I had to do. I rushed at my desk, grabbed the Red Binder, and threw it at the wall. I enjoyed seeing the rings pop open and the pages spill out. It felt satisfying, like watching an explosion at the end of a car chase. But the satisfaction was temporary. I couldn't just leave the binder lying there; it would give my parents the evidence they needed to confirm something was wrong. Clenching my jaw, I bent down to pick up the pages. I didn't bother putting them in order as I had a month ago when I'd first been burdened with the damn thing. Instead, I shoved the pages in willy-nilly and nipped a finger as I forced the rings shut. I sucked on the injured finger and glared at the Red Binder; it knew how to retaliate. I slid it across the floor and under my bed. My oversized navy quilt hid it nicely. Out of sight, out of mind. At least for now.

As I sat on the floor feeling sorry for myself, I could swear I heard a thumping coming from under my bed. I flashed back to reading Poe's *The Tell-Tale Heart* at the beginning of the year. It was the sound of a hideous heart! I had tried to hide from my guilty conscience, but it was no good. My own heart beat faster, and I broke out in a cold sweat. Which is when my sister poked her head around the corner of my doorframe. She was out of breath and annoyed. "Didn't you hear me dragging my amp up the stairs? You couldn't lend me a hand?" I was so relieved that I wasn't going crazy, that the thumping had been perfectly ordinary and not at all supernatural, that I started to giggle. The giggle turned into a guffaw as the absurdity of it hit me. Annie rolled her eyes as I tried to catch my breath. It was the kind of laughing that got worse the more I tried to stop it. After Annie left, exasperated at me as usual, and once my laughing fit finally subsided, I felt lighter. I still had no clue how I was going to fix things with Becca, but at least I felt like it might be possible.

CHAPTER 16

"You keep saying you've learned your lesson, but I don't think you have," Annie said, trotting to keep up with my determined stride. The quiet after-school hallways made it easy to build up a good head of steam. Maybe I couldn't fix things with Becca yet, but I could fix another one of my problems.

"I *have* learned my lesson—from the fake date! I'm not going to act as an intermediary anymore. I'm going to get Jenny and Mr. Evans in the same room so they can talk to each other. No more getting in the middle!" I felt good for the first time since Friday. The beginning of a new week meant a chance to turn things around. I took a deep breath, and the stale institutional air felt like clean mountain air in my lungs.

Annie grabbed my arm to stop me. "Isn't there something else you should have learned from the fake date?"

I was genuinely puzzled. "That I have trouble eating when I'm nervous?"

Annie sighed. "No, dummy. You shouldn't trick people into spending time together! *Sheesh.*" Annie let go of my arm, apparently convinced that I wasn't going to run away.

"This is different." I stood before her, sure of my plan.

"Oh yeah? How?"

I ticked a finger on my right hand. "Well, first, I'm only tricking one of them, not both of them."

"Now that you put it that way, I'm totally convinced," Annie retorted.

I didn't let Annie's sarcasm stop me. I ticked off a second finger. "Also, the ruse is temporary. I'm coming clean once they're both in the same room."

Annie threw up her hands. "Fine. Whatever. But I am not getting involved."

It was my turn to grab Annie's arm as she turned to walk away. She shook me off but waited to hear me out. "I need you to get Jenny for me."

"Why?" Annie faced me, hands on hips.

I needed her help, so I tried my best to keep my tone even. "Because I'm not exactly her favorite person right now."

"And why's that?" She made exaggerated eye contact with me and spoke slowly, like I needed things spelled out for me.

"Because she thinks I'm a liar."

"And you're solving that problem by…" Annie was not going to make this easy for me.

"Telling a little white lie."

"Fine. You are completely delusional, and I think this is a terrible idea, but I'll do it. And you're doing the dishes for a month!" I nodded my agreement, and Annie went on, "Tell me what you want me to say."

I thought about hugging my sister but changed my mind very quickly. It would only embarrass both of us. We weren't huggers. "Thank you, Annie! Just tell Jenny that the vice principal sent you to get her, then take her to the drama room."

"When this blows up in your face, I reserve the right to say 'I told you so.'" Annie pointed a finger at me, then started walking in the direction of the art room, her graffitied canvas sneakers squeaking on the linoleum floor.

"Won't be necessary," I called after her before continuing to the drama room. My sister's warnings had shortened my stride just a little. The air seemed less mountain-fresh and more Clorox-clean, but I was still breathing deep. The knot in my chest wasn't as tight as it had been all weekend. This still felt like a good idea. Maybe not a perfect idea, but definitely better than the fake-date fiasco.

I knocked on the open door to the drama room, waiting for Mr. Evans to look up from the script he was notating. The room was darker than usual. Mr. Evans was using his desk lamp instead of the overhead fluorescents that turned everyone's skin sallow. I couldn't blame him for choosing ambience over brightness. It was nice to escape the white-noise hum of the fluorescents. When Mr. Evans finally looked up, he smiled and asked, "What can I do for you, Alison?"

I entered the room and stood before his desk, hands clasped in front of me. Time to confess. "Mr. Evans, I have to tell you something. I've messed things up." The knot in my chest eased a fraction more, though I held my breath as I waited for his reaction.

"Oh?" Mr. Evans cocked his head to the side, the warm light from his lamp gleaming on his bald spot and highlighting the red fringe around it like a ring of fire.

"I promised Jenny that she would have full control over her designs." Mr. Evans opened his mouth to say something, but I rushed on before he could interrupt me. I needed to get this out. "I know I had no authority to tell her that. I thought I was doing the right thing for the show, but I know now that I should have spoken to you."

"Yes, you should have." Mr. Evans didn't sound mad, but he didn't sound happy either.

"I get that now. So instead of acting as a messenger between the two of you, I thought I should bring you together to talk." I took a step closer to his desk.

"That sounds reasonable," Mr. Evans said. "Let's set something up. Maybe I should come to the production meeting on Wednesday."

I cleared my throat and looked at the ground. "I think we should have the meeting today. You see, Jenny sort of quit, so she won't exactly be at the production meeting on Wednesday."

"Why didn't you tell me our set painter quit?" Mr. Evans seemed genuinely confused at this point.

Time for some more honesty. I blushed as I admitted, "I

was afraid you'd think I was doing a bad job if I told you she quit. I thought I could fix this on my own, but I can't. I'm sorry."

"Alison, I have worked with a lot of people in my many years in the theater. I know how fragile the egos of artists and actors can be." Even in my depressed state, I couldn't help but find the humor in this. Didn't he think directors had egos too? "I would not have been disappointed in you if you'd told me the truth about what happened with Jenny. I would have used my experience to help you."

I wanted to say something more, to tell Mr. Evans that I had learned my lesson and that I was sorry, but at that moment Annie and Jenny walked in. At first, Jenny looked puzzled, but when she saw me, her confusion turned to an angry scowl. "What's going on?" she demanded.

"I was hoping—" I started to try to explain, but Jenny cut me off.

"I don't care what you were hoping. I'm outta here." Jenny spun around, but before she could leave the room, I got some unexpected backup.

"Give Alison a chance to explain," Annie said, blocking the doorway.

"Why should I listen to anything she has to say?" Jenny asked Annie, pointing at me without deigning to look at me.

"Because she was acting on my behalf. I think you and I should speak," Mr. Evans interrupted. He stood up from his desk and invited Jenny to come into the room. He pulled up a chair so she could sit down at his desk.

I could not have been more grateful to both Annie and Mr. Evans. They were trying to help me clean up my mess, even though they were both disappointed in me. I didn't deserve their help, but they were giving it to me anyway. I knew I had endangered my chance at getting Mr. Evans's vote for valedictorian, but that worry seemed petty in the face of the second chance I was being given.

"Annie and Alison, will you excuse us? Jenny and I are going to talk, one creative visionary to another." Good ol' Mr. Evans. He might be self-aggrandizing and delusional, but he was willing to try to fix my mistake. I only hoped he didn't mention anything about Bollywood.

Annie and I left the room quietly. She checked the clock on her phone and started hurrying toward the front doors of the school. Without Becca to give us a lift, we needed to hurry to catch the bus. "Hey, Annie?"

"Yeah?" Annie didn't slow down, which was just as well. It would be easier to say this to her back than to her face.

"Thanks for…you know. In there." Yup, more evidence of my great eloquence.

Annie might have slowed a fraction before hitching her worn canvas backpack higher onto her shoulder. "No problem."

CHAPTER 17

Walking into rehearsal the next day felt like walking onto a minefield of social awkwardness. (Though maybe I shouldn't compare my First World problem to the horrific experience of trying to walk through a field of landmines. Like I needed to add "insensitive, privileged Westerner" to my list of character defects.)

I sat at my little producer's desk in a quiet corner of the room. Under the cover of my bangs, while pretending to read texts, I tried to scan the space. (Still nothing from Becca.) Charlotte was nowhere to be seen, but she often entered at the last minute. She seemed to enjoy making an entrance. Jack was chatting with one of the other actors in the far corner. His back was to me, and I wondered if that was on purpose. He looked tense, his shoulder blades protruding sharply in his thin cardigan. I spotted Ben trying to flirt with a fairy who, judging by her smile, seemed to be enjoying the experience. No accounting for taste. Finally, I tried to use my peripheral vision to find Mr. Evans. There was too much hair in my way, so I attempted to blow some of the bangs out of my face. Instead, I managed to spit on my phone. Lovely. I wiped the screen on my jeans and looked up in time to see Mr. Evans giving me a funny look. Oh god! Had he seen me spit on my phone then wipe it on my jeans like some grimy toddler smearing a booger on her leg? Or was he wondering why I was even here? Did he think it was clear that I was fired? Should it have been clear? The easy breathing of the day before was replaced by a tight, rasping feeling that transported just enough oxygen to my brain to keep me from passing out.

Before I could figure out what to do, Charlotte breezed into the room, tossing her jean jacket on top of a pile of backpacks with a coordination and confidence I could only admire. She grinned at the room, and this somehow worked as a signal to the other actors, who all gathered in a circle. Mr. Evans joined them, but I hesitated. Mr. Evans had insisted I join the circle in past rehearsals, but would he want that now? Was this my chance, if I continued on as producer, to skip the circle? Or was it an opportunity to show Mr. Evans my commitment to producing the play? Did I want to join the circle or not? I looked down at my phone again, hoping for an answer. It was, as usual, totally unhelpful. *Smartphone, my ass*, I thought. *You're just as bad as that stupid binder.*

"Alison, you know phones aren't allowed in rehearsal. Put it away and join us." Mr. Evans stepped back to make room for me to squeeze between him and Ben, who was standing beside him. I was so happy to know I was still part of the team that I didn't mind his mild rebuke. I didn't even mind having to stand next to Ben. At least, I didn't mind standing next to him until I was accosted by his heavy cologne. Things got even worse when Mr. Evans asked us all to hold hands. Ben and I seemed to come to an unspoken agreement; we moved our hands so they hovered close to each other without actually touching.

"Now close your eyes. Listen to your breath." The room was silent except for the sound of the prehistoric ventilation system rattling away above our heads. "Try to match your breathing to the people next to you. If we can breathe together, we can create art together."

How could I match two different people's breathing? I unintentionally held my breath while trying to listen to the breathing of my neighbors. The room gradually got louder as some people shifted uncomfortably and others tried to help those around them by inhaling and exhaling loudly. Mr. Evans either didn't notice or didn't mind. "Excellent work! I can feel our energies coming into alignment." Our energies coming into alignment felt a lot like a class of kids trying to suppress giggles, but who was I to judge? "Now open your eyes and find a partner for our warm-ups."

Ben practically ran over to the fairy he'd been flirting with. I held back as I watched the other actors pair off. Even the freshmen seemed confident enough to make overtures to near-strangers. I chanced a glance in Jack's direction, but he'd already found a partner. I hadn't expected anything different, yet I still felt a pang. It looked like everyone else had paired off, and I was about to tell Mr. Evans that I would skip the rest of the warm-up when a pair of cool blue eyes froze me to the spot.

"Looks like we're the odd ones out." This close, I could see that one of Charlotte's incisors protruded a little.

The nervous feeling from the fake date returned. This time, I couldn't even swallow my own saliva. *So this is a thing I do now*, I thought. My saliva tasted acidic, like warm diet soda. I nodded at Charlotte, unable to think of anything else to do. I couldn't speak, and it would be unutterably rude to just walk away. I was going to have to partner with Charlotte for whatever mad "game" Mr. Evans made us play next.

At a signal from Mr. Evans, all the actors sat on the ground. Charlotte sat cross-legged in a single, fluid move. I made my way down in increments, like my arthritic grandmother: First I bent my knees a little, then I put a hand down to balance myself, and finally I lowered myself all the way. At least I didn't grunt or groan like an old person. Of course, that was probably only because I couldn't make a sound unless I wanted to drool all over myself like some over-excited bulldog.

I craned my neck to look at Mr. Evans, pretending that I needed to see him to properly follow his directions. Charlotte's Medusa-effect seemed to work only when I was looking directly at her, so I swallowed the saliva I'd been hoarding while gazing up at Mr. Evans.

"We're warming up with a classic today. You're going to act as mirrors. The job of the mirror is to reflect exactly what its partner is doing. The leader's job is to make sure that the mirror can follow its movements. Use eye contact to help you com-municate. This warm-up is about building bonds and paying attention to how we move. I'll tell you when to change so that the mirror becomes the leader." What was with these stupid warm-ups requiring people to make awkward eye contact? Theater people were baffling.

Mr. Evans switched on some weirdo spa music, and people shifted so that they were facing each other. It looked like the other pairs were staying seated on the floor, so I turned my body to face Charlotte and forced myself to look directly into her eyes. Her cool blue irises were outlined in midnight blue. They reminded me of coloring books I'd had when I was a little kid. I would follow the lines with my crayon, pressing down to create a satisfying dark outline, then I would lightly fill in the center.

"Want to be the leader first?" Charlotte offered. I shook my head no. "Okay. I'll go first."

Charlotte slowly raised her right arm, long fingers splayed in a languid hello. I tried to match her loose-limbed move-ments, but everything in me felt too tight. To an outsider, she must have looked like a cool ballerina, and I, a robotic facsimile of a human being.

Charlotte lowered her arm, and I followed her as she rested her hand on the floor. It was difficult to concentrate on the outer edges of my body. It felt like every atom of my being was drawn to the point where our eyes met. Charlotte smiled, and my brain reminded me, a beat too late, that I was supposed to do what she did. I smiled back, and her smile grew almost imperceptibly. Was it possible I had made Charlotte happy, even in some small way? I could now feel my heart as well as the hot point between us.

Charlotte reached her left hand forward, fingertips at the very edge of our imaginary boundary. I moved my own hand without thinking. In the periphery of my vision, I could see the contrast between my pale skin and her lightly tanned skin. Then she twitched her index finger forward, and every atom in my body rushed to that point of contact. Emptied of my atoms, I forgot to breathe. The next moment, she slid her hand up, as if it rested against the mirror between us. My entire palm was now pressed against hers. My fingers were shorter, and I wondered vaguely what it would feel like if she wrapped her hand around mine.

"Everyone up! Mirrors are the leaders now!" Mr. Evans's peppy instructions jarred me out of my reverie.

When Charlotte stood up, I followed her, still attuned to her every action. I almost mirrored her raised eyebrows until I realized she was reminding me that it was my turn to lead. Though I wanted to touch her again, I couldn't bring myself to be that forward. Instead, I modestly nodded my head yes. She followed, frowning. I panicked, thinking I had somehow disappointed her, but then it came to me: I must be frowning. Why would I be frowning? Did I normally frown? I made an effort to smile. Her lips turned up, but no protruding incisor. I told myself to smile big, and there it was. I took a deep breath, and so did she. So this is what it was like to breathe with someone. Maybe Mr. Evans had been on to something.

Mr. Evans clapped his hands together. I didn't break eye

contact with Charlotte until he instructed the actors to take their places for Act 1. At that point, I reluctantly made my way to the table. Only when I was seated did I notice I had somehow managed to swallow like a normal person during the mirror exercise. Miracle!

The rehearsal seemed to drag, probably because I had to ration my glimpses at Charlotte. I didn't want to act like a stalker, so I made myself look at six other people before looking back at her. She was in character, which meant she seemed more regal and untouchable than ever. But I had touched her. My stomach clenched at the thought.

When Mr. Evans finally instructed the group to give themselves a round of applause, I thrilled at the sight of her walking toward me.

She stopped in front of my table. "You make me look much better than my mirror at home. Can you come to my house every morning to make me feel hot?" She laughed. Her laugh was a bit hiccup-y. I loved it. I wanted to hear more of it. "Sorry. That's a terrible line."

I smiled and considered flirting back. (She had to be flirting, right?) And then, with the worst possible timing, Mr. Evans interrupted. "Alison, can we speak?"

"Of course," I said. The reality of the last few days came flooding back. I had to make sure things were okay with Mr. Evans. And when I was finished with that, I had to figure out how to get Becca and Jack to talk to me again.

I turned back to Charlotte, desperate to say something, anything, to let her know I was interested. "I'll be sure to *reflect* on your offer." It was a terrible pun, and I regretted it the second I said it, but then Charlotte laughed again. I sketched an awkward wave as I turned away from her and readied myself for producer work.

Mr. Evans rambled on about props and costumes, but I kept thinking about Charlotte. I wondered if she was gay. Then I wondered if she knew I was gay. Maybe I had imagined the heated moment between us when we were playing the mirror game. Maybe I was just seeing my desire reflected back at me. Maybe it had all been performance. But wasn't all flirting a kind of performance? If that was true, then maybe I was a bad actor. Maybe I didn't know the right cues, the subtle signs I was supposed to use to communicate my attraction and gayness to my audience.

I left rehearsal feeling out of place with myself.

CHAPTER 18

By some miracle, Mr. Evans—who had never before shown an understanding of teenagers—managed to talk Jenny into staying on as set painter. When I asked him how, all he said was, "I have my ways." If Becca were still speaking to me, she would have said that his "ways" must have involved animal sacrifice or blackmail. I missed Becca. Her sarcasm helped keep things in perspective. She was the yin to my yang. But what was I was to her?

I took the late bus home, relieved that Mr. Evans was planning to keep me on as producer. I closed my eyes and rested my head back on the hard bus bench, passing the time by reliving those amazing moments with Charlotte. I felt guilty for being happy when I still hadn't made up with Jack or Becca. I was emotionally exhausted when I got home, but that didn't make a difference to my sister. I was taking my shoes off in the entryway when Annie shouted down the stairs to me, "I am not taking the bus again tomorrow. Make up with Becca!"

I kicked my shoes off, plunked my backpack on the entryway bench, then stomped up the stairs.

"If I knew how to make up with Becca, I would have done it by now!" I shouted at Annie, even before I was through the door to her room. She was curled up in her comforter watching YouTube videos on her laptop. Without her school makeup, she looked younger, a little like the kid who used to follow me around.

"Whoa. Calm your horses, cowboy!" Annie joked in a bad southern drawl. She scooted over, and I sat on the edge of her bed. "Have you tried apologizing to Becca?"

I tried to keep the exasperation out of my voice. "Of course, I've tried apologizing! I sent her a text Friday, and she hasn't responded."

"Maybe this is one of those times when a phone call is better than a text?" Annie seemed genuinely unsure. She was always texting; I couldn't remember the last time she'd used her phone to make an actual call. Not that I was much better. Phone calls just felt so intrusive. They felt a bit like waving your hands in someone's face. A text, on the other hand, was like nodding at someone from across the room at a party. When they had time, they knew where to find you. A phone call was more personal than a text, though. And it allowed for more subtlety in delivery and tone. Of course, I wouldn't have a chance to carefully edit my words, without which I had a tendency to say the wrong thing.

"Maybe." I picked at a loose thread on Annie's comforter. It was a crazy fuchsia color. I would never have picked bedding so bright. I would worry I'd get tired of it, but Annie didn't worry about what might be. She focused instead on things that would make her happy now, like a colorful comforter.

"This has been a nice visit and all, but I've got some pimple-popping videos I've got to get back to." Annie ran her fingers across her trackpad to wake up her laptop.

I pushed myself off the bed and made my way back to my room. I dug my phone out of my jeans pocket. I needed to start somewhere. I scrolled through my contacts and pressed *call*. I paced my bedroom and waited to find out if I'd just be sent to voicemail.

"Hello." I had never heard Jack's voice sound so formal.

I stopped pacing, took a breath, and started. "Hi, Jack. It's Alison."

"I know."

"Right. Of course. Caller ID." I chuckled awkwardly to cover up the silence, then I forced myself to keep going. "I, uh, wanted to talk about what happened Friday."

"No need."

I could feel my resolve weaken. Jack obviously didn't want to talk to me. But I knew I had to at least try to apologize. Even if he didn't forgive me, even if it didn't make things better, I still owed him an explanation. I took a deep breath. "Yes, need. I'm really sorry about Friday. I should have been more honest with you."

"You don't need to do this. I get it. You don't like me." Jack's tone was clipped. "You could have just told me you didn't want to go on a date with me. You didn't have to bring Becca with you."

"It's not that I don't like you!"

"Yeah? So then why did Becca come on our date?"

I chewed on my thumb. It was a fair question. "It's hard to explain, Jack."

"You're the one who called me."

"Right. You're right." I took another deep breath. "Jack, you're one of my best friends." I paused, gathering my thoughts.

"So you didn't want to ruin our friendship?" Jack sounded hopeful, and I felt all the guiltier for misleading him. He was still willing to believe the best of me. He was hurt and angry, but he was still willing to give me the benefit of the doubt.

"I don't want to ruin our friendship, but that isn't exactly why I didn't want to go on a date with you. I should have told you this a while ago, but it felt kinda awkward to bring up. And then I didn't realize you'd asked me on a date, so that made it harder."

"You didn't realize that it was a date?" Jack asked. I was messing this up. I started pacing again.

"My sister had to tell me it was a date, but that isn't the point," I rushed on, then stopped. *Why is this so hard?*

After I'd been silent for a few seconds, Jack asked, "What *is* the point?"

"I'm gay," I said. I slowed my pacing and tried to interpret the silence. *Jack is open-minded*, I reminded myself. *He's just surprised. It's taking him a moment to digest what I've said, but I can trust him.* I believed everything I was telling myself, but still felt nervous. I wondered if it would always be like this.

Finally, Jack said, "Oh."

I rushed to say everything else I needed to tell him. "So it's not that I don't like you. It's that I don't like boys. At least, not in that way."

"Why didn't you tell me before?" He wasn't being accusatory. He sounded almost...sad.

I tried to explain. "I haven't told that many people. I don't see why it's anyone's business."

"Did you think I would judge you? Stop being your friend? I'm not that kind of person, Al."

"I know!" I said, though I couldn't help but think about how just a few moments before, I'd been nervous when I came out to him. I felt a little guilty that some part of me had been worried. My logical brain knew Jack was a good person, a good friend. Too bad my logical brain couldn't always be in charge. "I just haven't felt like making a big deal of it. I figured it would come up naturally. I didn't know you liked me that way." I looked out the window into the dark front yard.

"I think I get it," Jack said.

"Yeah?" Maybe he could explain it to me.

"Yeah. You're not out."

"I'm out!" I felt defensive.

Jack was confused. "But you haven't told anyone."

"I've told Becca and my family."

"Does that count as out?" Jack sounded like he was genuinely asking, and I wished that I had an answer for him, and more importantly, for me.

I was honest. "I don't know. Why can't it be?"

Jack chuckled softly. "Fair point. At least that explains Friday. Well, most of Friday. Becca seemed pretty angry. Was she in on the plan?"

I hung my head. "No."

"Ah. So she's…" Jack paused, waiting for me to fill in the blank.

"Not talking to me right now," I admitted.

"Sorry to hear that."

"Yeah. It's my own fault. She's next on my list of people I need to apologize to. Any tips for me? Ways to improve the service?"

"The honesty thing works. Maybe try to get to it faster."

"Where were you with that advice last Thursday when I finally got that I'd agreed to go on a date with a dude?"

Jack laughed, and I felt relaxed enough to chuckle at my own joke. We hung up on good terms, and I hoped my practice tonight would help me with what I knew I had to do next.

CHAPTER 19

I tried to lean casually on the wall outside the drama room door, but I couldn't get comfortable. For one thing, the concrete wall felt clammy on my skin. For another, I was the awkward person making, then quickly breaking, eye contact with everybody who walked by the room. I wanted to make sure I grabbed Becca before she went in for the production meeting, so I kept staring any time someone entered my peripheral vision. The tension and social pressure kept me pretty rigid, which also prevented me from looking the least bit casual. No wonder when I finally did see Becca coming down the hall, she stopped in her tracks for a moment. Everything about my stance must have screamed "uncomfortable social encounter this way!"

As Becca came nearer, I could see that her jaw was clenched and her heavy eyebrows were drawn together. When she was a good body-length away, she stopped, crossed her arms, and stared at a spot just to the left of my head. "Hi."

"Becca, can we talk before the meeting?"

"About what?" She was still staring at the spot beside my head. I resisted the urge to look over my shoulder, though some survival instinct had the hairs on the back of my neck on end. My limbic system was sure there was a predator over my left shoulder. For the sake of our friendship, I had to ignore the vampire that might be sneaking up behind me.

"I want to talk about Friday."

"I'm only here because I promised to help with lights and programs. I don't want to talk about Friday."

"Then let me talk. Please, Becca. I'm so sorry. I should have told you Jack was going to be at the restaurant." I took a step toward her, and she stepped back. It hurt to see her back away from me.

"I told you, I don't want to talk about Friday. So can we go in?" Becca jerked her head at the drama room.

"Not until you hear me out." I stood my ground.

Becca looked me in the eye. "You don't get to make all the decisions, Al! I don't want to talk. I'm not going to talk. I'll find someone to do the lights and I'll finish the program and then I'm done." With that, Becca spun around and stalked off. I wanted to call after her, but I could feel tears burning at the corners of my eyes. If I tried to do anything more than breathe right now, I would cry. I did not want to cry at school. Annie poked her head out of the drama room at that moment and asked what was taking me so long. With an unsteady breath, I headed into the meeting.

The production team was crowded around Mr. Evans's desk. Mr. Evans wasn't planning to attend any of the minor production meetings, so his chair was empty, but no one wanted to sit down in it. This was not a group of people who would feel comfortable sitting in a teacher's chair. Looking at them all gathered in one place, I could see what a rag-tag team I had managed to stitch together. Our costume designer, Zach, was almost a foot taller than anyone else. His thick wavy hair was styled in a funky pompadour, and his white, leather sneakers looked pristine. Jenny was just as pale, brooding, and pierced as ever. Annie looked a bit like a rainbow had thrown up on her, especially in contrast to Jenny's monochromatic goth-look and Zach's clean palette of blues and grays. This was my team, minus Becca of course. I couldn't help but feel that Becca would have made the group look more normal.

I made my way over to them. "Hey. I think you all know each other, right?"

Nods from Annie and Zach. Silence from Jenny.

"So maybe we should start by sharing some ideas to see what people are thinking. I mean, we can't have the costumes and set clashing. Or the props, for that matter. I'm no expert on color schemes, but clashing colors would look terrible and—"

Annie cut me off. "You're rambling."

I smiled to show I wasn't ruffled by my sister's bluntness. "Right. Um, why don't you start, Zach?"

Zach spread some sketches on the desk and also brought

up a series of photos on his phone. He explained that he'd been looking through the costumes left over from previous shows, the ones we had painstakingly dug out of the dusty storage room, and that some of them could be repurposed. Zach had also done some reconnaissance work at a local thrift store. Not only had he come up with a couple different concepts, he'd also priced out the options, and they were all affordable. I had lucked out with Zach.

I looked through his sketches and photos and paused when I reached his choice of shoes for the fairies. The dainty, strappy heels he'd picked looked like death traps to me. "Zach, are you sure the actors are going to be able to walk in these things?"

He took the photo from me. "They're only two-inch heels."

I had no idea what that meant. Was that a normal height for high heels? I looked at Annie for help, but she shrugged. We were sneaker gals, through and through. "But they're so flimsy," I tried. I felt on surer ground with this argument. The heels, though "only" two inches high, looked about as sturdy as twigs.

Zach said, "Wait here." He left without any other explanation.

We couldn't wait in uncomfortable silence, and I couldn't handle Jenny just yet, so I asked Annie how she was doing with props. "Fine. Not much to do yet. Mr. Evans hasn't decided on many of the props." She paused and rolled her eyes theatrically. "Other than a ukulele. He keeps insisting Puck needs an electric-blue ukulele."

Jenny snorted. "Good luck with that."

Zach returned just before I had to ask Jenny how her plans

were coming along. A pair of sparkly heels dangled from the fingers of his right hand. "Here you go!"

"Okay. Well, they still look kinda flimsy to me," I said, confused.

"Put them on." Zach held the shoes out to me. I took a step back, hands plastered to my sides so Zach couldn't make me touch the terrifying things. Jenny laughed at that. A genuine laugh, not a sarcastic snort. When we all looked at her, she scowled even harder to make up for it.

I tried to refuse, but Zach insisted that I wouldn't know how comfortable they were until I tried them on. I argued that I knew fire was hot without sticking my hand in it, but that did nothing to convince Zach. Realizing he wasn't going to give up, I unlaced my canvas sneakers, slipped off my socks, and held onto his shoulder as I balanced precariously on each foot, fastening the ridiculous things to my feet.

"Now walk."

"No thanks. I'm good like this." My voice was embarrassingly high-pitched.

"You'll be fine. I'll walk with you." I didn't have a chance to argue because Zach started to walk. Unless I wanted to lose my balance, I had to go with him. The shoes didn't pinch like I thought they might. And the heel, though slender, was a marvel of physics. Tiny as it was, it was holding up all 140 pounds of me. But I did not feel steady.

"Why are you bent over like that? You look like my bubbe after she's had a few glasses of wine." Zach tried to shake me off, but I wouldn't let go. To appease him, I stood straighter.

"Ow!" he complained. "You're pinching my shoulder!" There was no pleasing some people.

Just then Annie laughed. I turned around and caught her pointing her phone in my direction. "You better not be taking a picture of me!" I warned her.

"I'm not."

"Then why is your phone out?" I asked, trying to pick up a little speed so I could take the phone from her.

"I'm taking a video." Annie grinned at me, looking just like the bratty baby sister who cut the hair off all my Barbies.

"That's worse!" I let go of Zach's shoulder so I could stretch out my arm to grab the phone. Big mistake. My right ankle rolled, and I tripped forward, barely catching myself on the edge of the desk. By the time I was standing straight again, Annie had hidden her phone.

I rubbed my ankle after returning the devil shoes to Zach. Despite my near-death experience, he was still insisting that the fairies would be fine in the shoes. "They'll just need to practice walking in them at home. Plus, most girls have worn heels before." He looked at me pointedly, and I was too ashamed to argue anymore, so I said if the fairies and Mr. Evans were fine with the shoes, then they were okay by me. Secretly, I hoped at least one of the fairies would sprain an ankle. Petty? Yes. But I didn't want to be the only one who couldn't handle a pair of shoes.

Costumes and props sorted, I had no choice but to speak to our set painter.

"So, Jenny, do you think Zach's costumes will work with

your designs?" *Please let her like at least some of what he's picked out*, I begged the universe.

I guess the universe felt it owed me a little luck after the heels debacle, because Jenny seemed to be in a less-foul-than-usual mood. Without looking at any of us, she said, "I guess so. I'm going to add some jewel tones to my paintings, so the colors should work." Miracle! Mr. Evans had managed to get Jenny to compromise.

"Great!" I sounded maybe a little too enthusiastic because Annie raised a knowing eyebrow in my direction. Before anything else could go wrong, I decided to call the meeting to an end. Jenny left without saying good-bye, and Annie waved as she rushed out to catch a ride with a friend. I waited as Zach gathered his drawings and the shoes. It felt rude to leave him, plus, I had to make sure we locked up.

I was wasting time on my phone when Zach asked, "Isn't your friend also part of the production team? You know, the one with all the curls?"

I stopped scrolling but kept my eyes on the phone. "Oh. Uh, Becca had somewhere she had to be."

I guess I didn't sound as casual as I thought because Zach stopped zipping his messenger bag. "Lovers' quarrel?"

I lowered my phone and shook my head. "Becca and I aren't a couple."

Zach's eyes widened. "Wait. Are you gay?"

"Yes?"

"Is that a question?"

"No?"

Zach laughed. "Sounds like a question."

I sighed. "It isn't. Sorry. I'm just not any good at talking about this stuff."

"Gay stuff or personal stuff?" Zach leaned against the desk, crossing his feet at the ankles.

I leaned against the desk beside him. It was easier to talk if I didn't have to make eye contact. "Both." I looked at my feet. "Becca and I had a fight. I've tried apologizing, but she doesn't want to hear it. It's totally my fault and I get why she's mad, but I feel like crap, and I just want to make it up to her."

Zach gently poked me with his elbow. "You're sure you're not a couple?"

"Just friends. But that doesn't seem to make this any easier."

"Don't be so sure. Sex makes everything more complicated." Zach rubbed his forehead.

I got the feeling we weren't talking about me anymore. "Boy troubles?"

"Closeted boyfriend troubles."

"Oh."

"Oh is right. You can do the whole 'out and proud' thing, but if your boyfriend is closeted, then so are you…you know?" Zach turned to look at me. I wanted to say I understood, but the truth was that I didn't. I didn't have a girlfriend, closeted or otherwise. But I didn't want to get into that now, so I just nodded and sat with him in companionable silence for a couple minutes. Eventually Zach shook it off and finished packing away his things.

We walked out of the drama room together. I stopped to check that the door was locked and waved good-bye to Zach. It was nice to have someone to talk to about gay stuff. Not that Becca and my parents (and even Annie, in her own way) didn't try to understand, but there was something different about talking to someone who *knew* what it was like to grapple with the different levels of out. It felt like I was less alone in a way.

CHAPTER 20

"Alison, can I have a word with you?" Ms. Merriam asked as she erased the whiteboard. It was the end of the school day, and I wasn't exactly looking forward to lining up for the bus. I decided on the spot that I would wait for the late bus since it would at least be less crowded.

When Ms. Merriam finished cleaning the whiteboard, she came and sat down at the table next to me. She angled her chair so she could look at me, then leaned forward, concern in her eyes. "Alison, you seem a bit distracted lately. Is everything okay?"

"Just busy," I lied.

"That's all? Because I have to say I was surprised today when you said that the storm scene in *King Lear* is an example of pathetic phallus instead of pathetic fallacy." Ms. Merriam looked away as she said this, giving me a moment to wallow in shame for the mistake I'd made so publicly.

I felt my stomach clench. *So that's why the class laughed. How did I miss that?* I rested my head in my hands. "I can't believe I said that. I can't believe the class didn't laugh more!"

Ms. Merriam chuckled. "I don't know that everyone caught the mistake. The words sound pretty similar. And to be fair, it is an interesting interpretation."

At least one of us found this funny. I was trying to remember exactly who had laughed at my blunder. Had Ben caught it? I couldn't handle it if Ben knew I'd confused a penis with a literary device. "Oh god."

Ms. Merriam tilted her head and gave me an understanding smile. "It's really not that bad, Alison. But it did make me wonder if you're stretching yourself a little thin."

"Things are busy with the play right now. I know that's not an excuse, and I shouldn't let an extracurricular get in the way of my studies—and I won't! Today was just a fluke. I'll be back on track next class." I spoke fast, trying to fix my mistake with words.

Ms. Merriam looked at me without speaking. After a moment, I had to break eye contact because I was afraid her compassion would break me. "Alison, it's okay to mess up. I just wanted to check in with you, not to scold you for a small mistake." She paused. She looked like she was considering what to say next. I braced myself. "I think sometimes you may be too tough on yourself. Nobody expects you to be perfect."

I wanted to tell her that *I* expected myself to be perfect, that valedictorians are perfect, or as close to perfect as a person can get. I wanted to tell her that I had made too many mistakes lately and that most of them weren't small at all. I thought about Becca and had to squeeze my eyes shut to keep from crying. Instead of saying any of the things that were true, I said, "I know. Thanks, Ms. Merriam. I'll be fine. Really."

Ms. Merriam sat back, still looking at me. "Okay." Another pause. "Just know that I'm here if you need to talk."

"Thanks again." I stood up, pulling my bag by its straps. It felt too heavy for me, but I knew I had to carry it anyway. "I better get going."

I left the room at a brisk walk. By the time I'd reached the end of the hall, I was trotting. I had a plan. At least, I had the outline of a plan. The core concept was rudimentary and childish, but it was all I had.

I swung open the scarred metal doors to the parking lot and stood there, scanning the cars until I spotted the familiar, aged, blue Honda. Taking long strides to the car, I kept from running by reminding myself that many of the people in this parking lot were still learning to drive. And that the rest of them might have a reason, at the end of a long day, to want to run over a teenager.

I was in luck. Harvey was empty. I patted him affectionately and scooched myself up onto his hood. The metal was uncomfortably warm after a full day in the sun, but I didn't budge. I noticed Becca's curly hair as she came out of the double doors. She walked toward Harvey, head bent over the phone in her hand. If we were on speaking terms, I would have warned her not to walk and text in a school parking lot. But we weren't. And I needed another minute to steel myself.

I knew the moment she saw me. Her pace slowed, and she tucked her phone into her back pocket. As she drew closer, I debated whether I should be the first one to say something or not. When Becca was eye level with me and only about three feet from the car, I opened my mouth to speak, but Becca walked right past me. I didn't turn but heard her unlock the driver's-side door. I heard some squeaking as she opened it and sat down, then I felt and heard the door slam shut. I chanced a glance over my shoulder. Becca was glowering through the windshield.

"Becca, we need to talk," I started. But my voice was drowned out by the combination of Harvey's old motor turning over and a Coldplay song blasting on the stereo.

Becca glared at me some more. I held her gaze, hoping she'd see my resolve and my apology.

She revved the engine. It was a warning.

I looked forward, but I didn't move.

Becca revved the engine again.

I scrabbled at the hood with my fingers, but there was nothing to hold on to.

I heard the engine shift into drive and closed my eyes. The car gently edged forward, and my stomach turned. I was unmoored.

Harvey eased into a turn, and I slid a little along his hood. I tensed my legs, trying desperately to find purchase.

The car stopped, and I heard a window creak open. I looked back. Becca stuck her head out of the driver's window and said to me, "Get off Harvey. Now."

I was too nervous to speak, so I just shook my head.

"Your choice," Becca said. I gulped.

Becca picked up speed. A steady speed meant I could maintain my balance on the hood. It felt almost exhilarating. The car wasn't moving at a speed that could be described as creating a breeze, but I did feel fresh air waft by my face. Becca saw that this tactic wasn't working and started to swerve in big, terrifying loops. I slid from one end of the hood to the other. I thought I might throw up.

Becca braked, not as suddenly as she usually did. It was comforting to know that my best friend didn't actually want to harm me.

I looked back, and she stuck her head out the window again. "Alison, get the hell off my car!" she yelled.

"Ladies, is there a problem?" Neither of us had noticed the vice principal approaching. Nervous as I was, I jumped, then tried to cover it up by casually crossing my legs. *Yup. I sit on moving cars all the time. Nothing to see here, Mr. Patel.*

Becca turned off the music and answered tersely, "Nope." I shook my head and smiled.

"Is that so?" he asked. He swung his heavy key ring around his pointer finger three times, then said, "Might I suggest that you ride *inside* the car then, Alison?"

I was thrilled that the vice principal knew my name. I'd never been sent to the office or suspended, so why did he know my name? Maybe because it had come up in conversation with teachers. Maybe as a potential candidate for valedictorian. But then I remembered he was reprimanding me for joyriding on the hood of my friend's car, and I jumped down. I chuckled, pretending we were all in on a joke, and walked to the passenger's-side door. I yanked on the handle, but nothing happened. I yanked a second time. It was locked. I chuckled again, but Mr. Patel's face remained completely impassive. I looked in through the closed window at Becca. She was staring straight forward. I tapped on the window, and when she finally looked at me, I nodded my head in the direction of the vice principal. Nothing happened for what felt like an eternity, and I started to panic that Becca was so mad at me, she'd chance a suspension just to keep me out of her car. Then I heard a click and clambered into Harvey before Becca could change her mind. I was careful to buckle up since Mr. Patel was still staring at us. I gave him a little wave, and off he went.

I waited until he was in his own car before saying to Becca, "Want me to get out?" My voice was small. I was about to repeat myself when Harvey started forward. I smiled.

CHAPTER 21

To say the ride home was awkward would be an understatement. I decided to follow Becca's lead. She stayed mum, so I did too. She didn't hum along to the music, so I didn't either. Halfway home, she still hadn't said a word, and I felt like all the blood in my body was pooling in my head. I opened and closed my hands, hoping to covertly redistribute some of it. It didn't seem healthy to have that much blood concentrated in one place, plus I could feel the beginnings of a massive headache building in my temples.

When we were five minutes from my house, my right leg started to jiggle. I couldn't hold it in anymore. "Becca, I—"

"Not yet, okay?"

"Okay." I had to respect what Becca needed, so I let more blood pool in my head, fantasizing about a cold compress when I got home.

When we got to my house, I slowly opened the passenger door, every creak in the old hinges audible as I waited for Becca to say something. I was even more slowly closing the door when she said, "See you tomorrow."

"For sure!" I gushed.

I watched as she answered a text before driving off, wondering if the smile was for me or for whomever had sent the message.

At supper, Annie was briefly happy to hear that Becca and I were patching things up, but that only lasted until she figured out she'd missed a ride home. She glared at me as she chewed her steak so aggressively and thoroughly that she could have fed it to a baby bird. (Not that baby birds eat steak, but you get my point.) Sisters. They hardly seem worth the bother.

Although I had an enormous pile of homework that I needed to get started, I went to my room right after supper and lay in the dark, letting the calm and quiet soothe my headache. When my phone buzzed on the bedside table, I was tempted to just ignore it, but the thought that it could be Becca with further communication got me to reach out an arm for it. I opened one eye to read the text. It wasn't from Becca. It wasn't from anyone in my contact list. *heard u went car surfing!?*

I closed my eyes again. Of course, the rumor mill had started its work already. By tomorrow, everyone would think I'd done somersaults atop a moving car. I decided to ignore the message.

Then my phone buzzed again. I propped myself up on my pillows, leaning my head against the headboard as I read the new message. *srsly. u didn't actually car surf in the school parking lot, did u? ;)*

This was weird. I decided I needed to be direct. *Who is this? How do you have my number?*

lol. sorry. should have said. its charlotte. got your # from zach. hope thats ok!

I remembered giving the crew my number in case they needed to get hold of me urgently, but why would Zach give some random girl my contact info? It took me another embarrassing minute of staring at the phone before my brain, burnt out from too much emotional work and still suffering from a headache, figured out that this was THE CHARLOTTE. Charlotte of the bluest eyes and the protruding incisor and the coolest hair. That Charlotte was waiting for me to say something. *That's ok*, I texted back. Worst. Banterer. Ever. I hadn't even bothered to include an emoji.

Charlotte didn't respond right away, and I was desperately trying to think of something clever or flirtatious to say when my phone vibrated in my hand: *u 2day*. I'd received a cheesy gif of a corgi riding a skateboard. It made me laugh, partly because corgis are ridiculous animals that obviously are popular only because they're the pets of weirdo royals, but also because I was giddy with the pleasure of texting the girl of my dreams. I texted back: *Ouch. I can't believe you're comparing me to a stumpy dog with oversized ears! I'm insulted. ;)*

I held my breath and clutched my phone in both hands as I waited for her response. I hoped the winky face was enough to convey that I was joking. *corgis aren't stumpy!* Uh-oh. I was about to respond with a lame explanation that I was just joking when another text came in. *theyre adorable, just like u.*

This was obviously flirtatious. I needed to say something flirty back. Or did I? Hadn't I promised myself that I wouldn't get distracted this year, that I would focus on becoming vale-dictorian? Wasn't my future more important than a crush? The answer wasn't as clear as it had been just a week earlier. I mean, how often does your crush hit on you? This very cool girl, who should have been out of my league, seemed to be pursuing me. Wouldn't I be a fool to pass this up? I was poised to answer when she texted: *g2g. ttyl.*

I was a little disappointed, but also a little relieved that I didn't need to think of something clever to say. I texted back: *ttyl.* A second later, I added a smiley face.

CHAPTER 22

I woke up smiling. Things were looking up for ol' Alison. I hummed as I brushed my teeth and even let Annie use the toaster before me. I wasn't usually a morning person, but this day was different. Becca was talking to me again, Charlotte was flirting with me, and I knew the essay I'd written on *King Lear* was good enough to reassure Ms. Merriam that I was back to my old self. Yes, things were looking up.

I practically floated through all my Friday classes. I multi-tasked at lunch, eating my sandwich while I prepped a review sheet for a history test the next week. I'd been sitting alone at lunch since the Fake Date Incident, but today was different. I knew Becca had an appointment with the guidance counselor at lunch to go over some university application stuff. How did I know this? Because she'd texted me to say so. She'd added that she'd give me a drive home after school. Communication had progressed to texts.

The drive home was mostly silent again, but the music wasn't quite as aggressively loud today, and after I asked, Becca told me her meeting with the guidance counselor went well. Things weren't normal, but the silence didn't feel as oppressive today. When she stopped to drop me off, Becca put Harvey in park instead of just braking long enough for me to get out the door. I took this as a sign and sat still after I unbuckled my seatbelt.

"Want to come over tomorrow to watch a scary movie?" Becca asked. She was a horror movie aficionado. I wasn't into scary movies, but I recognized the peace offering for what it was.

"Sounds great. I'll bring some kettle corn." I grinned at Becca, and she gave me a half smile. More progress.

Walking in the front door, I felt so good, so on top of things that I decided this was the weekend I was going to tackle some of the scholarship essays I'd been putting off. I was like an athlete on a winning streak: There was no stopping me now!

At supper, Annie talked about an open mic night she was planning to play next Saturday. She was thinking about performing one of her own songs, something she'd never done in public before. Our parents were both appropriately supportive and made a point of taking out their phones and marking the date and time in their calendars. Annie then turned to me. "Are you going to come?" I was surprised Annie wanted us there, but if that's what she wanted, I was happy to oblige.

"Count me in!" I said, and Annie rolled her eyes at my enthusiasm, but I could tell she was pleased we were all making a fuss.

Before bed, I organized myself so I'd be ready to start writing the essays the next morning. I printed out all the instructions and arranged the applications according to due date. Pleased with myself, I was about to head to bed early when a sudden urge stopped me. I sat on the corner of my bed and pulled out my phone. I hadn't heard anything from Charlotte since last night. Maybe it was my move. Before I could over-think things, I decided to send a pic of a sloth snuggled in a fuzzy blanket and hugging a teddy bear. I followed up with *goodnight*. Only a few seconds later, she sent me a pic of a corgi sleeping on its back, legs splayed. It was a good day.

When I woke up the next morning, I could remember snippets of my dreams. They featured Charlotte in her fairy queen costume, though there was much less of it than I recalled from Zach's sketches. I checked my phone. No more messages from Charlotte. I wasn't surprised; our texts from the night before had been just to say good night, but it was still a bit of a letdown. I shook the feeling, reminding myself that *she* had asked for *my* number. She wasn't playing hard to get.

I reached the kitchen in time to ask Dad to double his smoothie recipe. Full glass in hand, I returned to my room and opened my laptop to start my first essay. Question: Give an example of a time you took on a leadership role. Were you successful in the role? If you were, why? If you weren't, why not?

This was going to be easy. I started my essay: *This year, I volunteered to produce our school play.* (No need to tell a scholarship committee that I'd been tricked into "volunteering.") *The role required me to organize a team of weirdos and outcasts.* (Too honest. Would have to change that wording later.) *I liaised between the play's director and the production team.* (I didn't have to mention that my liaising was often ineffective, did I?) *As to whether I was successful in this role or not, the jury is still out. Our goth scene-painter may be planning to sabotage the whole thing from the inside. I still haven't figured out how to organize ticket sales, and I'm afraid of all the tech work coming up. I do not have a good track record with power tools, as the birds who survived the great birdhouse disaster of Grade 8 can attest to. I mean, the play is still weeks away, so there's time to get things done. But not that much.*

Maybe this wasn't the right question to answer first. I could feel my old friend Anxiety setting in. I remembered my good mood from yesterday and rolled my neck a few times. I decided to move on to the next essay. Question: What is your biggest weakness?

I am a perfectionist. I don't mean this in the way that most people do, as an attempt to sneak in a strength in the guise of a weakness. My perfectionism has cost me in big ways. I may have the chance to date the girl of my dreams, but I have to ace all my classes and produce the school play and write these ridiculous essays, so I'm probably going to screw things up. What kind of question is this anyway? Why would knowing my greatest weakness help you decide if I'm a good candidate for your scholarship? Don't you remember what it's like to be a teenager? Asking us to think of our weaknesses is like asking a cat to lick its butt. We're going to do it anyway, so why go out of your way to get us to do it?

This was not good. These essays were not going to win me any scholarships. But more worrying was the feeling that none of this mattered. I didn't want to write essays, no matter how important they had seemed just a few days ago. I wanted to text Charlotte. I wondered briefly if the Red Binder had any tips about romances between actors and producers. I shook my head. I had to be desperate if I was considering consulting the binder.

I lay back on my bed and stared at the ceiling. I had another flashback to my dreams of the night before. I snapped closed my laptop cover and took out my phone.

So I was kinda thinking about how useless corgis are. Their legs are so disproportionate. Just think of all the photos on the Internet of corgis falling over. They are an evolutionary aberration. I pressed send, even though I knew I was taking a chance by making fun of corgis. Maybe they were her favorite animals, which is why she kept sending me pictures of them. But Charlotte seemed like a girl with a sense of humor, so I felt the risk was calculated. I waited, even though I knew it was only eleven o'clock on a Saturday and plenty of my peers would still be in bed.

i was hoping id hear from u today.

I was floating again, the scholarship essays forgotten. We texted back and forth for hours. I thought about suggesting an actual phone call, but I felt safer with typed words. As fast as we texted, I always had time to think about what I was "saying." Real conversations didn't have that editorial moment; I got into trouble when I had to converse in real life. Plus, texting had the advantage of gifs, which were great conversation pieces and helped express things words alone could not convey. When she sent me a gif of Lily Tomlin saying "I'm engaging with all the people in Internet-land," I knew I was in love. What other person my age appreciated Lily Tomlin? My guess was only a fellow lesbian. I felt pretty certain at this point that Charlotte was into girls—was into me, in fact. Of course, neither of us had come out to the other, but maybe it went without saying. I felt relieved to think that might be the case. Maybe not every new friend or crush meant I had to declare my sexual preference.

Just before suppertime, Charlotte sent me a text telling me she had to meet some friends. The sad-face emoji at the end of the message gave me the confidence to respond: *We should get together some time.* I didn't think Charlotte would be so quick to take up the suggestion, but I shouldn't have been surprised given how open and self-assured she'd been since we first met. *how about next sat?* I didn't even pause before replying: *It's a date.*

CHAPTER 23

I was almost late getting to Becca's for our movie night but made it just in time, thanks to a bag of kettle corn my father had hidden at the back of the pantry. If I'd needed to stop to pick up snacks along the way, I would have been late for sure. It seemed the gods were still smiling on me.

We settled into the basement media room, an array of sweet and salty snacks laid out on the glass coffee table. We sat as far away from each other as we could on the oversized couch and didn't talk much. Every ten minutes or so, Becca answered a text. She angled her phone so I couldn't see anything, which was a bit strange, but given that I was on friend probation, I pretended not to notice.

The movie was gory, but I didn't mind. I had a date with Charlotte. After a particularly gross scene of dismemberment, Becca looked over at me to see how I was handling the blood.

I must have been smiling because she seemed a bit freaked out by my reaction. I tried to change my facial expression to disgust, but I couldn't maintain it for long. I was too giddy with my good fortune to pay attention to the movie.

When the movie was over, we sat through all the credits, neither of us quite sure what to do next. As the screen faded to black, I sat forward, signaling my readiness to leave if that's what Becca wanted. She sat back, settling into a corner of the couch. In this position, she was half facing me. I followed her lead and sat back.

Becca sighed and looked at the blank TV screen as she spoke. "I know you thought you were doing something nice with that whole third-wheel-date thing. I know you thought you were helping me get together with Jack." She paused, and I nodded my head vigorously. "But I also think you knew it was a bad idea, otherwise you would've told me about it beforehand. And that's what really bothers me. That you basically lied to me because you knew I wouldn't agree to do what you wanted." I nodded my head, less enthusiastically this time. "So I need you to promise you won't ever do something like that to me again."

"I promise, Becca. Honestly, I was an idiot and I know it. I didn't want to hurt Jack's feelings and I came up with a stupid plan. You're right. I knew you'd hate the idea and I shouldn't have lied to you." I reached out my pinky finger. "I pinky swear I will never trick you into a date ever again." Becca snorted and wrapped her pinky finger around mine. We raised and lowered our hands exactly three times, just as we had when we swore pinky oaths as kids.

"Okay. Now spill the news. I can tell you've been holding back." Becca turned to face me properly now. Talking to my best friend again felt a bit like coming home after a bad camping trip (not that I'd ever experienced a good camping trip, but that probably had something to do with my aversion to squatting to pee).

"Well, I kinda have a date with Charlotte." I could feel myself blushing and grinning. I had no control over my treacherous body. I would never be able to play it cool.

Becca was staring at me wide-eyed. "Like, a real date? With Charlotte Russell?"

"Hey! Don't sound so shocked." I was a little hurt that Becca was so incredulous. If my best friend thought Charlotte was out of my league, I was in trouble.

"It's just that you always act like such a…dork around her."

It was hard to argue with Becca's observation. In texts, it was easy to talk to Charlotte. In person, I did things like pet award cases and fumble with faucets. "Yeah." I picked at a loose thread on my sweatpants.

Becca nudged my leg with her bare foot. "This is great, Al. It is. I'm just surprised you kept your cool long enough for her to ask you out."

"I asked her out, actually," I said, proud of myself for showing some gumption.

"Well, this I need to hear. Tell me everything."

We ate the last of the popcorn, and I told Becca all about the texts. I even showed her a few, the ones I thought weren't too private. By the time I had finished the story, Becca was smiling.

"Al, this could only happen to you."

"What do you mean?" I felt defensive.

"I mean, you're always doing impossible things. Like getting me to publish an article in the school paper pointing out that basketball at our school is basically a violent entertainment sport."

"But you had to resign because of that article," I said.

"But it shouldn't even have been possible! Just like Jenny shouldn't have agreed to paint sets for the school play. And there's no way macho Ben Weber should ever, in a million years, have decided to play a fairy." Becca punctuated each of her points with a shake of the head. Her curls bounced around, and she tried to tuck them behind her ears.

"Ms. Merriam helped me with Ben," I reminded her.

"Not the point. Somehow, you get us all to do crazy things. Your sister even helped clean out the drama storage room! When was the last time Annie cleaned her room?"

I took a moment to think. "Probably last summer when Mom threatened to hold back her allowance if some of the missing plates and forks didn't make a reappearance."

Becca scrunched her nose. "Ew. Anyway, the point is that only you could get a date with one of the hottest girls at school, even though she's seen you at your worst. I mean, rumor had it she was dating the lead singer of some punk band. But you never give up, even when you should."

"A punk band?" I asked.

Becca nodded her head. I had so many follow-up questions I wanted to ask, like whether this singer was a guy or a girl and how Becca knew about this and I didn't, but I could see Becca had something else she wanted to say. I stayed quiet. This had to be about her.

Becca stared me straight in the eye. "How long would you have hung on to Harvey if Mr. Patel hadn't shown up?"

"I needed to show you how important you are to me," I said, leaning forward.

"I couldn't stay mad at you forever. If I did, I'd miss out on all the fun." There was a twinkle in Becca's eye, the same look she had every time we started out on an adventure.

Becca was not a hugger, but this called for a hug. I leaned forward and caught her up in a hug before she could stop me. She put up with it for almost five whole seconds before patting me on the back, a sign that I had better stop with this gushy display of affection.

"What about you? What have you been up to?" I asked. Becca proceeded to tell me all about her feud with a mechanic who wanted three hundred dollars to fix one of Harvey's many ailments. She paused every once in a while to respond to a text. When I asked who it was, she said, "Oh, just some guy I'm helping with math." I wiggled my eyebrows at her, and she punched me only medium-hard in the arm. It was a perfect end to the perfect day.

CHAPTER 24

For the first time, I was looking forward to going to rehearsal. The moment I walked into the room I could feel Charlotte's presence. She was like the sun; I could feel her light and warmth soaking into me. She was wearing a plaid shirt with rolled cuffs today. Her bare arms looked strong, though she was slim. We smiled at each other as the group gathered in a circle.

After his opening remarks, Mr. Evans asked us all to stand up and put our hands into the middle of the circle. "Grab hold of two other people's hands!" he instructed. There was a mad scramble as people tried to find the hands of their friends. I felt a warm palm press itself into my right hand and recognized the arm and rolled cuff immediately. I squeezed Charlotte's hand and barely noticed when someone else took hold of my left hand. "This game is called Human Knot," Mr. Evans explained as he circled us. "Your task is to untangle yourselves. At no point can you let go of each other's hands. This exercise will require you to communicate clearly and also to be patient."

"But Mr. Evans, this is totally impossible," a freshman whined.

Mr. Evans grinned, delighted that someone had fed him the expected line. "In theater, we do impossible things all the time. Now get to work!"

Some of the seniors took charge, directing people to move this way or that. It worked for a while, until they started bickering with each other. Then people pulled and pushed without any real sense of direction. Mr. Evans admonished us, "You need to communicate." But no one was listening. The person holding my left arm jerked me over, and I had to pull Charlotte along with me. I followed the left-hand-holder until I was face-to-face with a junior who was so tangled up that she couldn't move. She couldn't get her arm up to let me pass under, but the person holding my left hand kept pulling harder and harder until I had to shout, "Ow! Stop pulling. We need a second here."

Which was when I discovered that Ben was the person holding my left hand. He glared down his long nose at me. "Don't be such a baby. Let's get this over with." He tugged on me again, and this time I pulled back.

"Stop it, Ben."

He pulled harder, and I fell on top of the poor junior in front of me. I had to let go of Ben's hand, as well as Charlotte's, so that I could catch myself as I fell. The group froze.

"What is your problem?" I yelled at Ben as I got up.

"You're my problem! Why are you even doing the warm-ups with us? You're just the producer." He jabbed his finger at me. I could see the blue veins in his neck. He was mad and bigger than me, but I had put up with enough crap from Ben Weber.

"*Just* the producer? Do you have any idea how much work I do so you can prance around onstage?" Ben took a step toward me, but I refused to concede any ground to him. Things might have escalated if Charlotte hadn't stepped between us just as Mr. Evans put a hand on Ben's shoulder.

"Ben, maybe you should go take a walk," Mr. Evans suggested quietly. Of course, the big baby was being coddled. Teachers never saw him for the asshole he was.

Charlotte caught my eye, holding eye contact as I calmed down.

"Sorry, Mr. Evans," Ben mumbled. Such a suck-up. "I don't need to take a walk. I'm calm."

"Passion is important for actors, but you need to channel that passion into your performance. You can't let it take control." Mr. Evans looked over at me. "Isn't that right, Alison?"

I looked at Mr. Evans, then back to Charlotte. Was I getting in trouble for yelling at Ben because *he'd* been a jerk? Charlotte shook her head almost imperceptibly. I knew the warning was for my benefit, but I was still disappointed that she wasn't as outraged as I was. Would she be so calm if Ben had implied that she didn't belong here? That all her hard work was unnoticed? As usual, though, I knew I had to rise above, to be mature. "Yes, Mr. Evans," I said.

Mr. Evans decided that "after all the excitement," we should take five minutes to meditate and "find our centers" before we started rehearsal. I chose a spot as far away from Ben as possible, and Charlotte sat nearby. I liked that she gave me room to cool down while still staying close enough to show her support. I knew I had to calm down, so I pictured my thoughts as clouds in the sky. I wanted to let them pass by, but they felt like gathering rain clouds. They were too dark and heavy to drift away. Ben Weber was a sexist scumbag, but he wasn't usually so aggressive. What had gotten into him? The only time I'd seen him mad before was the day I'd spotted him arguing with Zach.

What was I doing? Why was I trying to understand the motivations of Ben Weber, certified jackass? I listened to the nature sounds Mr. Evans was playing for us and focused on breathing in and out. By the time the meditation was over, I was feeling much cooler. When Charlotte looked over at me to check in, I gave her a real smile. She smiled back before taking her place in the opening scene.

We started blocking, so I sat at my little desk and took notes. It was my responsibility to help the actors remember where they were supposed to stand. It felt a bit silly to be noting where everyone entered and exited, but the Red Binder had insisted that the promptbook was crucial to a "professional-looking production." I didn't know if we should aim so high as "professional-looking," but I could see how important my notes were when Mr. Evans reran bits of the first act. A number of the actors had already forgotten their cues. It felt good to be useful during a rehearsal. *See, Ben Weber? A producer is important.* A small part of me hoped Charlotte noticed as well.

Though we were a few weeks into rehearsals, it was obvious that some of the actors were still struggling to get their lines right. Charlotte, Jack, and, to my great disappointment, Ben seemed to have the easiest time with the Shakespearean language. Listening to the stilted dialogue of the other performers, I remembered that Annie had nicknamed this Ye Olde Shakespearean Disaster. I had to find a way to sell tickets to this thing. Watching Mr. Evans run the actors through simple lines again and again, I worried about having to sell tickets to three performances. At least we had a big cast, which meant a bunch of parents and friends buying tickets just to be supportive.

The last hour of rehearsal passed quickly. I alternated between taking notes for the promptbook and brainstorming ideas to get people to come see the show. So far, my best ideas were to either bribe people with cupcakes or get the actors to beg people in the hallway. I remembered the last time I'd tried to make vanilla cupcakes from a mix. Through some weird alchemical reaction, they had burned on the outside while remaining raw on the inside. So that was out. Actors didn't seem to embarrass easily, so maybe the begging thing could work, if they could manage to look pathetic enough.

At the end of rehearsal, Charlotte stopped by my desk. She wasn't wearing makeup today, and she looked gorgeously androgynous. Her slim hips were boyish while her long lashes and pouty lips were distinctly feminine. I was jealous of her ability to look great with so little effort. She smiled at me, that protruding incisor catching on her lip. "You know, I think you need to give corgis a break. How can you not think they're cute?"

I leaned back a little in my chair. "They aren't cute. They're too weird looking. Sorry. I stand by my position on corgis."

Charlotte laughed her hiccup-y laugh and said, "I'll change your mind yet, Alison Green." I liked how my name sounded when she said it. She made it sound exciting, like the name of an international spy, or at least a meteorologist on a popular local radio station.

"We'll see about that. I wish I could walk you out, but I need to stay to go over some notes with Mr. Evans."

"Call of duty, I get it. Text me later." One more dazzling smile and Charlotte left. Thanks to Charlotte, my earlier confrontation with Ben was forgotten. Well, nearly forgotten. I couldn't help glaring at him as he left the room, hating everything about him, right down to his trendy backpack. But the thought of Charlotte kept me from throwing something heavy at his head, which showed just how much power she had over me.

CHAPTER 25

I still wasn't having much luck with the scholarship essays. The unfiltered truth thing wasn't working, but I couldn't seem to turn it off. I had a couple of months before most of the applications were due, so I set them aside and decided to focus on another problem: the play's budget. I couldn't count on the show selling out (or even selling well at this point), and the five hundred dollars the school had given us as "seed money" was almost all spent, so I needed to find another source of revenue. I scowled at the Red Binder as I picked it up. I could almost feel it gloating in my hands, like it knew I'd already conceded that it was right about the promptbook. "You don't have to be such a know-it-all," I whispered, flipping through the pages to see what advice it had about money.

When I found the relevant page, I laughed out loud. "While it is the responsibility of the director to put together a play the audience will want to watch, it is the producer's job to fill the theater seats." So basically, it would be my fault if the show didn't sell out. Is that it, Red Binder? "The producer of a school play has three sources of money: school budget (always tight), ticket sales (unpredictable), and ads for the program. Obviously, the surest revenue source is selling ads for the program." The Red Binder wasn't even trying to disguise its contempt for me at this point. But I wasn't going to take its sass. I would show it I could do this job. I kept reading. "As soon as possible, approach local businesses with the opportunity to both improve their visibility in the community and show their support for the arts." Calling a school play "the arts" seemed a bit much, but the argument otherwise made sense. "If the producer fails to procure the support of local businesses, s/he may resort to imploring parents of cast members to place congratulatory messages for a fee, but this should be the last resort of a desperate producer." I wasn't desperate. I would get that ad revenue. So there, Red Binder.

I brought up the topic of selling ads at our next production team meeting. No one was exactly enthusiastic.

Zach looked at the ground as he apologized. "Sorry, Al. I've been dealing with some personal stuff lately and I've fallen behind with the costumes. I can't help with the ads if we want to start fittings soon." I remembered our conversation about the closeted boyfriend and told him not to worry about it. He was looking a little rough, now that I took a second glance. He had dark under-eye circles and his sneakers were scuffed.

Jenny didn't even try to make an excuse. "I'm not doing

that," she said. You had to give the girl credit for being straightforward.

That left Annie and Becca. I looked at them both, and they looked at each other. I could feel another "no" coming on, so I decided to break out the puppy dog eyes. Becca laughed and Annie rolled her eyes, but I could tell they felt sorry for me. I was not beyond using pity to get the job done.

"I can't this week," Annie said. "But maybe next week I can go grovel for money for you." Her tone told me she was serious, so I didn't push her. I was hoping to get the ads sorted this week, but if that didn't work out, it would be useful to have backup for the week after. Anyway, Annie's blue hair might turn off some of the more conservative business owners.

We all looked at Becca who put her hands on her hips but eventually conceded. "Fine. I'll knock on some doors this week. Maybe my dad will want to buy an ad for the store." Becca's father owned a local hardware store where all the suburban do-it-yourselfers went for advice and supplies.

"Great! Maybe he'd even be willing to help us build some of the set pieces?" I knew I was pushing my luck, but Ms. James still hadn't been able to find me a student volunteer who knew anything about building. Obviously, having had just one shop class in Grade 8 was insufficient. None of my peers could build anything more useful than a birdhouse.

"Maybe." Becca sounded skeptical, but I knew Mr. McArthur liked a challenge. I just had to present the set design as a creative experiment, a way to test his skills in a new way. Helping clueless homeowners build decks got boring after a while. Jenny's designs and Mr. Evans's unusual requests would certainly keep Mr. McArthur on his toes.

The rest of the meeting went well, if I do say so myself. Jenny showed us some pictures of the backdrops she was outlining. As usual, she dismissed our compliments but blushed under her makeup. Zach really was behind. He hadn't made any progress since our last meeting, but at least he had a plan for how he would catch up. Costume fittings for some of the actors could start as early as next week, so I made a note to ask Mr. Evans to let the actors leave rehearsals for their fittings. Annie had managed to find an old ukulele a musician friend was willing to give away for free and had painted it bright turquoise. She was also collecting fake flowers and greenery for the fairy scenes. Finally, Becca said she'd been able to talk a couple of her acquaintances into helping out with lighting and sound at the show. I wondered what kind of persuasion that had required. We needed them, so I chose not to ask about her methods.

"We're in pretty good shape," I told my team. I was proud of them and I wanted them to know it. "Thanks for everything you're doing."

"Happy to do it," Zach said before he left. He seemed down, but it appeared like the meeting had distracted him from his worries, at least for a little while.

Jenny grunted at me and stomped out the door. Her rudeness didn't bother me anymore. I was starting to suspect it was a cover for extreme shyness.

Annie, Becca, and I left the meeting. It was nice to know we were driving home together without having to say anything.

It felt like things were back to normal. I asked Becca if maybe we could go see her father at his store after we dropped off Annie.

"You don't waste time, do you?" Becca twirled Harvey's keys in her right hand as we made our way down the empty school hallway. I grinned at her. "At least the store isn't too busy on Wednesdays. He'll probably have time to talk to us." I grinned some more, and Becca warned me, "But don't get your hopes up."

After we dropped Annie at home, Becca took me to her father's store. She parked Harvey at the back of the parking lot. He wasn't always well-behaved in parking lots, so it was usually best to park far away from other cars. He didn't exactly accelerate smoothly, and the soccer moms in their SUVs didn't like it when a car came mere inches from their bumpers.

McArthur Hardware smelled like wood and glue and paint. There was something wholesome about the smell, though that feeling was maybe influenced by my childhood memories of playing hide-and-go-seek in the aisles. We wound our way through shelves stocked with screws, nails, and bolts. Becca waved at a few of the employees wearing the blue-and-red-striped apron uniform. At the back of the store, Becca knocked at a door marked Employees Only. I remembered how important we felt walking through that door when we were little.

At the end of a short hallway, Becca's father was seated at his desk, his office door open. He smiled wide when he saw us, setting aside a stack of papers he'd been reviewing. He was a big man with a smile to match. "Hi, girls! I can't remember the last time you visited me at work. Are you here to ask for money to go get ice cream?" Mr. McArthur teased us, hearkening back to the days in middle school when we would take the school bus to the strip mall where his shop was located just so we could get enough money to go to the convenience store next door to get Popsicles. "I don't have any screws that need sorting today, unfortunately."

"Darn." Becca's sarcasm was half-hearted. Mr. McArthur had never made us sort screws for long. He would put us to work for five minutes before giving us the money we needed and shooing us out. It might have had something to do with our singing. Time might have passed faster for us when we sang while we worked, but it probably slowed to a near stop for everyone else.

Becca plopped down in a chair across from her father. She mostly looked like her mother, her dark hair and brown skin part of her Moroccan heritage, but she had her father's eyes, right down to the sparkle of humor. I took the empty seat beside Becca.

"So. To what do I owe this pleasure?" Mr. McArthur pushed his reading glasses to the top of his head. He was a little chubbier and a little balder than he used to be, but he still had the muscled arms of a man who had always worked with his hands.

"Alison has something she wanted to talk to you about," Becca explained.

They both looked at me, and I stuttered, "Well, ah, Mr. McArthur, you see, we're working on the school play, you know?" I sounded like an idiot. Not the kind of person who persuaded others to do them favors.

But Mr. McArthur was kind. "Yes, I do know that. Is there something you need help with?"

"Well, actually, yes. See, we need to build some stuff for the set. I think they're called platforms. Also, trees. Well, not real trees, but things that look like trees that our set painter can, uh, paint. And maybe some other stuff that the director hasn't thought of yet." I paused. "You know how the birdhouses went in Grade 8." Mr. McArthur nodded. Becca still had a scar on her right thumb thanks to that project. "I don't know anyone who can build stuff that's safe. Except for you. So I was kinda hoping you might, you know…help us build the sets." The rambling was embarrassing. This is what happened when I didn't rehearse what I wanted to say. I probably should have written a letter and passed it along to Mr. McArthur via Becca. It was too late now, though.

"I don't know, Alison. I'm awfully busy." Mr. McArthur gestured at the paperwork on his desk, proof that the owner of a small business didn't have time to volunteer to build sets for the high-school play.

"I totally understand, Mr. McArthur. But it will be such an interesting project! Think about it. Have you ever built a tree? It'll put your creative juices to work." Creative juices? I was starting to sound like Mr. Evans, which was truly terrifying. But I couldn't stop now. "Plus, you're so good, I'm sure it'll hardly take you any time."

Mr. McArthur held up his hands in surrender and chuckled. "Okay, okay, okay. You can stop with the flattery. I'll do it."

"You will?" I looked at Becca, who seemed just as surprised as I was.

Mr. McArthur shrugged his shoulders. "Why not? Might even be fun."

"Thanks!" I stood up and reached out to shake his hand. Mr. McArthur chuckled again and took my hand. I could feel the calluses he'd earned through years of physical work. Much like Becca, he came across as tough, but underneath he was kind and generous. Before we left, I agreed to send him the "specs" as soon as I had them. I also made a note to myself to figure out who would have the specs.

When we reached Harvey, Becca performed the car-starting rituals. As we pulled out of the parking lot, she said, "See? You get people to do shit. It's like some kind of weird magic power."

I thought that it was probably the gift of getting people to feel sorry for me, but I wasn't about to give up any power I had in this battle royale against the Red Binder.

CHAPTER 26

The brass bell over the glass door tinkled. Again. The first dozen times, I thought the sound was musical. That was before the infuriating conversation with the gum-chewing clerk who couldn't figure out how to page the manager for me. It was also before I roamed the aisles of Avon Craft Supplies looking for the manager, only to find her back at the front cash, chatting with the gum-chewer, who hadn't bothered to tell the manager I was looking for her. And it was before said manager insisted on having me make my pitch standing at the front counter in front of her gray-haired customers, all of whom seemed to think I was "adorable," but who kept interrupting me to ask for a particular knitting needle or to argue the price of a glue gun. At this point, I wanted to rip the brass bell off the wall and run it over with my father's Volvo. But I didn't. I kept my cool and asked the manager if she would be interested in buying a quarter-, half-, or full-page ad in the program.

The manager looked up from a stack of cross-stitch patterns long enough to say to me, "Oh, I don't think so, dear. We have commitments to other organizations, and we don't have the budget to support any more causes this month. Why don't you leave me your phone number, and I'll call if things change." She was trying to be nice, but I knew she was brushing me off.

This was my fifth store of the afternoon, and they'd all given me the runaround. The Laundromat owner had to "consult" with his wife before committing. The king of used car sales wasn't sure about buying an ad to a Shakespeare performance when there were "more popular" avenues open to him. The grocery store manager and the florist just told me to leave the price list with them and walked me out, darting looks left and right as they shooed me out the door. It was like they were afraid to be seen with me, which sounded completely paranoid. I knew that. And yet…I didn't know how else to explain it. I'd done my share of fundraising for walk-a-thons. When people said no to a kid asking for money, they were usually apologetic. But they weren't nervous.

I hoped Becca was having more luck than I was. We'd agreed it would be too much to ask her father to both volunteer his time and buy an ad, so Becca was targeting the other businesses in the strip mall where McArthur Hardware had been a mainstay for twenty years. Becca knew all the owners and managers. We hoped they'd remember the little girl in braids who liked to follow her daddy around.

Becca called me as I was leaving the craft store. I sat on a bench on the sidewalk and kicked at some pebbles. "Al, this is seriously weird. Old Mrs. Lawrence had zero interest in buying an ad. She used to buy out almost all my cookies when I was in Brownies, just to be helpful. I thought it might just be an off day for her, but I got a no at every store I went into."

"Yeah, I'm not having any luck either. Do you think our prices are too high?" I stood up and paced the sidewalk.

"I don't think so," Becca said. "Mrs. Lawrence didn't even let me show her the price list. No one has said anything to me about the prices. You?"

I stopped pacing and sat back down on the bench. I leaned forward, elbows on my knees, and stared at the concrete. "No. You're right. No one has said anything about the prices."

I could hear the creaky sound of Becca opening and closing her car door. "Maybe it's just a bad time to ask," she suggested. "We can give it another shot next week."

"Maybe. Thanks for trying, Becca. Now get off the phone before you start driving!" Becca wasn't an attentive driver at the best of times. I would not have her getting into an accident because she was on her cell talking to me.

"Yes ma'am." Becca chuckled and ended the call.

I might have stayed there feeling sorry for myself, but my phone buzzed. It was another message from Charlotte. Over the last two days, she had inundated me with photos of corgis doing "cute" things like attacking empty bottles and chasing their own tails. She was on a campaign to get me to love corgis. I wasn't any fonder of corgis, but I was falling hard for the girl sending me the texts. I smiled like an idiot as I texted her back. Even though I was sitting on a splintery bench looking out at a drab suburban street, I felt great.

I decided Becca was right. We'd probably have better luck next week. In the meantime, I had texts to answer and an outfit to pick out for Saturday night.

CHAPTER 27

By Saturday afternoon I was reduced to googling "What do lesbians wear on dates?" The results weren't all that helpful. I went from worrying about what to wear to agonizing over who would pay for the date. I had technically asked Charlotte out, so some websites suggested I should offer to pay. But that seemed weirdly old-fashioned. Would she think I was pushy if I paid? Or would she think I was rude if I didn't offer to pay? I checked my account balance to make sure I had enough cash left over from my summer job babysitting the Pratchett twins to buy supper. I breathed a sigh of relief when I saw that I had a good chunk of change sitting in my checking account. But then I remembered I still hadn't decided what to wear and went back to worrying.

Thanks a lot, Google. You're about as useful as the Red Binder today. The cursor blinked at me, completely unfazed by my criticism.

I stared at my closet for the hundredth time that week. I owned three pairs of jeans and an embarrassing number of T-shirts—too basic. I had a couple of cocktail dresses for family functions—too dressy. At the back of the closet, I found a jean skirt Becca had talked me into buying, despite the pastiness of my legs. I tried it on. My legs were so white they nearly blinded me. Otherwise, though, the skirt looked pretty good. My legs had a nice shape, despite their terrible color. Unfortunately, the one time I'd tried my mother's self-tanner, I ended up looking like a streaky Oompa Loompa, so that wasn't an option. The evenings were getting chilly. I wondered if I could wear the skirt with a pair of tights. It seemed worth a try, only I didn't own any tights.

I knocked on my sister's bedroom door. "Come in!" she shouted. I opened the door and gaped. Her room was even messier than usual. Annie was sitting on a chair in the middle of her room, her guitar resting on her lap and papers strewn on the floor around her, most of them crumpled. She looked like a tree losing its leaves.

Annie seemed frazzled, so I thought it was best if I didn't say anything about the room. "Annie, can I borrow a pair of tights?"

Annie was so distracted by something she was writing on a fresh piece of paper that she took almost a minute to look up at me and say, "Huh?"

"I just wanted to know if I could borrow a pair of tights for tonight?"

"Sure. Whatever." Annie waved her hand at her dresser. Three of the drawers were already open. I could see tights snaking their way over the edge of the top drawer. I walked over to the dresser on tiptoes, trying not to step on any papers.

"Can I take the purple pair?" I asked as I held them out to her. I thought they'd look cool with my red Converse sneakers.

"Yeah, yeah." Annie clearly wanted to get back to whatever she was doing, so I tiptoed my way back across the room.

At the doorway, I turned around. "Thanks, Annie." She grunted and crumpled another piece of paper. "Are you okay?"

"Just stressed about tonight."

I leaned on the doorjamb. "Tonight?"

"Yeah. I have a new song I want to play, but the bridge is giving me trouble. I know it's just a dinky open mic night, but a lot of my friends are going to be there, and you and Mom and Dad. I don't want to embarrass myself."

I felt panic rising in me. How could I have forgotten that tonight was Annie's show? How, how, how had I agreed to a date on the night my sister was playing in public for the first time ever? I'll tell you how. I was twitterpated. I was so excited about my first date with a girl that I'd become a forgetful airhead.

Annie was looking at me, waiting for a response. I couldn't let her know I'd forgotten about her big night. I had to play it cool. Time for a big sister pep talk. "Annie, I hear you playing your stuff through the wall all the time. It sounds great. You'll be awesome tonight."

"Whatever." Annie picked up a fresh piece of paper and strummed a chord. She frowned. My pep talk might not have worked, but at least Annie didn't know about my massive screw up. And she wasn't going to. I just needed to do a little creative problem solving.

In the hours leading up to my first real date, I googled local restaurants, distances, and panic attacks. I drew up a detailed itinerary thinking it might give me a sense of control. It didn't. I was about to google panic attacks again, when my mom knocked on my door and offered to lend me her Mini for the evening. Her way of showing support. My solution to a huge problem. Now I could pick up Charlotte, have time to eat, *and* get to Annie's performance on time. Furthermore, after a quick check, Google assured me that as the asker-outer, I was expected to choose the restaurant. I texted Charlotte and told her I'd pick her up at seven and got a smiley face back. Everything was suddenly working in my favor. I should have known better.

That night, dressed in an almost sexy, short-ish jean skirt, funky, borrowed purple tights, and a nearly trendy cropped jacket, I felt as close to cool as I ever had. Taking one last look in the hall mirror, I felt hopeful that when people saw me with Charlotte, they wouldn't wonder why she was hanging out with such a nerd.

I pulled into Charlotte's driveway a minute early. Google might not know much about how to counsel a young lesbian on her first date, but it did know its driving times. *I take it back, Google*, I thought. *You're way more useful than the Red Binder.*

At that moment, I spotted a corgi barreling toward the car, its tiny legs pumping hard and a demented doggy-smile plastered on its face. I opened my door and stepped out of the car. The corgi ran in tight circles around me. I bent down to pet the frenzied creature, hoping to calm it down before it had a doggy aneurysm. It licked my hand and plopped onto its back, stomach exposed for a belly rub.

"You wouldn't survive in the wild, would you?" I cooed. I crouched down and patted the stomach. "A predator would just bite this belly. Yes, it would."

"I see you've met Princess Sunshine." I looked up to see Charlotte grinning down at me. She looked beautiful, as always. I noticed that she had replaced the navy laces in her Docs with hot pink ones. Even with my purple tights, I couldn't hope to be as cool as her.

The dog nudged my hand. I had stopped petting it, and Princess Sunshine was having none of that. "Oh my god." I stood up as I came to a sudden realization, then started to babble nervously. "You have a corgi. This is your corgi. Princess Sunshine is a corgi."

"Excellent powers of observation."

"I've been making fun of corgis. A lot." I reached into my jacket pocket, feeling for the phone that documented all the offending texts.

Charlotte nodded, yet she was still smiling. "Yes, you have. Princess Sunshine would be hurt if he knew how much you make fun of corgis. Good thing the only words he knows are cookie, walk, and sit." Princess Sunshine cocked his head to the side. He didn't know how to react when a person used all three of his favorite words at once.

"He's cute," I said. And I meant it. He might be useless, but he was affectionate, and petting him had briefly lowered my blood pressure.

"You don't have to pretend to like corgis." Charlotte bent down to pet the dog, and he leaned into her leg.

"I'm not! I still think they're a stupid breed." *Smooth, Alison.* "I mean, they wouldn't survive in the wild. But what domesticated animal would? Princess Sunshine is super cute."

"He is at that," Charlotte agreed. "Just let me put him in the house and we can head out." She pulled gently on Princess Sunshine's collar, and after looking back at me once, he followed her to the house.

I got back into Mom's car, cursing my inner censor, who seemed to go on break at the most inconvenient times. I rested my head on the steering wheel for a moment, then looked at my watch. We were already behind schedule.

When Charlotte was settled in the passenger seat, I suggested we eat at an Indian restaurant that was only a block from where Annie was performing. I told her the reviews looked good, which was true, and that I'd been dying to try it, which was true in a way. I'd been looking forward to eating there since I learned about it that afternoon. I even managed to casually mention a show I thought might be worth catching. I didn't specify that my sister was in the show and that I'd already committed to going. I didn't want Charlotte to think I was bossy or punctilious; she could learn about those unfortunate characteristics later. Thankfully, Charlotte was game for all of it, and I felt hopeful as I backed the car out of her driveway.

I made my way through quiet suburban streets, and the silence seemed to drag. I checked the dash clock. Only two minutes had passed. Still, I felt the need to keep the conversation flowing.

"Princess Sunshine is an interesting name."

Charlotte chuckled and picked a white dog hair off her black pants. "My little sister named him. My father freaked out. I tried to explain to him that gender is a social construct, but he thinks I'm corrupting my little sister and that she'll turn out gay too. My mom had to convince him that a five-year-old isn't making a political statement when she names her dog. But he refuses to call the dog by name."

"My parents let us name our pet fish Snot and Fart," I offered. I felt guilty that my parents were so accepting of me and didn't know what to say about her homophobic dad. So I rambled on. "Snot and Fart didn't live long. It's probably not a good idea to put a six-year-old and a four-year-old in charge of feeding fish. Or naming them." I was regaling my date with the tragic story of two dead fish. I was hopeless at dating.

"Which one did you name?" Charlotte asked.

"Fart," I admitted.

Charlotte laughed. "I wish I could have met Fart."

"Well, I'm glad I got to meet Princess Sunshine. Maybe not all corgis are useless."

"He's pretty useless. But we love him."

"Even your dad?" I ventured. I didn't want to force her to discuss something awkward, but I also didn't want to seem like I was brushing off something important that she'd shared with me.

"Deep down, yeah. He just thinks it's his job to 'create boundaries.'" Her voice deepened as she imitated her father.

"What happens if you cross a boundary?" Without thinking, I'd slowed down. The car behind me was tailgating us in frustration. I pushed the gas a little.

Charlotte sighed. "Well, then he's disappointed in you. If you're a dog, you grovel for his approval. If you're his daughter, you learn not to tell your father that you're going on a date. You let your mom run interference."

I felt doubly grateful to my parents for being supportive and understanding. I also felt guilty for having things so easy.

"What about your parents?" she asked.

I pretended I didn't understand Charlotte's question. "It's kinda hard to create boundaries for fish."

Charlotte snorted. For the rest of the drive we talked about pets, and I felt like things might be going, if not well, at least not disastrously. That warm feeling followed me into the restaurant where we were seated at a quiet table in the corner. It even stayed with me as we both perused the vegetarian-friendly menu. Charlotte said she appreciated that I'd picked a restaurant where she could find more than one meal option. I grinned. Our server, a young man in black pants and a white T-shirt, asked if we had any questions about the menu. I said we were ready to order, thinking of my itinerary. Charlotte ordered first, and I noticed how the server leaned toward her, smiling and nodding enthusiastically. He was just as taken with her as I was. But his attention wasn't what ruined my feeling of well-being; I couldn't blame him for noticing how beautiful Charlotte was. No, what brought me back down was a flashback to my last "date."

What on earth was I going to do if I couldn't swallow my food again?

CHAPTER 28

I ordered saag paneer and naan bread, not wanting to alert Charlotte that anything weird might be going on. I couldn't invite her out to supper and then refuse to eat.

As soon as the server left to place our orders, I excused myself to go to the washroom. I locked myself in a stall and pulled out my phone. I called the only person I could think of.

Becca answered without saying hello. "Aren't you on your date right now? Why are you calling me?"

"I am on my date. I don't know if I can swallow my food." I held the speaker close to my mouth, practically whispering. This was not a conversation I wanted a stranger to overhear.

"What? Why wouldn't you be able to swallow your food?" Becca sounded puzzled, and I remembered that we hadn't discussed the date-which-should-not-be-mentioned, so she didn't know I had this swallowing problem.

"Sometimes when I get nervous, I can't swallow."

Becca chuckled. "Only you, Al. Only you." I did not find this helpful.

"Yeah, yeah. I'm a freak. But what do I do?"

"Stay calm."

"That's not useful advice. If I knew I could stay calm, I wouldn't be calling you." I stared at the graffiti on the stall door. *The future is in your hands.* It was like the graffiti was conspiring with Becca to feed me useless platitudes.

"Well, it's the only advice I have. Take some deep breaths and go back to your date!" She hung up before I could say anything else.

I left the safety of the stall and splashed some cold water on my neck. I looked at myself in the mirror and said, "Get it together, Alison Green." The pale-faced girl looking back at me seemed skeptical. I took one last deep breath and walked back into the dining room.

At the table, Charlotte was sipping an iced tea and looking at her phone. Her hair fell over her right eye in a funky swoop, and she tried to blow it out of the way. She might have been wearing lipstick, but it looked to me like her lips were just naturally coral pink. How was I lucky enough to be on a date with this girl? And how could I keep myself from screwing it up?

I sat down and took a tiny sip of my water. I swallowed it, but it seemed to take more effort than usual. I couldn't be sure, though, since I wasn't normally aware of how much effort it took for me to perform this basic human function.

Charlotte put away her phone and was now looking right at me with those frost-blue eyes. "Rehearsals seem to be going well," she said.

"Yes!" I clutched on to the topic like a drowning person grabbing hold of a floatation device. We were able to chat about the play as we waited for our food. I felt almost calm for a few minutes.

And then the food came. The warm smell of curry and ginger made my mouth water, but I was not fooled by this reflex. I couldn't trust that I would be able swallow any of the delectable dishes once I started eating.

Charlotte ripped a piece of naan bread and dipped it in her curry. I stared at my plate and moved the food around, a trick I had learned when eating my grandmother's burnt meatloaf and soggy mashed potatoes.

"This lentil curry is delicious," Charlotte told me between bites. "Want to try some?" She pushed the plate toward me, and I shook my head.

"I don't like lentils," I lied.

"Oh, okay," she said, digging into her food again with gusto. I was jealous of how easily it came to her. I ripped up some naan and dunked it into my saag paneer, hoping it looked like I was letting it soak up the sauce.

My charade couldn't last forever. Charlotte's plate was clearly getting emptier, while mine just looked messier. Eventually, Charlotte noticed. "Not hungry?" she asked.

"Not really."

She put down her fork and wiped her hands on a napkin.

"We didn't have to go out for supper if you weren't hungry."

"I was hungry," I hurried to explain.

"But you aren't now?" Charlotte was confused. I couldn't blame her.

I looked down at my plate, but there were no answers there. Instead, I thought about what Jack had said to me after I'd called him to apologize for the fake date. Maybe it was time to try the honesty thing. Still looking at my plate, I told Charlotte, "I'm nervous. This is kinda my first date with a girl and I really like you, and I don't want to screw things up." There it was. The naked truth. I felt exposed. Maybe Charlotte would think I was too immature or inexperienced to date.

Then I felt her hand take mine. I chanced a glance at our hands on the white tablecloth. Charlotte had long fingers, long enough to wrap my whole hand in hers. I felt warmth spread through my hand and up my arm. I felt it radiating throughout my whole body.

"Everyone's nervous on a first date. Do you know how many times I changed my outfit this afternoon?" she asked. She pressed my hand, and I looked up at her. "I really like you too." I felt like something had just squeezed my heart, but it felt good, not panicky. "Now are you sure you don't want to try some of this lentil curry? It's yummy." She let go of my hand to pick up her plate and offer it to me.

"Maybe a bite," I said, reaching my fork across the table to try the curry. Charlotte was right, it was delicious, creamy, and gingery. And I was able to swallow it, which felt like a major triumph.

I shared my saag paneer with Charlotte, and we lingered over a pot of chai, chatting about the play and our favorite books. I admitted to Charlotte that I reread the Anne of Green Gables books anytime I was feeling down, and she told me that for years she had lied and told people she was named after *Charlotte's Web*, when the truth was it was her great-grand-mother's name. "I just loved that spider so much, you know?" I thought there might not be a more perfect person in the world than Charlotte Russell.

I was so caught up in our conversation that I completely lost track of time. When the waiter placed our bill on the table, a subtle suggestion that maybe we'd overstayed our welcome at the now bustling restaurant, I remembered to check my watch. Annie's show had started half an hour ago! I prayed that she wasn't one of the first performers and snatched up the check, telling Charlotte I would pay at the cash. When she offered to pay half, I told her, "Why don't you get the cover for the show?" She nodded, and the money issue had been resolved quite simply, mostly because I was distracted by a more press-ing problem.

Annie's show was taking place at a quirky café/art space/organic bakery. The owners liked to support young artists, and they hosted an open mic night once a month so teens and twenty-somethings could perform their poetry, music, and stand-up comedy for an audience of mostly friends and family. The five-dollar cover went to charity, because that's just how community-minded the owners were. I made a mental note to hit them up for an ad-buy as I drove over.

I was locking the car doors when Charlotte asked me if I knew anyone performing. "Yeah, my sister," I admitted.

"Cool," she said, following me to the Odd Duck Café.

The hipster seated on a stool at the front door asked us for the cover. As Charlotte pulled money out of her wallet, I scanned the room. The place smelled of fresh bread and coffee. In the daytime, the café was lit by funky Mason jar chandeliers. Tonight, the mood was set by fairy lights and candles. Most of the small tables were occupied. The "stage" at the back of the room was just an Oriental rug with some stools and a drum set. At the moment, a trio of banjo players was performing. I wasn't unhappy that we'd missed some of their set. In fact, I hoped this was their last song.

Charlotte came to stand beside me, her arm pressed against mine in a very pleasant way. I would have stayed standing like that, but Charlotte tugged on my hand, pointing to a free table at the back. I was happy that the chairs were all pushed together so the audience could face the stage; it meant I had to sit close to Charlotte, her heat radiating through my body.

I looked around again, hoping to find my sister. Her face would tell me if she'd performed yet or not. But instead of my sister, I saw my parents, my dad's salt-and-pepper hair and my mother's perfect posture as familiar to me as the feeling of panic flooding my body. I was going to have to introduce Charlotte to my parents. On our first date. After she'd basically told me that she couldn't tell her father she was going on a date, I was going to introduce her to my super supportive parents? This was not good.

I pulled on the hem of my skirt, uncomfortable showing quite so much leg when my parents were in the room. I tried to focus on the stage, hoping my mother and father wouldn't see me. A young slam poet paced up and down. I didn't catch what he was saying, partly because he spoke so fast and partly because my attention was torn between him, my parents, and the beautiful girl beside me. When everyone applauded for him, I did too. It was an automatic reaction drilled into me by years of politely listening to classmates' presentations.

Annie walked up to the mic, a guitar hanging from her shoulder. I leaned forward, nervous for her.

"Is that your sister?" Charlotte asked.

"Yeah." I could tell Annie was nervous because she was looking over the audience, not at it.

"This is a song I wrote. It's called 'Cat Nap.'" Annie closed her eyes and started playing. Her voice was shaky at first, but it got stronger after just a few bars. It was a good song—funny, but not silly. When she finished "Cat Nap," the audience cheered louder than they had for the slam poet. I clapped loudest, but my parents clapped longest. I saw Charlotte glance at them and hoped she wouldn't notice that my sister had the same smile as my father.

"That sounded good, didn't it?" I asked Charlotte, hoping to draw her attention away from my parents.

Charlotte smiled. "Look at you, proud big sister. Yeah, she sounded good."

Annie played her next song, a cover of a Florence + the Machine track we both loved. The audience applauded warmly when she finished. Annie beamed as she left the stage.

An emcee came up to thank everyone for coming, and I stood up. "We should go," I told Charlotte.

Charlotte gestured at Annie. "Shouldn't you stay to say something to your sister?"

I waved at Annie. "Nah. I'll talk to her at home."

Charlotte stood up just as my parents approached the table. I wanted to grab her hand and pull her out of there, but I knew it was too late. There was no mistaking that they were coming to speak to us. I could see Charlotte looking from my mother to me, probably noticing that I have the same button nose.

My father spoke first. "We were afraid you weren't going to make it, Al."

"Wouldn't miss it for the world." I forced a smile. "I'll see you at home." I turned around and pulled Charlotte with me toward the door.

I was grateful my parents didn't follow or try to say anything else.

When we got outside, Charlotte asked, "Were those your parents?"

I nodded.

"Were you embarrassed to introduce me?" Charlotte crossed her arms, and I knew I had to explain.

"Yes. I mean, no. I mean, I thought it would be awkward to introduce you to my parents on our first date." I was rambling.

Charlotte raised an eyebrow. "More awkward than pretending I wasn't there?"

"Now that you mention it, no. I'm sorry. I didn't think about them being here when I said we should come to the show." I walked toward the car, and Charlotte followed, though I noticed her arms were still crossed.

"Are you out?" Charlotte asked before I could get in the car.

I looked at her over the top of the car. "Yes, I am. I told my family last year."

"Are they not okay with it?" She looked sympathetic.

I looked at the ground. "They're totally fine with it."

"Oh." Charlotte got into the car and I followed, remembering that her father wasn't "fine with it." I put the keys in the ignition but didn't turn the car on. I had to ask Charlotte something.

"Did you think I was in the closet?"

"I wondered."

"I didn't know if you were gay," I retaliated, even though Charlotte hadn't accused me of anything.

Charlotte remained calm. "I'm not."

How had I gotten things so very wrong? "Oh. But…Isn't this…?" I trailed off.

Charlotte saved me. "I identify as pansexual."

I nodded, pretending I knew what that meant. But then I remembered I was trying the honesty thing. "I, uh, I'm not exactly sure what that means."

Charlotte explained, "For me, it means I'm attracted to the person, not to their gender or sex." She reached for my hand.

"I really like you, but I don't want to be with someone who's ashamed to be with me."

I squeezed Charlotte's hand. "I'm not ashamed to be with you! I was just embarrassed to introduce you to my parents. I figured you'd think I was a weirdo who skips from first date to meet the parents." I paused. "Plus, it sounds like things aren't exactly cool with your dad, and I didn't want to rub it in your face that my parents are supportive."

Charlotte squeezed my hand back. "I'm happy your parents are supportive. Listen, my mom is great. And my dad is old-school, but I don't hide who I am from him, so I'm definitely not going to hide it from anyone else."

I nodded. "Of course. I get that."

Charlotte ran her thumb over my hand, and I shivered. "So you'd be okay holding hands at school?"

My brain was slow to process words; it was too preoccupied with the sensation of her skin on mine. "With you?" I asked.

Charlotte chuckled. "Yes, with me." She was tickling the palm of my hand now.

I caught my breath. "Absolutely. Yes. For sure."

"What about kissing?" she whispered, her voice huskier than a moment before.

"Well, that would be nice," I stammered. "I mean, I don't like it when people full-on make out in the hallways, but a tasteful public display of affection seems cool. I mean, if you wanted—"

Charlotte cut me off by leaning forward and kissing me.

At first, I felt stiff. I didn't know what to do, where to put my hands, how to move. But soon I couldn't think anymore. I closed my eyes and kissed Charlotte right back.

CHAPTER 29

This morning called for a Pop-Tart. I wasn't usually one for sweet breakfasts, but I felt like celebrating. After all, it's not every day you make out with your crush. I dug around in the cupboards to find my sister's stash of Pop-Tarts. Instead of choosing between Strawberry or S'mores, I decided to have one of each. I was humming as I waited for the toaster to finish its work when Annie slumped into the kitchen, her hair knotted from sleep.

"Good morning!" Even to my own ears, I sounded much too peppy for this time of day. But I couldn't help it.

"*Hmph*," Annie grunted back, digging around in the fridge for the orange juice.

The toaster popped, and I plucked out my breakfast. Annie squinted at my plate, the orange juice carton halfway to her mouth.

"Are you eating my Pop-Tarts?"

"I felt like Pop-Tarts this morning. I can get you more, if you want."

"You should've asked." Annie slammed the orange juice down on the kitchen counter, and it splattered.

"Sorry. I didn't want to wake you up." Annie wasn't usually this possessive of her foodstuffs. So long as you didn't finish the supply without replacing it, she was generally happy to share her junk food. In fact, Dad counted on Annie's generosity to survive Mom's occasional juice cleanses.

"This is so typical." Annie marched over to me and tried to grab the plate from my hand. Instinctively, I pulled it away.

"What's the matter with you this morning?"

"You're the matter with me this morning!" She grabbed for the plate again.

Annie seemed so angry that I decided the Pop-Tarts weren't worth the fight. I handed the plate to her, and she tossed the Pop-Tarts in the sink.

"Hey! I wanted those."

"Yeah? Well, you can't always get what you want, Al." Annie's fists were clenched.

"Why are you being such a brat? Your gig went well last night. You should be happy."

"How would you know? You were barely even there." Annie turned her back on me.

"I was there. I waved to you." Had Annie not seen me?

"Oh, yeah. You wandered in at the last minute, made moon-eyes with Charlotte during my set, then left without saying anything to me. Is that what counts as 'there?'" Annie stomped over to the counter, picked up the juice, and poured herself a glass. I noticed the carton shaking as she poured.

"Annie, I'm sorry I didn't stick around. I thought it would be awkward to introduce Charlotte to Mom and Dad on our first date." I took a step forward but decided not to get too close.

"Then why did you bring her? Huh? I bet you forgot about my show. I'm helping you with the stupid play, and you can't even make the effort to show up on time for my gig." Annie closed the carton, jammed it into the fridge, and slammed the door.

I didn't want to admit she was right, so I fought back. "You're only helping me with the play because I threatened to tell Mom about what happened to her car."

Annie spun around and jabbed her finger at me. "I'm pretty sure Mom already knows it was me! I'm done with the play. Find someone else to be your prop master." Annie stormed out of the room, abandoning her orange juice.

I stood rooted to the spot for a moment before walking over to the counter and tipping the orange juice down the drain, then putting the empty glass in the dishwasher. I wiped down the counter and threw the Pop-Tarts into the garbage. It was hard to remember why I'd wanted them. Annie was right. I had forgotten about her show. I felt guilty about forgetting and even guiltier about pretending I hadn't. Was I the kind of girl who dropped everything just because her crush fluttered her long eyelashes?

Annie wanted me to be more supportive. Charlotte wanted me to be more out. My parents wanted me to be happy. My teachers wanted me to stay focused on my studies. My guidance counselor wanted me to fill out endless scholarship applications. Mr. Evans wanted me to help him realize his crazy vision. My production crew wanted me to have all the answers. It was too much.

I was sitting slumped at the kitchen table when my parents came back from the market. My mother unpacked the fruits and vegetables as my father put coffee on to brew. I couldn't leave the kitchen without talking to them, not unless I wanted to trigger their parental worry alarms, so I stayed seated at the table. Looking over her shoulder, my mother said, "I think Annie was disappointed that you didn't stick around last night."

Oh, great. Like I hadn't been feeling guilty enough. Now my parents were piling on. I picked at the grapes in the bowl on the kitchen table. "I know. I told her I was sorry." No need for them to know she hadn't accepted my apology.

"Why didn't you introduce us to your friend?" Dad asked. He leaned on the counter, feet crossed casually at the ankle.

More guilt. "Uh, well…" I trailed off.

My mother turned around and looked at my father. "Honey, that was her date," she explained.

My father looked from me to my mother and back again. "Really?"

I nodded.

My father still seemed a little confused, so my mother asked him, "When you were a teenager, did you want to introduce your dates to your parents?"

"No, but we're not like my parents. Remember when you finally met them?"

"Yes," Mom replied in a flat tone. "Your mother referred to me as 'that girl.'"

"We're not like that," Dad said. He asked me, "We're not like that, right?"

"No, you're not like that," I reassured him.

He looked like he wanted to say something else but wasn't quite sure how to say it. "It's not because she's a girl, is it? That you didn't introduce her? Because we want you to feel comfortable bringing home anyone who's important to you."

There was that stab of guilt again. This was too easy for me. Charlotte couldn't even tell her dad she was going on a date. My dad was hurt just by the thought that I might see him as anything less than completely understanding. I put aside my feelings and explained, "It was a first date, Dad. I didn't want her to think I was jumping straight to meeting the parents."

"It was a first date?" Dad's eyes opened wide in surprise. Great. Even he knew how awkward it was to take a first date to a place you knew your parents were going to be.

"Honey, why don't we get started on the yard work?" my mother suggested. It looked for a second like my father was going to object, but she raised her eyebrows and he finally took her meaning.

"Right. Yes. Good idea. We should get to work." Dad busied himself with pouring their coffee into travel mugs, and Mom gave me a little nod. I took that as my cue to get out of the kitchen before any more family drama could take place.

CHAPTER 30

I'd told Charlotte I was comfortable holding hands with her at school. And I was more than comfortable holding hands. Any contact with her made me feel tingly. I was even comfortable kissing her at school, at least when there weren't any teachers around. She tasted like the weird gum she chewed, Sour Strawberry. What I wasn't so comfortable with were the stares. Maybe Charlotte was used to being the center of attention, but I wasn't. I felt paranoid. Were people staring because they were surprised a geek like me was with the coolest girl in school? Or were they staring because we were both girls? Most of our classmates might be theoretically open-minded, but it wasn't as if there were many gay couples engaging in PDA every day at our school. I wanted to ask Charlotte if she noticed it too, but I wasn't sure how to put into words what I was noticing. Could I even call us a gay couple? Since she was pansexual, did she believe in the term "gay relationship?" Was this a relationship, even? I had so many questions I wanted to ask, but I was worried she'd take it as more proof that I wasn't comfortable being out. So I kept the questions to myself. I hated being stared at, but who doesn't?

Actors, that's who.

At our rehearsal that week, the whole lot of them agreed to wear unitards. What normal human being would agree to being squished into a piece of clothing that needs to be completely stripped off every time you have to pee? As Zach handed out the black spandex torture devices, the actors smiled and laughed together. Even the boys. They teased each other, but they still toddled off to the washrooms to get changed. Charlotte winked at me before she left, and I had to admit I wasn't entirely unhappy at the prospect of seeing her in something tight-fitting. Still. Unitards! Puck was right: "What fools these mortals be!"

"They'll have costume pieces to wear over the unitards, Alison. No need to look so scandalized," Zach reassured me. He pulled wings and tutus and colorful streams of gauzy fabric out of the boxes he'd brought to today's rehearsal. I tried to look more blasé. If I was going to date Charlotte, I couldn't be so easily shocked.

Mr. Evans was giddy as he touched each piece. "This is all so perfect. Excellent work, Zach."

"Thanks, Mr. Evans. You haven't even seen our *pièce de résistance* yet." Zach opened another box and wrestled out a giant papier-mâché donkey head. I snorted, and Mr. Evans clapped his hands.

Mr. Evans and I helped Zach lay out the accessories so that when the actors trickled back in, pulling at their unitards and giggling uncomfortably, we were able to hand them their costumes right away. The fairies wore multicolored tutus and sparkly wings. Not one of them objected as Zach handed them the spindly heels. I wondered if I was missing some girl gene that made high heels appealing.

Next, Zach gave the human characters billowy tunics, leather vests, and tall boots. I had to admit that the unitards looked less ridiculous as the actors accessorized. I could even see how helpful the unitards would be for the actors who had to perform quick-changes backstage.

Finally, Zach dressed our main characters. The costume for Puck reminded me a little of Peter Pan. Jack's unitard was brown, to go with the mossy greens of his long tunic, which Zach belted at the waist. The actor playing Bottom donned the donkey head and walked around with his hands out, trying not to bump into anything. Everyone laughed, and he hammed it up even more, pretending to trip on his own feet. Finally, Charlotte was outfitted as the regal Titania. She wore a long gown with bell sleeves that reached the floor. The peacock colors brought out the blue of her eyes. Even Bottom stopped his clowning to look at her.

Mr. Evans clapped his hands again, his grin so wide that his pale blue eyes looked like sparkly little slits hidden in the folds of his wrinkles. I smiled, happy to see him so pleased.

"There's one costume left," Zach said, looking around the room. "Where's Oberon?"

Zach was right. Ben was missing.

"Mr. Evans, do you know where Ben is?" I asked.

He was so distracted by the costumes that he barely registered my question. "He must still be changing into the unitard. Can you go find him, Alison?"

"Uh, Mr. Evans, if he's still changing, that means he's in the boys' washroom," I pointed out. Some of the actors sniggered.

"I can't send any of the actors." Mr. Evans swept his arms around, indicating all the actors in their costumes. "What if someone sees them? We can't ruin the surprise for our audience."

I could tell it would be useless arguing with him, so I went off to search for Ben Weber. I walked as slowly as I could, hoping Ben was just taking his sweet time getting changed. If I was lucky, I'd see him walking down the hall in his unitard. Not that I was looking forward to even glimpsing Ben dressed that way. Maybe if I stared at the floor as I walked, I'd see his feet before I saw the rest of him.

Unfortunately, I made it to the boys' washroom without meeting Ben in the hall. I stood at the door for a moment. What was I going to do now? I could barge in, grab Ben by the ear, and pull him out. That might be satisfying. But what if I saw him naked? Naked was definitely worse than a unitard.

I hesitated for another minute before I knocked on the heavy bathroom door. No answer. I knocked louder. Still nothing. "Ben," I called through the door. "Mr. Evans needs you for rehearsal." Silence. I was turning around when I thought I heard a…snuffling? That couldn't be possible. I pressed my ear against the door. It definitely sounded like someone was crying in there. I wanted to walk away, to tell Mr. Evans that I'd tried to find Ben, but that he was MIA. However, some part of me that I wished didn't exist felt bad about leaving anyone, even Ben Weber, crying alone in a bathroom.

I pushed the door open a tiny bit. "Ben? Are you in there?"

The person inside blew his nose.

I opened the door a little wider. I kept my face pointed at the doorjamb so I wouldn't catch even a glimpse of naked white skin. "Are you okay?"

"I'm fine. Go away." It was Ben. And he definitely wasn't fine. His voice cracked, and he snuffled.

"Ben, please don't be naked. I'm coming in." I pushed the door open, shielding my eyes with my left hand just in case Ben was too upset to worry about the social convention of clothing. I stared at the tiled floor. *What are you going to do now, smartypants?* My brain had a fair point. What *was* I going to do now?

"Can I go get someone, Ben?" *Please say yes*, I thought at him.

"No!"

So much for that plan. "Is there something wrong with the costume?" I asked, unable to think of why Ben could possibly be crying in the second-floor boys' washroom during rehearsal.

"You think I'm crying because of some stupid costume?" He made it sound like I was an idiot for suggesting this. Here was the old Ben I knew and hated.

"Then why are you crying?" I tried to be empathetic, but I couldn't help sounding exasperated.

Ben sniffled and mumbled, "I can't be in the same room with *him*."

"Him who?" It was like a game of twenty questions I didn't want to play.

"Zach."

In my shock, I lowered my hand. Thankfully, Ben was dressed in his unitard. I never would have thought that I'd be grateful to see Ben's "package" outlined in black spandex. Weirder still, I never thought I'd see Ben Weber sitting on a bathroom floor—eyes red from crying, snot dribbling out of his nose—and feel sorry for him. I walked over and awkwardly patted his shoulder. He stiffened, and I backed away.

"Why can't you be in the same room with Zach?"

"Because…because…because…" he repeated, trying to catch his breath between sobs.

"Take a deep breath, Ben," I instructed him, reaching into the paper towel dispenser and handing him a sheet. He honked his nose into the paper towel and passed it back to me. I threw it in the garbage as fast as I could and wiped my hand on my jeans. "Why can't you see Zach?" I tried again.

"Because we broke up," he mumbled, hanging his head.

"Oh." I remembered my conversation with Zach and the argument I'd witnessed between the two of them. This certainly explained some things. But it didn't leave me any less shocked.

Ben looked up at me. "He didn't understand. It's great that he's out, but I can't do it. I have a reputation to uphold."

It felt like Ben was pleading with me to understand. And to my great surprise, I sort of did. I knew what it was like to be with someone who was more out than me and who was pushing me to catch up.

"Trust me, I get it. I've been getting stares from people for just holding Charlotte's hand. But I gotta tell you, it's worth it."

"But I'm not like you! I care what people think about me," Ben said. "You've always been okay with people thinking you're the nerd obsessed with being valedictorian. It's like you don't care that everyone thinks you're weird."

There was some more of the old Ben. I resisted the urge to point out that he was the one wearing a unitard. "Well, I don't exactly *love* the idea of people thinking I'm weird."

"But you keep acting weird! How do you do it?"

He didn't have a clue he was insulting me. He looked so pathetic that I didn't feel angry. I tried to find an answer to his question. "I guess I just don't think about it. If I stopped doing things because I was embarrassed, I'd just stay at home all the time." Sadly, true. But living with the embarrassment meant I was now dating Charlotte Russell, so it wasn't all bad.

Ben sniffled. I guess embracing embarrassment wasn't the answer for him.

"Maybe people won't care that you're dating a guy," I suggested. Ben snorted and wiped his nose on the shoulder of his unitard. I tried not to gag. If possible, I was growing to hate pathetic Ben more than I hated regular Ben. "Well, you seem pretty miserable this way, so maybe having people gossip about you would be better than being heartbroken." Perhaps a little tough love was what he needed.

Wrong. The tears started again, and I felt like a heartless jerk. I stood in silence for a few minutes, unsure of what to do next. "I think Zach misses you."

Ben looked up at me, his beady little eyes brimming with hope. "How do you know?"

"I don't *know* exactly. But he said he'd been having trouble concentrating lately, and I got the feeling it was a heartbreak thing." I hoped I wasn't sharing something Zach would want me to keep private. It seemed like the two of them needed a little help finding each other, though, so I thought it was okay for me to say this much.

"Yeah?"

"For sure." At this point, I would have said anything to stop having to comfort Ben Weber in the smelly boys' washroom. (Why did the boys' washroom smell so much worse than the girls' washroom? Did they pee directly on the floor?) "Now why don't you wash your face and come to rehearsal?"

Ben pulled himself up off the floor and splashed his face with cold water. I handed him another paper towel. He walked out the door and I followed him, looking at the floor so I wouldn't need to see his backside in the unitard. As we were about to enter the drama room, Ben mumbled what sounded like "Thanks," without turning around to look at me.

CHAPTER 31

"Did you make Ben Weber cry?" Becca stood on my parents' porch with her hands on her hips. I stood back to let her come in, but she didn't budge. We were going to have this conversation right there, despite the nippy evening temperature.

"Why would you think that?" I stalled, leaning against the doorjamb and zipping my hoodie closed.

"Because that's what people are saying." Becca didn't seem to notice the temperature, maybe because she was outraged or maybe because her massive head of curls kept her warm.

"Oh, no." I rubbed my forehead. What was I supposed to do about this rumor? I couldn't tell anyone the truth, because that would mean outing Ben. But I couldn't let the world think I'd made him cry. Could I?

"You did, didn't you? You made him cry, and you didn't

think to call me!" Becca stomped her foot like a cranky toddler. "Tell me you at least took a picture."

"It wasn't like that, Becca." This conversation wasn't helping my headache. It had been a long day already, and it was just getting longer.

"So you didn't take a picture." Becca looked incredulous.

"No. I mean, I didn't make him cry." Ben wouldn't thank me for letting that rumor spread.

"But he *was* crying, right?" Becca sounded suspicious now, like she knew I was holding something back. She was too perceptive for my own good.

I tried evading the question. "He was having a bad day."

"Such a bad day that he was crying like a baby?" Becca leaned in, hope carved into her face.

I tried humanizing Ben. "We've all had bad days."

Becca flapped her hand at me, dismissing the comment. "Yes, but the rest of us are normal people with normal emotions. This is Ben Weber we're talking about."

I sighed. "Becca, I can't talk about it. I'm sorry. It wouldn't be fair to Ben."

Becca was shocked silent. She was my best friend, and she knew I was holding back. I tried to wait her out.

"Becca, if I could tell you, I would. All I can say is that I didn't make him cry."

Silence again. This time, Becca squinted her eyes at me.

I tried another tack. "If someone was going to make him cry, wouldn't you want to be that person?"

There was another half-second of silence, then a grudging, "Maybe."

I smiled. "There you go. Something to look forward to before graduation. Or maybe at graduation?"

"That's not a bad idea," Becca conceded. Her eyes took on a dreamy, far-off look. "Getting Ben to cry in front of the whole graduating class might just make up for the years of bad innuendo. I wonder if pantsing him would do the trick. Do you think they would withhold my diploma if I pantsed someone?"

I chuckled. "I don't know, Becca. I'm not sure it's worth taking the chance, though."

"Says Miss Valedictorian. I don't care about this whole high-school-graduation thing, so long as I have the grades to get into a decent engineering program." Becca was a bit of a physics and math whiz, so I wasn't worried for her. But I didn't like that she assumed I would be valedictorian. I didn't consider myself superstitious, but I also didn't want to tempt the fates, if they did happen to exist.

"Becca, you know I might not be valedictorian."

Becca rolled her eyes. "Yeah, yeah. Whatever."

I shivered. "Can we go inside now?"

Becca checked the time on her phone. "I don't think I can. I told my dad I was just going to get some tampons. If I take much longer, even he will get suspicious."

"See you tomorrow, Becca."

Becca waved as she walked back to Harvey.

After Becca left, I climbed into bed and pulled the comforter up to my chin. I thought back to the glimpse I had caught of Ben talking with Zach after rehearsal. I hoped they would make up. I liked Zach and, for some unfathomable reason, he liked Ben. I wanted them to be happy. I also never wanted to comfort Ben Weber again.

I worried that Ben might think I was behind the crying rumors, but there wasn't anything I could do about that. I was about to open my math binder to start studying when my phone rang. The number was blocked. I thought about letting it go to voicemail before I remembered all the businesses I'd been trying to woo. Maybe one of them was finally calling to offer us some much-needed ad revenue. I put on my best peppy voice, which sounded a tad like Minnie Mouse on speed. "Hello. Alison Green speaking."

"Is this the girl who's trying to sell ad space for the high school play?"

"It is. To whom am I speaking?" I hoped the correct use of *whom* sounded polite, not snobby.

"Let's just say I represent the interests of the Upstage Players." The voice was muffled, like the person was holding the phone away from her mouth. Or like she was trying to disguise her voice, which seemed just silly.

"The community theater group?" I asked.

"So you've heard of us."

"Yes. I saw your production of *The Scarlet Letter* last year. It was very…interesting." The Upstage Players were known for their over-the-top productions. I occasionally went to their shows with my parents because summer in the suburbs was boring enough that a post-apocalyptic version of a classic play sometimes seemed more appealing than another night of meeting Becca for ice cream.

"Then you should know we don't take kindly to people asking *our* sponsors for money."

"I'm sorry. I don't understand." I didn't sound peppy anymore, just confused.

"This is a small town. There isn't room for two theater troupes here." There was definitely an edge in the voice now. I felt pretty sure I was being threatened, though the idea was so absurd that I couldn't accept it.

"We aren't a theater troupe. We're just doing a high-school play," I tried to explain.

"That's not the point!"

I considered hanging up but made one last attempt at communication. "I'm sorry, but I still don't understand."

"You can't just go around asking businesses for money," the voice explained. She spoke slowly, as if I was an idiot who didn't understand a basic concept.

I was starting to feel like an idiot who couldn't understand a basic concept. "I can't?"

"No, you can't. There isn't enough ad revenue here for two shows. We were here first, and we have relationships with all the local businesses. They won't buy ad space from you, so stop asking them." The line went dead. I stared at my phone some more. It felt like a foreign object now, like it had somehow betrayed me. How could it have let this crazy person call me? I put the phone away in the drawer of my bedside table and tried to get back to studying. I gave up less than an hour later when I noticed I was repeating practice questions I'd already answered. I put my stuff away and went to bed. In one day I'd seen Ben Weber cry, found out he was gay, and received a threatening phone call from a local theater troupe. Things like this never happened when I was editing the school newspaper.

CHAPTER 32

At lunch the next day, I told Becca and Charlotte about the threatening call. Charlotte laughed so hard she choked and squirted water out her nose. It was adorable, though not at all helpful. Becca looked cynical and said she'd ask her father if he knew anything about this. They both agreed that I shouldn't say anything to Mr. Evans yet. They argued it was probably just a prank call. I couldn't shake the feeling that a prank caller wouldn't sound so hostile, but I kept that to myself. Their explanation was reassuring. Still, I decided to postpone my canvassing of local businesses until after Becca had a chance to speak with her father.

Instead, I focused on another problem. Before our next production meeting, I needed to figure out if Annie was still mad. She often needed a cooling-off period after a fight. I didn't want to find a new prop master so late in the game. If Annie wasn't going to forgive me, though, I needed to start begging people soon. I hoped four days was long enough for her to cool off.

After school, I made my way to Annie's locker. "Hey." She didn't even look at me as she packed her backpack. "Want a drive home?" Annie had been taking the bus, which is how I knew she was pissed at me.

Annie kept her eyes on her bag. "No."

"Come on, Annie. The bus sucks." Annie hunched her shoulders. I didn't know if she was girding herself for the ride or if she was getting ready to punch me. I had to take my chances. "Listen, I'm really sorry about Saturday. Your song was awesome, and I should have stayed to tell you that."

"Too late." Annie slammed her locker door shut. The metallic crunch reverberated as we stood in painful silence. Annie still wouldn't look at me. Instead, she stared at the closed locker.

"How can I make it up to you?" I wanted her to hear the apology in my voice.

"I don't know," Annie whispered.

"You can have the front seat," I offered.

Annie looked at me from the corner of her eye. "For how long?"

"A week?"

"I'm still not going to work on the school play," she said.

I nodded. I knew a week of shotgun wouldn't be enough to get her to forgive me, so I was prepared for this. The first step in negotiations was to open the lines of communication. "Will you at least talk to me?"

"Fine." Annie finally looked at me. I smiled at her, and she gritted her teeth at me. It was progress.

On the drive home, I tried to tell Annie all about the weird phone call from the night before, figuring a funny story might help ease the tension. "No play talk," she said before I could get to any of the good stuff. I shut up.

Becca shot me a look in the rearview mirror. As an only child, she often found my fights with Annie both amusing and confusing. The twist to her lips said she was amused this time.

I stared at the back of Annie's head, contemplating possible topics. I noticed her roots were showing but didn't think she'd appreciate my telling her so. I decided to find neutral conversational territory. "Can one of you explain how it is that our basketball team might actually make the playoffs this year?"

Annie and Becca were happy to explain the bizarre confluence of events that meant the Otters were having their best season ever. From what I understood, which was very little, it had something to do with other teams experiencing unlucky injuries and one of the better schools being moved up a league. It didn't matter, ultimately. I was just happy to have Annie talking to me again.

Unfortunately, the détente lasted only until we walked in the front door. Annie went up to her room without another word to me, and I wandered into the kitchen a little deflated. I opened the cupboard to see if my sister had accepted my other peace offering. The new box of Pop-Tarts remained unopened, so either she was refusing to eat them, or she hadn't noticed them yet.

I didn't want to go upstairs to study. I didn't want to see my sister's closed door. I settled at the kitchen table with my school supplies spread out around me. I set the table with highlighters to my left, pens to my right, and binders stacked in front of me. I tucked into my academic meal and managed to stay occupied until my parents got home and asked me to clear my things so they could set the table for supper.

I silently thanked Mom and Dad when I saw what we were eating for supper. It was Annie's favorite: vegetable lasagna from Nonna's Kitchen, a tiny restaurant just down the street from my parents' firm. If anything would put Annie in the mood to forgive me, this was it.

Over supper, Dad told a funny story about a client who was convinced he could sue his neighbor for property damages because her dog kept pooing on his lawn. Annie was smiling. This was my chance.

"Mom, there's something I have to tell you. I've been feeling guilty for months about it."

The whole table turned to look at me. My mother raised a groomed eyebrow, waiting for me to continue.

"You know that thing with your car last year?"

"You mean the mysterious dent that appeared in my brand-new Mini Convertible that no one seemed to know anything about?" I couldn't tell if she sounded mad. She had been furious at the time. So furious that Dad had taken us out for the afternoon while Mom stomped around the house and called body shops to get quotes on how much it would cost to repair her car. Breakfasts and suppers had been tense for weeks afterward.

I could feel Annie's eyes boring into me, but I didn't look at her. This needed to happen. I squared my shoulders and looked my mother straight in the eye. "It was my fault. I dented your car. I'm so sorry."

I heard my father drop his cutlery onto his plate, but otherwise the room was silent. I didn't break eye contact with my mother, afraid that any weakness on my part would make things worse.

My mother wiped her mouth with a napkin, even though her face was spotless. It was a stalling technique meant to make me more nervous. It succeeded. I felt my pulse racing. "Is that so?" she asked.

"Yes. I wasn't thinking, and I tossed my backpack onto the hood. I forgot how heavy it was." I stopped myself. Over-explaining would make her suspicious.

"Your backpack dented my car," she repeated. My mother was well-known for her cross-examinations. There was something about her calm demeanor that witnesses (and her daughters) found off-putting. Witnesses (and daughters) had cracked under her intense gaze and quiet skepticism. But this would not be one of those times. If I wanted Annie to forgive me, if I wanted to prove to her that I was really sorry, then I needed to convince my mother the accident was my fault. At least, I needed to make sure she couldn't prove it wasn't my fault.

I nodded. If I'd learned nothing else from listening to my parents talk about their work, I knew that when you were under cross-examination, you should keep your answers short.

My mother looked at my sister, and I chanced a quick look her way. Annie's mouth was hanging open.

"You know, the body shop said the dent looked a lot like a basketball had hit the car." My mother paused and looked from me to Annie, hoping to draw one of us out through silence. It didn't work. She turned her gaze back to me. "You don't own a basketball, Alison."

It wasn't a question, so I didn't know if I had to say anything. It felt like a trap, but I didn't see how a simple confirmation could hurt anything. "No, I don't."

Mom looked first at me, then at Annie. Her tone remained eerily calm. "But Annie owns a basketball." Annie's eyes widened, the dark eyeliner making the whites of her eyes even whiter. I prayed she wouldn't crack.

That's when we got unexpected reinforcement. "But the repair shop wasn't sure what caused the dent, were they?" Dad asked, his voice steady and composed.

Mom nodded her head slowly. "True."

"So it could have been a backpack, as Alison said," he continued, his long hands folded in his lap. Annie and I watched them closely, looking for clues about how this was going to play out. The problem with parents who are lawyers? They have excellent poker faces.

"Yes." Mom's answer was terse, but she didn't seem angry.

"Why would Alison lie about this?" Dad asked. The question was directed at my mother, but he looked at me. They both looked at me. I knew that they'd long suspected Annie was responsible for the dent. Without any proof, though, my mother had dropped the matter after a few failed interrogations.

"Exactly! Why would I say I did it if I didn't?" They both studied me a moment longer, then my mother nodded. She was accepting my story, not because she believed it, but because I was insisting she accept it.

"All right. For starters, you're grounded. No social outings for the next two weeks." Mom had transitioned from lawyer to judge. I tried to look contrite, hoping I might manage to commute my sentence if my mother believed I felt guilty. "You're also going to be washing and waxing my car."

I waited. This couldn't be it. But when my mother took a sip of her red wine and then went back to eating supper, I knew it was over. I slumped a little in my chair, relieved that the punishment wasn't worse, but even more relieved that I'd gotten away with the lie.

"That's it?" Annie asked, incredulous.

"Alison admitted to something she could have gotten away with. I appreciate her honesty," Mom explained. Annie blushed, probably because she knew Mom still suspected she was guilty. "Do you think she should be punished more harshly?"

"No," Annie mumbled as she inspected the half-eaten lasagna on her plate.

"Then the matter's closed." Mom took another sip of wine, and Dad picked up his fork.

We finished eating supper. Dad tried to start up another conversation, but it was apparent no one else was much in the mood for talking. I cleared the table and started dish duty without complaint. When Annie packed her own dishes away in the dishwasher, I hoped it was a sign that she was thawing. After all, she could have just left her stuff on the table, as she usually did when it was my turn to clear the table. It was a small gesture, but I held on tight to it as I texted Charlotte to explain I was grounded and wouldn't be able to go out that weekend after all.

CHAPTER 33

Jenny was drawing daggers and skulls on her left hand in black ink. Becca was watching Jenny and probably wondering, as I was, what she would do when she ran out of space on her hand. Zach was playing with the zipper on his jacket and checking his phone. I was mostly watching the door.

"Can we get started?" Jenny asked. She capped her pen, her hand a massive scrawl.

I'd kept everyone waiting for fifteen minutes in the hopes that Annie would show up for our production meeting. I had to let that hope go.

"Yes," I agreed. Zach tucked his phone away in his black skinny jeans, and Becca dug a folder out of her bag. "Becca, why don't you show us what your father's been working on?"

"Sure." Becca laid out a series of pages covered in meticulous measurements and drawings. "My father is building these moveable pieces for our set. He worked off your designs, Jenny." Jenny grunted in acknowledgment.

We all looked at the drawings. None of us knew much about building things, but the plans looked professional. We shuffled through the pages, pretending to understand what we were looking at and making vague sounds of approval as Becca texted. The upward twitch of her mouth made me wonder if there was something more to the boy she was "just tutoring," but I didn't have a chance to do more than register it as a vague possibility.

"Sorry I'm late." Annie stood in the doorway, her bag hanging off one shoulder like a question. She didn't come in any farther. I grinned at her, genuinely happy to see her, not just because I needed a prop master but also because this meant my sister had forgiven me. Annie quirked her mouth, not quite smiling, but not *not* smiling either.

Jenny, of course, didn't pick up on the tender sisterly moment. She said, "You kept us all waiting."

Annie smiled properly then. "Sorry, Jenny. I won't let it happen again."

Jenny rolled her eyes, her heavily mascaraed eyelashes exaggerating the movement. "Whatever."

Annie walked into the room, stood beside me, and looked at the pages. "These look good."

Becca nodded. "Yeah, Dad spent a lot of time on these. He's already started building a few of the smaller pieces in our garage. Mom's not so thrilled that he's putting off repainting the bathroom, but he's so happy that she's letting it go." Becca gathered the pages and tidied them into a stack before tucking them back into the folder.

"Great!" I said, clapping my hands together like Mr. Evans. Things were back on track, and I felt optimistic, even if it was a bit worrying that Mr. Evans was rubbing off on me. "What about you, Zach? Any progress on the alterations?"

"Yes and no." Zach rubbed his jaw and I noticed a hint of stubble.

"Why 'no?'" I asked.

"I need to buy some fabric, Al." Zach looked at the ceiling as he said this. I felt embarrassed for not realizing sooner that my team was running without funds.

Jenny, of course, decided to pile on. "And I need money for paint. Ms. James can't donate any more art supplies."

"Right." I thought about digging out the Red Binder, but it would just be a stalling tactic. "About the money." I took a breath. "We're having a hard time getting any ad revenue."

"Why?" Jenny asked. No beating around the bush with her.

"Well, there seems to be some kind of theater mafia in town," I mumbled.

Zach snorted. "What?"

The funny story didn't seem so funny anymore. It seemed ridiculous, like something a desperate producer would make up to avoid admitting she hadn't managed to raise any money. I pulled my phone out of my pocket and showed everyone the blocked number, as if that was proof that my story was true. "I don't know if it's a mafia exactly," I started. I paused, trying to think how I could make the story sound believable. "I got this kinda threatening phone call from the Upstage Players and…" I petered off.

Becca tried to help me. "Yeah. My father said a bunch of business owners he knows have been vague about why they won't buy ads from us."

Jenny looked outright skeptical. Zach seemed confused, his head tilted a little to the side. Annie watched us all; I couldn't tell what she was thinking.

"I know it sounds crazy." It did sound crazy. What else was there to say?

Jenny's eyes bored into me. Zach still looked like he was trying to follow what I was talking about. I could feel myself blushing at his pity and Jenny's contempt. I looked away from them. Annie was chewing on her thumb, a habit we'd both inherited from our mother.

Annie finally broke the silence. "Didn't Mr. Evans used to be part of the Upstage Players?"

Zach snapped his fingers. "Yes! He was in that ridiculous production of *Little Women*, where half the sisters were played by men in drag." This sounded familiar. I hadn't been involved with the drama department back then but I did remember some people from school making a big fuss about a teacher cross-dressing in a play.

Jenny, ever helpful, decided this was the moment she should chime in. "What does that have to do with anything?"

Annie, unlike her big sister, was not afraid of Jenny. She looked Jenny straight in the eye. I noticed they were almost exactly the same height. Annie explained, "Maybe Mr. Evans could talk to the Upstage Players for us. Or at least explain what's happening."

It wasn't much to go on, but it was all we had. I grabbed hold of the hope Annie offered. "I'll ask Mr. Evans what he thinks after rehearsal tomorrow. In the meantime, can you all try to make do with what we have?"

Zach, Annie, and Becca nodded. We all looked at Jenny. Outnumbered, she conceded. "Whatever. Fine." Without another word to the rest of us, she threw her bag over her right shoulder and stomped out of the room. Annie and Becca snickered. I prayed I wouldn't have to smooth things over with her. Again. All these artistic types were going to be the end of me.

CHAPTER 34

At lunch, I watched Charlotte running lines. Not all artistic types were so high maintenance. Some could even see past a person's bumbling exterior to the cool, sensitive, and funny person underneath. (Okay, I didn't see it either, but Charlotte insisted I was all those things. I wasn't about to argue with my ultra-cool and sexy girlfriend over something so silly as self-esteem.)

The Red Binder lay forgotten in my lap. I'd been searching for tips on how to run a show on a shoestring budget. Or how to cope with mafia threats. The closest I'd come was a page at the end entitled *When to Call It Quits*. The advice was sound. For once. "Not all shows make it to the stage. Some shows can't seem to raise enough audience interest or money. Others suffer from artistic differences. Yet others succumb to romantic dramas within the cast. A director needs to know when to call it quits." Our show had generated very little buzz, despite the gossip spreading about the unitards. We were out of money, and our male lead was heartbroken. At first, the sniffly and red-eyed king of the fairies had been entertaining to watch. But now he was just pathetic. Still, we limped along. I wasn't sure why. It was like Puck had sprinkled love potion on Mr. Evans's eyes, and the ass that was our play looked like a beautiful fairy to him.

At this exact moment, though, I didn't care. I didn't care that I was in charge of what might potentially be the worst school play in the history of all school plays. Because my girlfriend, *the* Charlotte Russell, was practicing her lines, and she looked just like a nervous little kid at a spelling bee, while still emanating cool. Her movements had a feline quality—long-limbed and graceful. But something in her face, something maybe only a girlfriend would notice, told me she didn't feel the confidence she was trying to exude. If only she could borrow some of the confidence I had in her, she would be unstoppable.

I thought for a half-second about the math quiz I had to take after lunch. I knew I should study some more, but watching Charlotte was just too mesmerizing. I knew how soft those full lips were and how blue those eyes looked in the sun. I knew how much she loved her little sister and Princess Sunshine, even when they were both getting underfoot. I knew how much she worried about freezing onstage, which is why she ran lines every lunch and most evenings. And I knew she liked me, though I still didn't understand why.

When Becca found us in a quiet corner of the library and

asked to borrow my chem notes, I wanted her to feel some of what I was feeling. I whispered to Becca, "You should ask Jack out."

Becca stopped flipping through my notes. She didn't think to whisper. "What?" she asked at full volume.

Charlotte was so engrossed in her practice that she hadn't noticed Becca. Still, I tried to keep my voice down out of respect for her process and also so as not to embarrass Becca. "You should ask Jack out. What's the worst that could happen?"

Becca glanced over at Charlotte, who was reading some tricky lines over and over to herself. Reassured that Charlotte wasn't listening, she answered me, "Total humiliation. Heartbreak."

"Okay, that would be pretty bad," I admitted. "But would it be that much worse than how you feel now when you see him?" I thought back to just a few weeks ago when the very sight of Charlotte hurt in a place so deep it didn't even feel like it could be part of my physical body.

"Yes, it would," Becca said matter-of-factly.

"Then what about that guy you've been tutoring? You can't tell me you aren't just a little into him."

She pointed at me. "You're not allowed to intervene in my love life anymore, remember?" She handed back my chemistry binder. "You're missing some notes."

"I am?" I asked. I flicked through the pages. "I was kinda distracted last week with play stuff. I guess I'll have to borrow notes from someone else."

Becca cocked her head. She moved to leave, but then turned back and sat down beside me. "Not that I don't think you deserve to have some fun for once, but are you maybe neglecting your schoolwork?"

"I guess I've been busy with Charlotte and the play, but I can catch up," I reassured Becca.

Becca stood up, her long fingers splayed on the table. "Okay." She paused. "Just. Well, you've wanted to be valedictorian since you found out what the word meant. Which, by the way, was weirdly early. I guess I just don't want to see you let the play get in the way of that."

I nodded in acknowledgment, and Becca left for real this time. I was touched that she was worried about me, but I knew I'd be fine. Thanks to mono, I'd missed three whole weeks in Grade 9 and still aced all my exams. So I could handle catching up after the play was over. And Becca was right: I deserved to have a little fun.

The bell rang and Charlotte packed her copy of the play away in her bag. She walked over to me and tilted my head up so she could kiss me. I felt a jolt of electricity course through me. I wondered vaguely if that feeling would ever go away. I hoped not, even if it left me a bit shaky. "We better get to class," she whispered. I nodded, though I wanted to stay here all afternoon. Even the neon lights in the library couldn't make Charlotte any less beautiful. Charlotte pulled on my arm. "Come on, slowpoke."

I followed her out of the library, my brain a little sluggish with love and, if I was being honest, lust.

The math quiz was a blur. I couldn't answer about half the questions, but I told myself it was just a quiz. I'd catch up before the unit test.

CHAPTER 35

Our Bottom was floundering. He was supposed to be a pompous jackass, but he was only pulling off the ass part, mostly because of a braying laugh that seemed to get worse the more nervous he felt. The actor, a junior with mousy brown hair, had no swagger. It wasn't funny watching a stuttering, awkward, pimply teen play a windbag. It was painful. And our Bottom knew it. You could see it in his eyes and in the way that he glanced at the clock every few seconds. Even worse, you could hear it in that awful laugh.

"Let's try that again," Mr. Evans said with more patience than I could have mustered if I were him. This was the fifth time they were running the same short scene. "Remember, your character is offering to play all the parts in the show, that's how confident he is. He's an idiot, but he doesn't know it." The problem was, our Bottom couldn't hide the fact that he knew his character was an idiot and that he was an idiot for taking the part. Most of the other actors avoided eye contact with him by pretending to study their lines. The ones who were in the scene with him found an excuse to get a sip of water or tie their shoelaces.

Bottom nodded his head at Mr. Evans's directions, jaw clenched.

They started the scene again. If possible, it was even worse this time. Bottom's nervousness was contagious. The other actors in the scene flubbed lines they'd had down pat only twenty minutes earlier. A few of them even flinched when Bottom laughed. Why, oh why, did his laugh have to sound like a donkey braying?

Halfway through the scene, Bottom stopped. He stood frozen for so long that the actor playing Quince tried cueing him again. Nothing. He tried the cue once again. Instead of saying his line, Bottom whispered, "I'm done." We all watched as he silently gathered his stuff and walked out of the room. We turned to Mr. Evans, who was now as frozen as Bottom had been.

When Mr. Evans remained quiet, the actors looked at me, like I would know what to do when an actor quit the show with only a couple of weeks to opening night. I had to try something, so I asked Mr. Evans, "Should I go after him?"

Mr. Evans shook his head. "No. When you've been in show business as long as I have, you know when an actor doesn't have it in him. I was hoping I could help him find his inner thespian, but sometimes the Muses just won't come to us."

Mr. Evans seemed oddly calm, especially given that we had no understudies.

After a few more moments of awkward silence, Jack spoke up. "Um, Mr. Evans, what should we do now?"

"That is the question we must always be asking ourselves," Mr. Evans answered cryptically. Jack looked at me, and I shrugged my shoulders. I didn't know if our director just needed a little time to process or if he was having a nervous breakdown. I'd always assumed that if Mr. Evans did lose it, it would be in a grand, dramatic style. When I'd pictured telling him just how broke we were, I imagined him needing to sit down because he felt faint. Or maybe shouting and throwing things. I never imagined him getting quiet. It was a bit scary.

Just as the actors were starting to shift in discomfort, Mr. Evans drew himself up. He wasn't a tall man, but he lifted his chin and squared his shoulders to make himself look more commanding than usual. (It was a bit like watching a kitten try to make itself big to scare off a predator. It didn't exactly have the desired effect, but you appreciated the effort and did your best not to laugh.) "The show must go on!" he declared.

The cast looked at one another. Then they looked at me. I had no idea when I'd become some kind of authority figure in their eyes, but I didn't like it. Someone had to say something. "Of course, Mr. Evans," I said soothingly, still not entirely convinced he wasn't having a nervous breakdown. I didn't want to make things worse if he was cracking. "Only, uh, what are we going to do about the part of Bottom?" Almost everyone who'd auditioned had a part in the show already. Unless we wanted to give the role to Charlie Egan, whose striptease still haunted my nightmares, we didn't have any backups.

"Simple," Mr. Evans replied, walking to the middle of the room where the scene had been taking place.

"Yes?" I asked, sure he was just waiting for his cue.

"I'll play Bottom," Mr. Evans told the room, taking a leisurely spin so he could look at each of the actors in turn.

You could tell the real actors from the talentless amateurs in this moment. Jack, Charlotte, Ben, and a few others kept straight faces. They were the pros. Some of the sophomores playing fairies giggled. Others glanced nervously at each other, not sure if this was a joke. A couple of the amateurs looked outright shocked—it was a good thing they had minor roles.

My brain stalled for a minute. Then a flood of images came to me: Mr. Evans wearing the donkey head as a theater full of teenagers gasped and snickered, Mr. Evans prancing onstage, Mr. Evans taking a bow to scattered applause. I felt torn. Who better to play the role of the over-confident, amateur actor who thinks he can take on all the parts in the show? But I'd grown to like Mr. Evans, and I immediately knew what kind of ridicule he'd be facing if he did this. I wanted to protect him from that, although I had absolutely no idea how.

"I can tell you're hesitant," Mr. Evans said to the room. Every once in a while he surprised me with his ability to read people. "But you have nothing to fear. Yes, I am more experienced than you. Yes, I have played on much bigger stages than this, but let me assure you all that I will not upstage you."

Yes, I thought to myself. *That is what's worrying us, Mr. Evans. That you'll upstage the rest of the cast.* My sympathy for him began to erode. I could tell I wasn't alone. Charlotte's eyebrows danced in amusement. Jack's mouth twitched. Ben looked less miserable than he had in days. The other actors were mostly staring at the floor. If Mr. Evans kept this up, he wouldn't need the donkey head to play the ass.

"It's been an exciting day," Mr. Evans told us. "I have lines to learn, as do most of you. Let's end rehearsal a little early today."

No one needed to be told twice. The room emptied out faster than it ever had before. The actors were silent as they left the room, but the hallway outside exploded with sound. I was grateful that they were all so loud that no single voice could be heard. I knew what they were all saying, but Mr. Evans would be spared that knowledge.

I was slower getting my things together. I still had a niggling feeling that I should fix this. Not for the first time, I wished Mrs. Abrams hadn't been lying when she said we'd be coproducers. A fellow teacher would surely have better luck talking Mr. Evans out of this terrible idea than I would.

Charlotte was leaning against the doorjamb waiting for me. When I reached her, she whispered, "You need to talk to him."

"I don't wanna," I whined.

Charlotte raised one eyebrow at me. "You need to talk to him."

I dug my toe into the floor, stalling. I kept my voice low. "What am I going to say? I can't tell the director he can't be in the play."

"I know," Charlotte said. I was surprised. "Don't get me wrong, I wish you could. I'm going to have to pretend I'm in love with him." She made a face. "But that's just the way it is. You need to talk to him about the money situation."

In all the commotion of the old Bottom quitting and Mr. Evans deciding he would take over, I'd completely forgotten about the theater mafia. What a simpler time it had been when I just had to deal with a threatening small-town theater troupe.

I nodded at Charlotte, and she gave me a peck on the cheek and a pat on the arm for encouragement. I turned around to see Mr. Evans pacing the floor, his forehead and bald scalp furrowed in concentration. He was running his lines.

I cleared my throat.

Mr. Evans looked up, somewhat dazed. It was like he was coming out of a trance. "Yes, Alison?"

"Um, Mr. Evans, I know it's already been a crazy day," I started. I walked forward, standing just a few feet away from him. "And I hate to add to the, uh, stress. But I kinda need to talk to you about something weird that happened last week."

Mr. Evans moved over to his desk, placing the script face down to save his page. "What happened?"

I stayed where I was, even though the distance was a bit awkward. It would be easier to say this if I didn't have to make eye contact. "I got a call from the Upstage Players. They kinda, well, threatened us."

Mr. Evans looked puzzled. Who could blame him? He bobbed his head, encouraging me to go on.

"They said that we couldn't ask local businesses for money. They said there wasn't room in this town for two shows." I spoke quickly, needing to get it all out.

Mr. Evans sat down heavily. I chewed on my thumb, waiting for him to say something. Would it be such a bad thing if I got fired at this point? I wasn't at all sure producing the school play was helping my case for valedictorian. I doubted very much producing Ye Olde Shakespearean Disaster made me seem like the kind of competent, intelligent, and driven student that deserved to speak on behalf of her classmates at graduation. If I was fired, I wouldn't see Charlotte as much as before, but I'd have time to study. By the time Mr. Evans finally spoke, I'd embraced my fate. "I didn't think they'd still be holding a grudge," Mr. Evans said, staring off into space.

"What?" I asked. If I was being honest with myself, I was disappointed. I'd been prepared to be fired. Being fired would have made my life so much easier.

Mr. Evans cleared his throat. "Alison, I'm sorry you got dragged into this. Let's just say I have a history with the Upstage Players. I never imagined they'd take it out on innocent students." He shook his head, either confused or saddened, or maybe both.

"But what happened?" I demanded. If nothing else, I deserved to know why I was being forced to continue working on this disastrous mess of a production. I deserved to know why I was getting threatening phone calls and why I couldn't raise enough money to pay for basic tech supplies.

Mr. Evans blushed. "It was a long time ago."

I stared at him, unwilling to let him off so easy.

He stared at the ceiling and told me, "Theater is a strange world. I think you're starting to see that." I nodded and he continued. "The intensity of the rehearsal process often leads to romantic entanglements." If possible, Mr. Evans blushed an even deeper scarlet. "In my last production with the Upstage Players, I was the romantic lead. My paramour was played by a very dramatic woman. Our scenes were powerful. I'd never felt such a strong connection with another actor."

As Mr. Evans paused, clearly caught up in memories of a different place and time, I tried to imagine what kind of person Mr. Evans would consider "dramatic." Nothing ever seemed too big or fantastic to him. I remembered the voice on the phone, the way the woman had been so quick to anger. I suspected this was the dramatic woman Mr. Evans was speaking about.

"Sometimes the line between fiction and reality blurs over the course of a show. You forget who you are. You think you've fallen in love." I was starting to understand what Mr. Evans was hinting at, and I wasn't sure I wanted to know more, but it was too late. "I had to leave the Upstage Players after that show. It wouldn't have been fair to keep taunting this poor woman with a future that couldn't be. She didn't understand that the spell of the show wasn't enough to change who I am, who I'm attracted to. She was angry, but I thought time would heal her. I had no idea she would still be so hurt and that she would take it out on my students. For that, I am very sorry, Alison."

It was my turn to blush. "It's okay, Mr. Evans."

"No, it isn't. And I'm going to take care of this," Mr. Evans reassured me. He stood up, hands planted firmly on the desk. He looked determined, and I was happy to have someone take some of the burden off my shoulders.

"Thanks, Mr. Evans." He smiled at me, which I took as my sign to skedaddle.

For once, I was almost happy to take the bus home. It gave me time to contemplate the ridiculousness of the day. Mr. Evans playing Bottom! Mr. Evans breaking a woman's heart! A few months ago, I wouldn't have believed any of this. Now? It all seemed part and parcel of life in the theater.

CHAPTER 36

Mr. Evans did not take care of things. Instead, he asked me if we could "make do" with our current budget when I saw him the next day. I told him we could not. He offered to pitch in a couple hundred dollars of his own. He looked so pathetic that I said we'd do what we could, but that he'd have to scale back on some of his "vision."

"No silk scarves draping the fairy bower?" Mr. Evans looked pained.

I shook my head.

"What about the colored lights?" His eyes were closed now, like he was braced for the worst.

"We can't afford new gels, so we'll have to stick to the basic lights."

Mr. Evans gave a terse nod without opening his eyes. "Do what you need to do."

I left Mr. Evans's classroom feeling a bit like I'd snatched a lollipop from a little kid. The guilt was uncomfortable, but I told myself absolute honesty was best at this point. The show must go on, but that didn't mean it needed to go on with silk scarves and expensive lights. Mr. Evans's requests had always been unrealistic. Without any outside revenue, his vision was absolutely unfeasible. Still, it was hard seeing the perky Mr. Evans brought low. The play might have squashed my spirits, but that didn't mean I wanted to see a fellow optimist give up hope. Without Mr. Evans's blind faith, I wasn't sure how we would keep going. At times his blissful ignorance seemed to be the only thing holding this production together. (His ignorance and my stubborn desire to please. And Becca's pragmatism.)

Things did not get better when I got to math class. That quiz I hadn't really studied for? I'd failed it. Spectacularly. The unit test was a week away, and I needed to set aside time to catch up, but I wasn't exactly sure when that would happen. I looked for Jack, who wasn't exactly a math superstar. I was hoping to find someone to commiserate with, but he smiled at me and waved his test, then came over to me.

"How'd you do?" he asked.

"Oh, fine," I lied. I could tell he wanted me to ask how he'd done on the test and though I didn't want to, I obliged. "How about you?"

"I got an eighty-nine!" His smile had been big before, but it somehow managed to get bigger. I wanted to be happy for him. I really did. But the best I could do was a forced smile. "You mind giving these notes back to Becca for me?" he asked.

243

I took the sheaf of notes he passed to me, too absorbed in self-pity to really hear what he'd just said. By the time I thought to ask which Becca, he was gone. I looked down at the notes and recognized my best friend's loopy handwriting. How? What? I tucked the notes inside my agenda and made a mental note to ask Becca about this later.

I shuffled my way to last period English, hoping for a respite. No luck. At the end of class, Ms. Merriam asked Ben and me to stay back. We remained at our desks as our classmates filed out. I snuck a look at Ben. His hair was still un-gelled, which suggested things with Zach weren't any better. I pitied him, which felt wrong, like I'd unintentionally swallowed gum.

Ms. Merriam turned a student desk around and sat facing us. She toyed with her dangly earrings. "I'm handing back the papers tomorrow, but I wanted to talk to the two of you today. I know you've both been under a lot of stress with the play, which is why I'm going to give you a chance to resubmit your papers."

Ben and I avoided eye contact, but I could feel shame radiating off both of us. Our papers were so bad Ms. Merriam wanted us to rewrite them. I traced the graffiti on my desk with my index finger. *Jennifer hearts Noah.* Oh, to be Jennifer, unconcerned about anything but her teen romance. I hated Jennifer a little. Her life must be so much simpler than mine. For one, a wannabe valedictorian couldn't chance getting caught vandalizing school property.

Ben broke the silence. "Thanks for giving us a chance to rewrite the assignment."

I piggybacked. "Thanks." My voice was flat. I was just observing the niceties.

Ms. Merriam nodded and seemed to think about what she wanted to say next. She spoke carefully, looking us each in the eye. "I think you both know your names have come up in discussions of who will be valedictorian this year." I nodded, but only barely. I didn't want to seem cocky. I avoided looking at Ben, though I could see out of the corner of my eye that he also nodded. Ms. Merriam continued, "You should know there's also been talk of your...erratic behavior lately. If you want to remain contenders, you'll both need to do some hard work catching up on your academics."

Ben stood up. As he walked to the door, he said, "Thanks, Ms. Merriam. I'll get that paper to you by Monday."

Ms. Merriam smiled. "Good luck, Ben."

And then there were two. I wished I had left with Ben, but I felt too heavy to get up from the desk just yet. I knew Becca was waiting to give me a lift home. I knew Ms. Merriam probably wanted to pack up and go home herself. But I couldn't get up. I didn't have the strength. I ran my finger over Jennifer's graffiti, hoping it might imbue me with some of her innocent enthusiasm.

Ms. Merriam got up and turned the desk back around, its metal legs scraping on the linoleum floor. I flinched at the sound, though I'd heard it almost every day of my school life. Ms. Merriam came over and sat at the desk next to mine. She leaned over, and I could smell her vanilla perfume. "Alison, are you okay?"

It was too much. The vanilla perfume, the ridge between her eyes getting deeper as she worried about me, the love message Jennifer had carefully engraved into the desk. I was either going to break down or I was going to toughen up. I clenched my fist on the table. "I'm fine. Just tired. I'll have the paper to you by Monday."

Ms. Merriam looked unconvinced. I forced myself to relax my hand and to smile. It felt more like a grimace, but it was the best I could manage. "We lost our Bottom," I tried to explain.

"You lost your what?" Ms. Merriam seemed genuinely confused by my non sequitur.

I tried to explain. "Not our butt. I mean, he was the ass, but I don't mean we lost our bum."

Ms. Merriam raised both eyebrows. I was making this worse.

"I mean, the actor playing Bottom left the play. So, Mr. Evans is going to play the part." If I'd thought Ms. Merriam's eyebrows were raised before, I'd grossly underestimated just how high eyebrows could go when a person was properly surprised. "It's a bit of a shit show," I admitted. Shocked that I'd just sworn in front of a teacher, I covered my mouth with both hands.

Ms. Merriam laughed outright, a hearty guffaw that made me smile. After she finished laughing, she said, "You've got your hands full, don't you?"

"You could say that," I responded, perhaps just a touch sarcastically.

"Alison, I know you're a perfectionist, but there are some things that are beyond your control." It was my turn to snort. It seemed like nothing was in my control these days. Ms. Merriam pressed on. "Sometimes the hardest thing to learn is how to be okay with things as they are."

I nodded and stood up. Having someone else acknowledge just how crazy things had gotten had lightened my load enough that standing was now possible. "Thanks, Ms. Merriam."

Ms. Merriam stayed at the student desk as I walked across the room. Just before I left, she said, "I think I'll buy an opening night ticket this year. It will be worth it to see Mr. Evans in a donkey costume."

At least we would have one person in the audience.

CHAPTER 37

I put my phone on vibrate as soon as I got home. I created a schedule and color-coded it using my favorite highlighters. If I used all my free minutes in the next week, I could get the paper finished and study for the math test. I ignored the occasional buzz from my phone as I reviewed my math notes and went over the quiz. The mistakes were embarrassing, now that I knew what in hell I was supposed to be doing. I remembered the notes Jack had asked me to return to Becca and was about to text her to ask how on earth Jack had ended up with her notes, since she never spoke to him, but then I reminded myself that I was supposed to be focusing on my schoolwork. I'd have to ask her later.

The essay was a write-off; I needed to start from scratch. I normally took detailed notes whenever I read a book for English class, but I'd been so far behind on my schoolwork that I'd basically just skimmed *King Lear*. I had nothing to fall back on except a few vague notes I'd taken in class: *fool = wise, king = fool*. Not exactly the stuff of an A+ paper.

My phone wasn't just buzzing with texts anymore. Someone had to be calling me because it was creeping its way to the edge of my bedside table. I picked it up, trying to ignore the messages and missed call notifications. But when I saw Charlotte's name, I couldn't stop myself taking a quick peek.

> *r we facetiming tonight?*
> *where r u?*
> *everything ok?*
> *2 missed calls from Charlotte Russell.*

I dropped the phone on my quilt and rubbed my eyes with the palms of my hands, trying to contain the tears that wanted to escape. Here was another thing I was messing up. I'd forgotten that I told Charlotte we could FaceTime. How was I going to cancel on her? I was grounded, so it wasn't like I could make up for it with a nice date later. But creating a study schedule had made something very clear: I had time for schoolwork, the play, and minimal sleep. Nothing else. Was I supposed to give up everything I'd worked so hard to accomplish for a girl I'd only just started dating? Hadn't I made fun of those girls, the ones who fawned over their boyfriends instead of pursuing their own goals?

How did Charlotte have so much free time anyway? Didn't she have lines to memorize? Didn't she ever do homework? I knew she wasn't applying for scholarships, but she was applying to universities. She couldn't get by on cool hair alone.

I grabbed my phone and angrily punched in a terse message: *I can't talk tonight. Sorry. Work to do.*

In seconds, Charlotte called. I should have ignored her call, should have left things alone until the irrational anger had passed. But I didn't. Instead, I answered the phone. "Hi." My tone was frosty. I wanted her to know the call was unwanted.

"Hi," Charlotte didn't seem to notice the tone. Or maybe she chose to ignore it. "You need to take a break at some point. Take it with me. I'll help you unwind." She was flirting! It was like nothing was ever serious to her.

"I can't take a break. I failed a math quiz, and I have to rewrite an essay." I could feel the tension in my jaw radiating down my neck.

"It's just a quiz," Charlotte said. She was so dismissive, so nonchalant about it.

"Failing the quiz means I'm not prepared for the unit test, which is next week. Plus, there's the essay!"

"Sorry. I just meant, it's not as if you failed some major assignment. You can catch up." I knew Charlotte was just trying to reassure me, but part of me felt like she was judging me. Here was the cool girl trying to get her nerdy girlfriend to chill.

"I know I can catch up!" I snapped. "But that takes time. I can't hang out with you all the time."

"We don't hang out all the time! What's your deal?" Charlotte wasn't trying to reassure me any longer. Good.

I started pacing my room. "I need to focus, okay?"

"Fine."

"What does that mean?" I knew I was picking a fight, and I didn't even want to stop myself.

"It means I don't appreciate you making it sound like it's my fault that you failed some stupid quiz."

"I didn't say it was your fault."

"You sure as hell implied it was."

"I don't have time for this!"

"Well, neither do I."

For the first time since our first date, the silence between us was awkward. No, not awkward. It was uncomfortable. We were holding back, but we could both guess at the things left unsaid.

Finally, Charlotte broke the silence. "I'd better go. Princess Sunshine needs his walk."

I wanted to feel bad for starting the fight, but I didn't. "Bye." We hung up, both obviously angry. I threw my phone on my bed and stared at it. As I calmed down, I wondered what had come over me. Why had I taken my anger out on Charlotte? I was angry with myself, not her. I sat on the edge of my bed, head in hands. Had I just ruined my first real relationship? Had we broken up?

I picked up my phone, but I couldn't think of a single thing to say or text. I knew how much acting meant to her. Why couldn't she see how much school meant to me? Was it because liking school was so uncool that she couldn't empathize? Could I be with someone who didn't respect how hard I worked? She didn't understand how much being valedictorian meant to me. She was cool and confident and beautiful and talented. She didn't know what it was like to feel like you were never enough, that you had to constantly prove yourself to people.

I picked up my copy of *King Lear*, intending to read it, but instead I found myself throwing the paperback across the room. It thudded against the wall in a satisfying way. *Screw you, Shakespeare!* I thought. *Why do you have to keep ruining my life?*

CHAPTER 38

To say things were awkward at the next rehearsal would be an understatement. Because Mr. Evans now saw himself as part of the cast, he insisted I had to lead the warm-up. I stared at him open-mouthed, imagining this must be some kind of joke. But his light-brown eyes looked just as sincere as ever. He was serious.

"Um, Mr. Evans, I don't know any warm-ups," I half-whispered to him, hoping not to draw any attention to myself.

"Sure you do!" Mr. Evans saw no reason to keep his voice down. Of course, nothing ever seemed to embarrass him, so I guess I shouldn't have been surprised. I blushed as the actors standing nearest to us looked over. "You know all the warm-ups we've done so far!"

"I guess so."

"Then it's settled." Mr. Evans grinned and addressed the

group. "Everyone in a circle! Alison will lead us through our warm-ups today." The usually spacious room suddenly felt claustrophobic. The ceiling seemed to be pressing down on me. My breathing grew shallow.

When they all looked at me, I stopped breathing altogether. And then I noticed one person wasn't looking at me. Charlotte was staring out the window, nonchalant as ever. I couldn't let her see how freaked out I was.

I cleared my throat. "Everyone spread out?" A few people hesitated, reading the question in my tone. But once Mr. Evans moved, the others followed.

I racked my brain for a warm-up. I looked at the floor, noticing, not for the first time, the mysterious brown stains. I couldn't make people play worms again. What other warm-up could I remember? They were all staring at me. Even Charlotte cocked her head my way. I couldn't tell if she was looking sympathetic or amused. Why did her eyebrows have to be so perfectly arched all the time? It made it damn near impossible to read her.

I suddenly remembered the moment I'd first touched Charlotte. Everyone's eyes were boring into me. Though I was in the center of the room, I felt like I was being backed into a corner. I didn't want to remember that warm-up. I didn't want to think about what it had been like to feel that electric moment between us.

"Alison?" Mr. Evans prompted.

I looked up at the ceiling and said, "Pair up." The actors looked at each other, a bit confused, but followed my instructions. I noticed that Ben was forced to pair up with Mr. Evans. Even watching Ben's rat eyes dart around searching for another partner didn't buoy my spirits. I pressed on. "We're going to play the mirror game. So, uh, choose who will go first and start."

I watched as people mirrored their partners waking up, dancing, and even picking their noses. I carefully avoided looking directly at Charlotte and her partner, a pretty little sophomore with strawberry blonde hair and freckles. Instead, I observed the pairs close to them, keeping Charlotte in my peripheral vision. She had eyes only for her partner. Her movements, as always, were languid and graceful. I tried to remember my anger from the night before, but it had fizzled out. I couldn't hate Charlotte, but I could remind myself that being valedictorian was more important than some high-school fling. I squared my shoulders.

Eventually, people started looking my way. I considered reprimanding them for losing focus, but I guessed they were waiting for more instructions. I hurried to tell the pairs to switch roles and forced myself to turn my back on the corner of the room where Charlotte was set up. I could still sense her, a tugging feeling at the base of my neck, but I fought against her gravitational pull.

After just a few more minutes, I decided we'd all suffered through the game long enough. I released the group with a quick, "That seems good."

I thought Ben would be relieved to no longer have to imitate Mr. Evans's exaggerated stretches and weird contortions, but he seemed nervous. He kept licking his lips. His rat eyes were darting around again. I wondered if he was going to cry. I did not have it in me to comfort him today. But then Ben stood a little taller and addressed the room. "Before we start, I was hoping I could say something to the group, Mr. Evans." Mr. Evans nodded, maybe because Ben seemed so serious or perhaps because he sensed drama in the air and he could not resist its sickly sweet smell. Ben looked down, then up. "You've all become like a family to me, and I wanted to tell you something very important." Now I worried that Ben was about to quit the play. I tried not to panic, though the room was feeling small again. Mr. Evans couldn't take on another role. And the only other person who knew the role was…me. Ben took a breath, then rushed on, "I'm gay."

I gaped at Ben. I was flooded with equal parts surprise, respect, and relief. After a moment, I scanned the room. I needed to know how everyone was reacting to Ben's announcement.

Mr. Evans gave Ben an awkward pat on the back.

Jack shook Ben's hand. Because he was Jack, it seemed totally normal and not at all forced. This was why Becca had a crush on him.

A number of cast members said things like "That's cool," and "You're so brave." Ben nodded, and I wondered if he didn't know what to say to that. I never did.

A couple of the freshman girls playing fairies looked disappointed, though they said all the right things. Basically, they were all supportive.

Finally, I turned to Charlotte. She was already looking

at me, and when we locked eyes, she raised her eyebrows. Nothing else. Her face remained impassive except for the raised eyebrows. Yet again, I cursed them. What was she trying to communicate? Surprise? Humor? Pride? I didn't know how to respond, so I looked at Ben, who was damn near grinning. When I glanced back at Charlotte, she was smiling at Ben. The moment between us was over. Instead of feeling pulled by her gravity, I felt like I might float away. My throat was tight. To keep myself from crying, I sorted through papers, even pretending to look for something in the Red Binder. As usual, it taunted me as I opened it to a random page: *Rehearsal Warm-ups.* Much good that did me now.

The rest of the rehearsal was uneventful, though awkward. Mr. Evans knew his lines and played his role with enthusiasm, but those were the only improvements over the last rehearsal's ass. His love scenes with Charlotte elicited muffled giggles from the cast. Mr. Evans seemed to think this was a tribute to his comedic timing, because his performance became even more over-the-top. Charlotte remained regal and cool. I admired her for staying in character as everyone around her broke, but I also felt like this was emblematic of our problem. I could never tell what Charlotte was thinking or feeling unless she told me. And I was an open book. I blushed and stuttered and tripped over my own feet whenever I got emotional. We would never have made it together.

Would we?

By the end of rehearsal, I'd decided that I had to talk to Charlotte. I needed to know if we had broken up. I stood up from my lonely desk and started walking toward her, but then someone stepped in my way. I tried to step around, but the someone grabbed my arm. It was Ben, and he was staring at me intensely. "Can you tell Zach I came out? He won't talk to me, and I need him to know." Ben's eyes bored into me. He was desperate.

"I don't know, Ben." I hesitated. I wasn't exactly friends with Zach or Ben, and I did not want to get involved in someone else's relationship. Look how my only relationship had turned out.

But then Ben managed to make his rat eyes look almost human. I caught a glimpse of Charlotte leaving, and I could feel my own hollowness echoed in Ben's desperate, pleading gaze.

"Okay. I'll try to mention it. But that's it." Ben was so happy that he caught me up in a tight hug. He let me go almost at once. Maybe it was because he felt me tensing up as he touched me, or maybe it was because he remembered our many years of rivalry. This new, vulnerable, honest, and less pervy Ben would take getting used to. I patted his arm awkwardly, and we parted ways.

I had to get home to work on that essay for Ms. Merriam.

CHAPTER 39

I was late for our last production meeting because I had to hand in my rewrite to Ms. Merriam. I'd spent most of my weekend hunkered down with ol' Willy Shakespeare, paging through the aged paperback for inspiration. Annie rolled her eyes at me when I refused to check SparkNotes for quotations. She thought I was being stubborn, but I wanted this paper to be mine. It had cost me so much that I needed to feel proud of it. It was satisfying to place the paper on Ms. Merriam's desk.

The room was silent when I walked in. Becca, Annie, and Zach were on their phones. Annie and Zach seemed to be scrolling through Instagram, but Becca had that faraway look that made me think she was texting her math tutee. Jenny was doodling in a textbook with a Sharpie. I briefly felt annoyed that they couldn't get things started without me, but there was enough leftover glow from the essay that the feeling soon passed.

I set myself up at Mr. Evans's desk. There was work to be done. "Our last production meeting before the tech rehearsal!" Becca, Annie, and Zach put their phones away in pockets and bags. Jenny continued to doodle. "Let's look over the schedule." I handed each of them a copy of the schedule I'd drawn up at lunch. (For once, the Red Binder had given a helpful suggestion: "Create schedules for tech and dress rehearsals, as well as show week, so everyone knows where and when they're expected.") Becca and Annie looked at each other and smirked. Here was bossy Alison back from her detour in a high-school rom-com. Well, it felt good to be in familiar territory again.

Jenny was forced to stop doodling in order to hold the paper I'd handed her. She glanced down, then frowned, the black eyeliner and shadow blending together to make her look almost eyeless. "Why do I have to be around for rehearsals?" She flapped the offending schedule at me.

"In case there are any changes, Jenny," I explained, careful to keep my voice even.

"There's no time or money for changes," she countered. It was a fair point.

"There won't be any major changes. But we may need some touch-ups once the backdrops are in place. It's the same for costumes," I added, hoping she'd be mollified that she wasn't the only one expected to attend the tech and dress rehearsals. "Actually, with possible costume malfunctions, Zach is there every show night, not just for rehearsals." In trying to placate Jenny, I could see I was upsetting Zach. His thin shoulders were hunched. His usual slim-fitting cardigan was hanging a bit loose, either because he'd recently lost weight or because he was dressing for comfort rather than style. Either possibility reminded me of my promise to Ben. I had to find a way to work Ben's big coming out into our conversation.

Annie chose that moment to help me out. "The dress rehearsal is going to be hysterical. I heard some of the actors aren't off-book yet. And Mr. Evans is playing the ass now that Corey quit the show!" Yes, my sister was using the draw of a possibly calamitous dress rehearsal to convince her fellow crew members to do their work. Sadder still, it seemed to be working. They looked intrigued.

I had to take every advantage I could. "There's been a lot of drama at rehearsals lately. Annie's right. Mr. Evans had to take over one of the leads when Corey quit in the middle of a rehearsal. Plus, some of the actors keep giggling whenever someone mentions 'making love,' no matter how many times Mr. Evans explains that in Shakespeare's time that wasn't a reference to sex."

"I heard some dude came out at rehearsal," Jenny added. We all stared at her, shocked that she had heard this gossip. Who could her source be? Who did she speak to? I never saw her with anyone. Maybe the spirits kept her informed.

"Seriously?" Annie asked.

The group turned to me to confirm or deny this bit of news. I felt torn. I didn't want to spread gossip, but Ben had asked me to tell Zach about his grand gesture. I nodded my head once.

"Who was it?" Annie didn't share my compunctions about gossiping.

I looked at Zach, willing him to understand what I was doing. He seemed confused by the intensity of my gaze. I spoke to him. "It was Ben. Ben came out at rehearsal."

"You mean the creep with gelled hair?" Jenny asked. "But hasn't he hit on basically every girl in the school?"

"I think that's an exaggeration," I responded, trying to spare Zach's feelings. I chewed on the corner of my thumb.

Becca and Annie were silent. Becca kept opening her mouth as if about to say something, then closing it again. Annie shook her head, her faded blue hair flopping around like a puppy's oversized ears. They were dumbfounded. I tried to remember what it had felt like to find out the macho dude-bro I'd known and hated for years was a closeted gay guy trying to throw people off by acting as straight as possible. To say it was a surprise would be an understatement.

Zach grabbed his messenger bag and stuffed the rehearsal schedule in an open front pocket. "I have to go," he said as he lurched toward the door. Before I could think of something to say, he was gone.

"That was weird." Jenny was as sensitive as ever. "If he's leaving early, so am I. I'll see you at the stupid tech rehearsal." She folded her schedule into quarters and stashed it inside the textbook she'd been defacing. I didn't try to stop her.

Once Jenny left the room, I slumped into Mr. Evans's chair and plopped my forehead on his desk, breathing in the waxy smell of the old wood. Annie and Becca still hadn't moved. I let them absorb the news as I reflected on what I'd just done. Ben had asked me to tell Zach he'd come out, but did that mean I was supposed to tell the whole production team he was gay? Ben had come out pretty publicly at rehearsal, so it was probably okay. But I wasn't sure I'd done the right thing outing him to the whole group. The image of Zach's pale face as he left our meeting floated in front of my closed eyes. I banged my forehead on the desk.

Becca let out a noise then. It sounded like someone choking. I looked up at her to make sure she was okay. Her shoulders were shaking, her curls bouncing. She was laughing! Becca's half-silent laughter seemed to unfreeze Annie, who laughed so hard she held her stomach, tears streaming down her face. The more one of them tried to hold back the laughter, the harder the other laughed. Soon they were both leaning on the desk, panting and wheezing.

"Oh, god." Becca finally gasped. "That explains so much."

Annie was digging around in her bag for a tissue to clean up her smudged eye makeup. She looked like a gleeful raccoon.

"I'm glad you think someone coming out is so funny," I said.

"Al, you know that's not what's funny. It's just…Ben! The boob inspector! The boy obsessed with lesbians!" She was laughing again, which set Annie off.

I rested my head on the desk. This was why I didn't want to make a big coming out announcement. What if someone I barely knew thought my being gay was hysterical?

When their second bout of laughter died down, Becca

poked me in the back with a finger. "Come on, Al. This is Ben we're talking about."

"Yeah. I know." How could I explain it to her? I raised my head from the desk but remained slouched. I whispered, "But what if people laughed when they saw me holding Charlotte's hand?"

"No one laughed." When I didn't respond, Becca repeated herself, drawing out each word. "No. One. Laughed. You two were too cute together. It was adorably disgusting." I plopped my head on the table again and groaned. I could hear Becca shifting behind me. Then I felt someone pat my back twice. The taps were so fast (and intense) that I wondered if Becca thought I was choking. But no. This was as close to providing physical comfort as my best friend got. Her feeble attempt was weirdly touching. I looked up in time to catch Becca motioning at Annie to do something.

Annie stuffed a blackened tissue in her front pocket. There was just enough of her runny eyeliner and mascara left to make her blue eyes more piercing than usual. "Al, did you two break up? I mean, you seem miserable and I haven't seen you together lately. Did she dump you?"

Of course, my sister would assume Charlotte broke up with me. She was too cool for me in the first place. I gritted my teeth. "No. She did not dump me. But yes, we broke up, okay?"

"That's stupid." Nothing like a little sister to give it to you straight. Becca was shaking her head at Annie, but Annie ignored her.

"It wasn't stupid. It was the smart thing to do. I was too

distracted when I was with her." I stood up, signaling to Annie that the conversation was over. She did not take the hint.

Annie looked from me to Becca and back again. Her mouth gaped open. "Wait. Are you saying you've been a sad sack for days because you thought the *smart* thing to do was to break up with Charlotte?"

I looked to Becca for help, but instead she said, "You couldn't have found a way to be with Charlotte *and* get your work done?"

They were ganging up on me. I was tired of having to explain myself to other people. I slammed my open palm on the desk. Annie stepped back, and even Becca flinched. "Not if I wanted to be valedictorian!"

Annie recovered herself and took two steps toward me. "Why does being valedictorian matter so much to you anyway?"

I was still angry, so I hissed at her, "Because being valedictorian means that hard work pays off! Maybe high school isn't so easy for all of us. Maybe some of us need to believe there's something better waiting after high school is finished." I felt myself deflating, the tension in my shoulders easing as I told the truth to both my sister and myself.

"You know no one likes high school, right?" Annie asked.

For once, I was the one to roll my eyes.

"Seriously. Some of us have a bit more fun than you. Probably all of us." She grinned, and I tried to smile at the joke, but my face felt frozen. "That doesn't mean high school is easy. Try being the younger sister of a school legend. There's no living up to that."

"Try sitting through years of science classes learning things you already know," Becca chimed in.

I wanted to believe them, but wasn't Charlotte proof that high school was easy for some people? That some people already had it all figured out? But high school had been torture for cocky Ben, so who knew what was going on with just about anyone?

"It's too late," I told them.

"You're giving up?" Annie was incredulous. "You're the most stubborn person I know. You won't even give up on this stupid play!"

I let Annie have the front seat on the drive home. I had a lot to think about.

CHAPTER 40

We somehow limped our way toward opening night.

The tech rehearsal was hamstrung when the vice principal informed us, ten minutes before starting, that we wouldn't be able to erect the full set because the caf was being used for a school assembly the next day. Our promises to strike any large set pieces at the end of the rehearsal did us no good. Mr. Patel, used to dealing with argumentative and recalcitrant students, firmly told us, "I can't stay to make sure that happens, so you'll just have to make do." Becca mumbled a few choice words at his retreating back, but I was too busy trying to decide how to run a tech rehearsal without major set pieces to give the petty bureaucrat a second thought.

As it turned out, we needed every minute of the tech rehearsal just to run through lighting and sound cues. With Mr. Evans now part of the cast, I was left to take notes, call the cues, and puzzle over the lighting board with our novice lighting tech, Sam. I remembered Mr. Evans's original lighting plan and felt grateful for our slashed budget. Sam couldn't seem to keep track of what fader controlled which set of lights, even though he was working with a grand total of six faders. I'd originally asked Becca to help him out, but when I caught her miming strangling him behind his back, I thought it was best if I called the rest of the show from the lighting booth (i.e., a corner of the caf blocked off to students). We eventually decided to label each fader with a bit of masking tape. At first I wrote upstage and downstage, but this system confused Sam, who might have been stoned given the pungent smell emanating from his long, greasy, surfer hair. So we settled on "close" and "far" for the labels. Things went marginally better after that. The actors got used to waiting a beat for the lights to come on before starting a scene.

As a director, Mr. Evans was unrealistic, dramatic, and relentlessly positive. As an actor, he was all those things, but also hyper-focused on his performance. He didn't seem to notice any of the technical problems, even when essential props didn't make it onstage on time. When I asked Annie why the props were showing up late or on the wrong side of the stage, she grumbled, "Because actors are stupid." I couldn't argue, given that many of them were still confused by the concept of a cue-to-cue rehearsal. They kept saying all their lines, even after I shouted repeatedly that we were moving on to the next cue. I asked Annie to throw the props at the actors if need be. She smiled in a way that made me worry for the actors.

By the time the tech rehearsal was over, I felt like a kindergarten teacher at the end of a long day. I craved silence and a stiff drink, but the crew and most of the cast members crowded around me, all demanding attention like grubby little kids who didn't know how to tie their own shoes. I sent the cast off for their last costume fittings as I tried my best to answer the crew's questions. I was able to help most of them, but a few stomped off, cranky that the best I could say was, "We'll figure it out at the dress rehearsal tomorrow." Jenny was the brattiest, unable or unwilling to understand that many of her painted pieces hadn't made it on today because of the VP's last-minute decree. To keep from snapping at her, I held my breath and counted to ten in my head. She pouted, but eventually left me alone.

The only good thing to come out of the tech run was watching Ben and Zach make tentative eye contact as they discussed Ben's costume. They still stood an awkward distance apart, but eye contact was progress. Charlotte wouldn't even look my way. Or maybe she snuck looks at me. I couldn't be sure since I couldn't chance looking at her for more than a few seconds at a time. In case she was sneaking peeks, I checked my ponytail a few times to make sure that my hair didn't reflect my harassed-kindergarten-teacher vibe.

One by one, the actors and most of the crew headed out. I bundled the last of my unruly kindergartners out the door when the cleaning crew started grumbling about overtime. I figured the VP wouldn't appreciate us costing the school any extra money. Plus, Annie and Becca had been waiting for me for almost half an hour at that point.

At the dress rehearsal the next day, Ben's hair wasn't at full-gel capacity, but it was obvious he'd put some kind of product in, so it looked artfully mussed rather than limp. Another sign of improvement, I supposed. I took comfort in Ben's hair progress as I prepared for the onslaught of questions and glitches. The highlights:

1. It turned out that many of the platforms were too heavy for our delicate little fairies to carry on- and offstage as originally planned. Mr. McArthur had made them a little too sturdy for our purposes, a problem I probably should have seen coming. Solution? The heavier platforms had to remain onstage for the duration of the show, even though this meant that the actors had to improvise new blocking. For the mid-sized platforms, Annie and Becca became running crew. I was a bit nervous about this, given that they liked to stage impromptu mime and dance performances while repositioning the boxes, but what choice did I have?

2. Budget cuts had forced Annie to cobble together some ramshackle props. Midway through the dress rehearsal, many of the smaller props, constructed from cardboard, Elmer's glue, and wishful thinking, were falling apart. Solution? Duct tape, leftover paint, begging actors to be gentle with their props, and yet more wishful thinking. At least the electric blue ukulele looked great, especially under the stage lights.

3. Some of the actors complained about shoes that didn't fit.

Solution? Zach and I raided the washrooms for brown paper towel. When stuffed into the toes of too-big shoes, they kept the shoes from flopping off. For the too-small shoes, Zach told the actors to "suck it up." There was something so charming, and just a little intimidating, about him that the actors accepted his decree. It was too late now, but I wished I'd let Zach deal with the theater mafia.

4. At the top of Act 4, a custodian wandered onstage with a mop. Mr. Evans, old pro that he was, pretended the man was just another of the fairies: "Good monsieur, our bower needs no cleaning. Go forth and pick us some flowers!" The custodian stared at him blankly and said, "Huh?" Solution? After a few more attempts at staying in character, even Mr. Evans could see the custodian wasn't going to take the hint. Finally, driven to frustration, Mr. Evans shouted, "The cafetorium is booked for our dress rehearsal until seven o'clock! You can mop up after we're finished." The custodian left in a snit while the cast tried to hide their laughs behind their hands and Mr. Evans straightened his ass head.

We had planned to run the show without stopping at least twice. We didn't manage to run it even once without stopping. At seven o'clock, the custodian returned with backup, our friendly neighborhood VP. We were kicked out.

Mr. Evans shouted that we'd go over notes at call the next night. No time for a pep talk tonight. Even the usually giddy bit-part actors seemed to droop as they left school. I watched as slump-shouldered teens piled into waiting cars, greeted by the worried faces of parents. Everyone moved sluggishly, even Becca, who seemed to be having trouble unlocking Harvey. As I waited for her to get the door-pushing-key-turning combination just right, I spotted our lighting tech, Sam, sneaking around a corner of the school. If he was going to get stoned, I couldn't blame him. I heard the driver's-side door click open, and just as Becca leaned over to unlock my door, I looked up to see a miracle in the making: Zach and Ben were kissing—in public!

If you'd told me a few months earlier that I'd soon be grinning because I'd seen Ben Weber kissing someone, I would have called you a liar and laughed in your face. Yet all the way home, I could not stop smiling. Maybe some of it was selfish. If Zach and Ben could reconcile, maybe Charlotte and I could work things out. But some of it was just pleasure at seeing other human beings so happy. More than the kiss, I kept remembering how their fingers had been intertwined. The image was enough to carry me through a night of triaging problems from "most likely to stop show in its tracks" to "will probably only lead to mild hysteria in the audience."

CHAPTER 41

Theater people say that a terrible dress rehearsal means a good opening night. The cast kept telling each other (and me) this as they passed each other in the hall during the school day. It became their mantra. I couldn't begrudge them whatever small comfort they could find.

I was calculating how many problems we might be able to fix before the curtains rose when Becca plopped her tray of food across from me in the caf and announced, "The Otters made it to the semifinals."

I stopped picking at my food. It's not like I was hungry anyway. "That's nice?" I had no idea why Becca was telling me this.

"It's a goddamn miracle is what it is," Becca said, folding back the spout on her chocolate milk carton. Becca only bought chocolate milk when she was studying for a big test, when Harvey needed major repairs, or when she was celebrating.

I put down my fork. "Wait. Did they win any games this season?"

"They tied two and won one last week through a technicality." Becca took a gulp of milk, licking the chocolate residue from her top lip.

"And that was enough for them to make it to the semifinals?" Even to someone who didn't care about sports, this didn't make any sense.

"One of the top teams got disqualified over some cheating scandal. I heard they got hold of a math exam ahead of time and made copies." Becca took another swig. "And then yesterday, another school had to drop out because half the team came down with mono. So now the Otters are in the semifinals."

"Oh. That's cool." I didn't care, but I knew Annie and most of the rest of the school would be psyched to see the Otters take their own violent brand of basketball to a big game.

"The semifinal game is tonight." Becca waited a beat. "The same night the show is opening."

The Otters were about to play a semifinal game for the first time in the school's history. Nearly every student, teacher, and parent would want to be there to cheer on and/or mock our team. That meant most of our potential audience had just disappeared.

I beamed. "That's great news!" Becca nodded, proud that I'd caught on. "The only people in the audience tonight will be cast parents and a few super supportive friends! Fewer people to witness the disaster."

"Exactly." She raised her milk carton in a mock toast and then finished it off.

We laughed, and I even initiated a high five. Becca was excited enough to humor me, slapping my hand so hard I rubbed it afterward.

That celebratory mood stayed with me through my afternoon classes. It got me through telling Annie that she couldn't skip opening night, even if it meant missing out on a historic day for our school. She glared and pursed her lips at me, but she must have known all along that she couldn't miss opening night, because she didn't put up much of a fight.

At call, everyone was buzzing about the big news. Most of the cast seemed disappointed that their opening night would be quiet, but I noticed that Jack, Charlotte, and the crew remained silent during the general complaining. I suspected they also saw the advantage of a supportive audience for our opening night. Mr. Evans reassured the group. "The size of the audience isn't what matters. Even if we were playing to just one person, it would be our duty to entertain and dazzle that person. The show must go on!"

And on the show went.

The audience trickled in. I insisted that our ushers, a pair of slackers who were being forced to "volunteer" with us in lieu of serving detention, seat everyone in the front. Our audience filled only three rows. It was a beautiful sight.

I checked in with my crew. Sam was reading over his lighting cues, Zach was pinning together a tutu that had fallen apart during the dress rehearsal, and Jenny was fussing over the backdrop, three different paintbrushes in hand. They all looked busy, so I didn't interrupt them. Annie was taping together a wreath with green duct tape while Becca was adjusting a few of the platforms. Annie and Becca were both dressed in black. I hoped this would mean their convulsive dance breaks would be less noticeable to the audience.

I snuck into the green room, gluing my back to the wall so I wouldn't be pulled into any weird prayer circle. The room buzzed with chatter and energy. The stage makeup gave the actors a cartoonish look. They were all feverish eyes and rosy cheeks. It was a bit like seeing people from your real life show up in a demented dream.

Mr. Evans called the group into a circle and asked everyone to hold hands. "We need to get centered. I want you all to close your eyes and take deep breaths with me." Despite the noise of just a minute before, the room went quiet eerily fast. I watched their faces be transformed by seriousness and concentration. I felt a wave of affection for these clueless weirdos who were about to make fools of themselves in a very public way. Sure, the show would reflect on me, but I didn't have to face the audience directly. These people were about to take the stage. I wanted to shield them from what was to come. That protective feeling extended especially to Charlotte, whose face looked both paler and more beautiful than ever. My heart ached to think that the audience might not appreciate how regal she was. I snuck out before any of the actors could see me and went to take my place in the lighting booth.

The curtain came up fifteen minutes after the show was supposed to start, but still it seemed too soon.

The first thing I noticed was that the lighting cues were on time! I sniffed Sam's hair. He gave me a weird look, and I couldn't blame him, but I was happy that for once his wavy, blond mop smelled like regular, unwashed boy hair. Sam was sober.

The next thing I noticed was that by the end of Act 1, no one had flubbed a line or lost a prop. It was the first time I'd seen the actors run a whole act without missing a mark or forgetting a line.

Partway through the second act, I could take full breaths for the first time in days. Mr. Evans had come onstage, he'd played the swaggering fool, and the audience had laughed, but in a way that was appropriate to the character. The awkward love scenes were still ahead of us, but at least the shock of his first appearance was over.

As we prepared for intermission, the last thing I noticed was how natural Jack and Charlotte looked onstage. I'd almost forgotten how much they both loved acting. They were playing characters, but they seemed more themselves than I'd ever seen them. I vibrated with pride and excitement.

During intermission, Becca and Annie came over to the lighting booth. They looked as shocked and pleased as I felt. My grandmother would have said they were both wearing shit-eating grins. On top of everything else that had gone well,

Becca and Annie had discretely moved platforms between acts, and I wanted to thank them. But before I could say anything, we had an influx of new audience members. Since our ushers had left as soon as the show started, Becca, Annie, and I tore tickets and directed people to take seats. I caught snippets of conversation and gathered that the Otters had already lost the game. I was pleased that the actors would have a proper audience for the last two acts. I wanted witnesses to this miracle.

The curtain came up. Within seconds, people snickered as Mr. Evans lounged in Titania's bower, his ass head sliding on his shoulders every time he shifted. *Okay,* I thought, *it's supposed to be a funny scene. They can laugh.* But the quality of the laughter had changed. This was not how a friendly audience sounded.

The next thing I noticed was one of the fairies waving at someone in the audience. I wanted to strangle the twit, but I didn't have time to build a full steam of anger because Charlotte had just lost her shoe. Unable to take the time to put her shoe back on, the queen of the fairies hobbled around the stage, shoe in hand. The snickers got louder. I wanted to strangle most of the audience now, but Charlotte acted as if she didn't notice. Head high and shoulders square, she finished the scene before hobbling offstage.

By now, though, the other actors must have noticed the shift in the audience because they started stepping on each other's lines. They were nervous. They rushed and cut their eyes sideways to watch friends' reactions. That did them no good. This was a crowd of people who'd gone out for a night of violent sport. They'd been conditioned to enjoy disasters, to cheer for fouls, and to revel in mistakes. They were happy any time the actors messed up and were bored during the brief moments when things were going okay.

Jack mustered all the dignity he could to deliver Puck's famous last speech, but then a bozo in the audience made a loud crack about the "Chinese fairy." Jack froze. Becca marched over to the heckler, pointed at the caf doors, and stared at him until he got up. Just before she closed the door on him, I heard her say, "By the way, he's Korean, you dumbass." She looked back at the stage, ignoring everyone who had turned around to get a good look at the commotion. She looked so formidable that the audience was silent for the first time since intermission. Becca ignored everyone else and smiled directly at Jack. He seemed to find some new resolve. He stood up straighter than ever and commanded the attention of everyone in the room. He promised the audience he would make amends, but we all knew there was nothing anyone could do to make up for this disaster of a play.

The cast came forward for their curtain call, and as I heard the sound of loud guffaws and sporadic applause, I thought, "Yeah, that's about right." Some of the family members and friends in the audience rose for the obligatory standing ovation, but even their applause was half-hearted. The show had, as Annie predicted, been a complete disaster. But when I looked at that stage, at the gaggle of misfits standing there—Mr. Evans trying to bow while holding his ass head; the fairies giggling and waving at parents; Ben standing stone-faced and square-shouldered; Jack taking a small, dignified bow; Charlotte flushing with pleasure or embarrassment or a mix of both of them—I felt nothing but pride. I whooped until my throat hurt and clapped until my hands went numb. I clapped longest and loudest, though Annie and Becca did their best to keep up. Becca even hooted, "Yay, Jack!" When he smiled at her, my slow, dumb brain finally connected the dots. Jack was the guy Becca had been tutoring in math. I checked her with my hip and she ducked her head; she knew that I knew. I clapped even harder.

That ragtag group of actors had done it. They'd gone out there and made fools of themselves and would do it again tomorrow night, even Jack and Ben and Charlotte, who knew the audience wasn't with them. To take a strange piece of fiction and tell some truth with it was a beautiful act of transformation, even if it was also ridiculous. And to be honest with strangers about a vulnerable part of you was an act of courage I could appreciate more than ever.

I kept clapping as the actors left the stage. Charlotte was the last to go, and I could have sworn that just as she exited stage left, she winked at me.

CHAPTER 42

I'd like to say that the show got better. But that would be an epic lie. We never got back to those magical moments of the first two acts on opening night. We didn't even get close. I therefore assumed that after closing night, everyone would just want to go home and lick their wounds. But no. These loveable weirdos were genuinely excited about their cast party. They were buzzing about it as they changed out of their costumes for the very last time.

I wasn't sure if the crew traditionally went to the "cast" party. What was the etiquette? If we weren't invited, should I host something? While we were cleaning up discarded programs, I asked Becca what she thought. She said, "I don't know. Jack invited me, but maybe that's because we're, you know."

"Dating?" I teased.

She rolled her eyes at me. After opening night, I'd inter-rogated Becca about Jack almost as thoroughly as my mother would have. When did she start talking to him? Were they dating or just friends? Were they going to prom together? She'd acted casual at first, like it was no big deal, but eventually revealed that Jack had called her after the disastrous "date." He felt bad about how rude he'd been to her when he just left the diner, and he wanted to apologize. She couldn't stay silent on the phone, so she'd been forced to talk to him. Their conversa-tion started out being about how infuriating I was, but then they'd talked about the play and school. He eventually asked for her help with math, and things had "progressed" from there. I refrained from crowing, "So I did make you two fall in love!" Maybe I was learning some things. I was going to apply some of my new wisdom to the cast party question. While Old Alison would have consulted the Red Binder or agonized over finding a subtle way to ask without asking, New Alison went to find Jack after the show. He was speaking to his parents, who were both beaming with pride.

"Hello Mr. and Mrs. Park! Wasn't Jack great?"

Jack ducked his head in embarrassment as his parents both nodded their heads. "Yes, he was," Mrs. Park said. "You also did a fabulous job, Alison. Your mother has been telling me all about how busy you've been with the show. Congratulations!"

It was my turn to feel embarrassed by the praise. "Thanks," I said. I was tempted to apologize for the poor lighting (Sam had been sober only the one night) and the bit in Act 3 when one of the actors skipped an entire section of dialogue, but I stopped myself. They'd gotten to see Jack shine in a starring role. That's all that mattered. "Jack, when you get a minute, can I ask you something?"

Mr. Park put on his jacket and said, "We're heading out. We know there's a big party tonight, and we don't want to keep you from it." He smiled at Jack. "Make sure you lock the door when you come in." Mr. Park patted Jack on the back, and Mrs. Park hugged first Jack then me.

When they were gone, Jack asked, "What's up?"

I took another chance on honesty. "Do you happen to know if the crew members are invited to the cast party?"

"Of course!" he said without hesitation.

"Great! No one told us much about it, so we weren't sure," I explained.

"Weird. Everyone probably just assumed someone else invited you. I'll text you the address. I just need to grab my phone from the dressing room."

I thanked Jack and texted Annie, Zach, and Jenny to let them know we were all invited to the cast party. I told them I'd have an address for them soon and could even give everyone a lift if they wanted. My parents had seen the show last night, and they must have felt sorry for Annie and me because they'd offered us the use of Mom's car again tonight.

I was tidying up in the wings when I heard someone clearing his throat. I turned around to see Ben looking mighty uncomfortable. "Do you, uh, need any help or anything?" he asked.

I was confused about what was happening. Ben gestured at the boxes of props. I opened my mouth to say I had everything under control, but then it dawned on me that he was trying to be nice. This was new territory for us both. "I guess you could help Zach organize the costumes."

Ben cleared his throat again. "Zach told me I should come help you."

Why on earth would Zach do this to me? I wondered. *I mean, it's fine if you want to make Ben work a little bit to get back in your good graces, but why drag me into this?*

I stared at Ben. He stared at me.

The silence got to him just a millisecond before it got to me. "I think Zach wants me to, you know, thank you." Ben cringed and buried his hands deep in his pockets. He looked more awkward with every passing moment.

"Oh." Now I was uncomfortable. I rearranged props in the box in front of me. I fluffed up some flower crowns while I wondered if I should say "You're welcome." It's not like I'd just passed him some salt at the dinner table. Do you say "You're welcome" for helping someone come out?

"So do you need some extra muscle to lift things or something?" Ah, there was the old macho Ben I was used to.

"Could you take those boxes to the storage room please?" I pointed at a couple Rubbermaid totes. They weren't heavy, and I could easily have taken care of them myself, but it was the least awkward way I could think of to acknowledge his thanks. Ben stacked the totes on top of each other and picked them up.

I don't know which of us was more relieved that he had an excuse to leave.

I was about to text Becca about this bizarro encounter

when my phone buzzed. Jack had sent me the address for the cast party. No wonder I didn't know about it.

Becca was giving Jack a lift to the party. Since I wasn't going to ruin their alone time by asking if Annie, Zach, and Jenny could tag along, I was stuck driving to a party I knew I couldn't attend. I told myself that this was Jenny's first high-school party and I was helping her make friends. She was as happy as I'd ever seen her, glowing from all the praise her set had garnered. How could I ruin that for her? And how could I deny Zach a chance to spend time with his boyfriend, even if his boyfriend was Ben? Plus, I'd never hear the end of it from Annie if she didn't get to go to the cast party. So that's how I ended up outside Charlotte's house on closing night.

I tried to be nonchalant when the others opened their doors. "Text me when you're ready to leave, and I'll come get you." I attempted to sound breezy.

Annie and Zach were confused. "You're not coming?" Annie asked me, one leg out the passenger's-side door.

"I don't think I should."

"Why not?" Jenny was as blunt as always.

"I don't think the host meant to invite me," I explained. Charlotte may have winked at me, but that didn't mean she wanted me in her house. Did it?

Jenny closed her door. "I'm not going without you," she declared.

A moment later, Annie and Zach closed their doors. "Neither am I," Zach said, catching my eye in the rearview mirror.

"You kept that shit show together. They wouldn't be having a party if it wasn't for you. I'll text Becca. Let's go get burgers." This was maybe the nicest thing Annie had ever done for me, and I started to cry.

We sat in the car, waiting to hear from Becca. Annie and Jenny pretended not to see me cry. Zach passed me his pocket square and patted my shoulder. I wiped at my eyes, touched beyond words.

By the time I'd stopped crying and Annie had turned on some music, the front door of the house opened. In the light of a stylish sconce, I saw my best friend's curly head appear. She was followed by someone with much shorter hair. I swallowed.

I resisted the instinct to escape, to press my foot to the floor and gun the car out of there. Instead, I forced myself to turn off the engine and get out of the car. Annie, Zach, and Jenny followed my lead.

Becca spoke first. "Don't be stupid. Come in to the party."

Annie, Zach, and Jenny looked at me. I was touched again by their loyalty. I trusted my best friend, so I nodded at them. Becca smiled at me and walked in with them.

Then it was just me and Charlotte. In her driveway. I remembered our first date and wished Princess Sunshine would come barreling out and cause a distraction. I looked at my shoes. I could hear the bass line of a dance song coming from inside the house, though I couldn't make out the tune.

"I can just come back to pick them up later," I tried. "I'm sorry for…God, I'm sorry for so many things, Charlotte."

My hand was on the latch of the car when she said, "What things?"

She could have meant the question as an accusation, but I thought it sounded more like an opening. I took it. "I'm sorry I pushed you away. I'm sorry I made it sound like it was your fault I failed a quiz. I'm sorry I got so caught up in the play and school that I was rude to you when you were only ever nice to me."

"And what about the corgis?"

"The corgis?" I was so confused that I finally looked her in the eye.

There was that quirked smile, the one I still couldn't entirely read. The one that was always challenging me to see the humor in things. I took a chance. "I already apologized for making fun of corgis. I won't do it again. Princess Sunshine is a good boy, but I stand by my position on the breed as a whole."

Charlotte laughed, took a step forward, and kissed me.

EPILOGUE

Essay question: Give an example of a time you took on a leadership role. Were you successful in the role? If you were, why? If you weren't, why not?

I produced our school play this year. I thought it was the kind of leadership role that would look good on scholarship applications like this one. I also thought it might help me become valedictorian. Little did I know how complicated it would be and how much heartache would follow. In hindsight, I'm happy I didn't know because I might not have agreed to produce it. And producing this show has taught me more than I can tell you, though I'm about to try.

First, I learned to accept imperfection, both in myself and others. I don't think I'll ever stop being driven or competitive, but I now know that if I stumble along the way, it won't break me. Maybe you want your scholarship students to excel at everything they try, but I can tell you I'm stronger now than I was before. Part of the reason is, I understand that disappointments are a part of life, even if we don't welcome them. I've learned that if I feel let down now and then by not meeting my own expectations, I won't fall apart. I know that I can work hard and find creative solutions to problems.

So, was I successful as a leader? In unexpected ways I think I was. I did help a quiet and detached painter find an outlet for her art. I'd say that was a success. I also helped a former foe feel comfortable enough with himself to speak his truth. I can't really take the credit for his finding the courage to do that, but the confidence and happiness he gained still felt like a success to me. My greatest successes as a leader involved giving other people opportunities to grow. My own success is pretty small by comparison: The show went on and I did the best I could with what I had. In the end, I guess that mattered too.

As for my failures as a leader? There were several, but I'll focus on the big one. Instead of being up-front, I avoided conflict and embarrassment. I wanted people to think I had everything under control. To maintain this facade, I lied to my best friend. I hurt my sister's feelings by running away instead of just facing an awkward situation. I almost ruined my first real relationship by getting angry with my girlfriend instead of addressing my fear of failure. I'm grateful to everyone who forgave me, especially my girlfriend, who taught me not to care so much about what others think of me.

I don't know if I'll be chosen as valedictorian or not, but it doesn't matter to me as much as it once did. It would be an honor to represent my classmates at our graduation, but I no longer see that honor as defining who I am. I know what I'm capable of, and I promise that if you award me a scholarship, you will not be sorry. I've learned to value hard work for its own sake, not just as a way to show off. I can't say it better than Shakespeare: "Things won are done; joy's soul lies in the doing."

Thank you for your consideration.

Acknowledgments

One of my favorite moments during a curtain call is when the cast gestures to the crew, orchestra, and director. This portion of the applause is for the people who do all the behind-the-scenes work, even though the audience still can't see them. It's a salute to the million little things directors, producers, and crews do to make the magic happen. It's a chance to acknowledge all the work, tears, laughter, and support of people who are usually invisible to the audience. Let me take this moment to recognize the people in my life who have made *The Year Shakespeare Ruined My Life* possible.

Thank you to Matthew and Brannon Flanagan for their love, support, and terrible senses of humour. (Brannon has the excuse of being a toddler. Matthew is just an unapologetic punster, and I wouldn't have it any other way.) Thank you for the tea, the squish hugs, the games of monster, and the many, many pep talks.

Thank you to one of my earliest readers, Beatrice Glickman. She started out as a student and over time has become a good friend. She took time out of her university studies to give me feedback, to correct me on how "the youth" (my phrase, not hers) talk these days, and to make sure Alison won some measure of happiness at the end of the story. I hope to repay the favor someday soon when she writes her first brilliant book.

Thank you to my colleagues for their encouragement, as well as their expertise. I work with many wonderful teachers, but I would like to thank two in particular. Donna Gold cried tears of joy when she learned my book was being published, and has been a thoughtful collaborator and a generous friend for over a decade now. Steph Blum read an early draft and asked to keep a copy because she was certain it would become a real book. Thank you.

Thank you to everyone I know who is in, or has been in, theatre arts. Many smart people let me ask them stupid questions and if there's anything in the book that doesn't seem believable, the fault is mine. (Or Shakespeare's. Probably Shakespeare's.) I'd like to especially acknowledge Romy Suliteanu, Candace Grynol, Julian Stamboulieh, and Adam Koren. I'll also be forever grateful to the students, faculty, and staff who let me join them onstage for glee. There's nothing quite so humbling as asking students to teach you how to reach that high note or how to make that last turn in the choreo. I loved every minute with G Major!

Lastly, thank you to my family and friends. Kathryn, thanks for keeping me from taking things too seriously. Tanya, thanks for plotting with me. Karen, thanks for the belly laughs. Christie, thanks for always believing in my writing. Mark and Mark, thanks for the pugs. Aaron, thanks for the music. Melissa, thanks for being a hugger. Mom, thanks for my love of books and for letting me borrow the car to get to all the extracurriculars I signed up for in high school. Dad, thanks for the gift of gab and the knack for spelling. Thanks, finally, to my grandmother, who was also a teacher and who loved words as much as I do.

About the Author

DANI JANSEN is a high-school teacher. She should probably be embarrassed to admit that she has performed as part of her school's Glee Club for eight years. She should probably also be ashamed to tell people that she named her cats after punctuation symbols…Ampersand and Em-Dash, in case you're curious. She lives with her family in Montreal.